SO NOT MY TYPE

DANA HAWKINS

Storm
PUBLISHING

Ebook ISBN: 978-1-80508-744-1
Paperback ISBN: 978-1-80508-745-8

Cover design: Leah Jacobs-Gordon
Cover images: Shutterstock

Published by Storm Publishing.
For further information, visit:
www.stormpublishing.co

ALSO BY DANA HAWKINS

Not in the Plan

In Walked Trouble

The Ex Effect

Any Girl But You

I Will Always Love You (Maybe)

To Papa Dave. Thank you for raising me to believe if I worked hard enough, I could accomplish anything.

ONE
SOPHIE

The rippling of whispers started in the back corner. An old-school game of telephone where one person whispered to the person next to them, then to the next, then to the next. People darted back to their sharp-white, open-seating desks with cool, yet impractical, teal LED lighting, when the ripple turned into a wave. "He's coming!"

Sophie Black launched into her rolling chair and scooted up to her desk. She straightened her ripped-edge pencil skirt and ran a flattened palm against her buzzed head. The tiny hairs prickled her skin and lowered her heart rate. She checked the bingo card on her smartphone. Only four left for a full blackout. All she needed was an "attagirl!," "working hard or hardly working," "rise and grind," and "let's turn that frown upside down."

Was playing office bingo based on what clichéd business jargon the CEO would next spew immature? Absolutely. A fireable offense? Probably not. Did it make the twelve-plus-hour workdays more palatable? Definitely.

George Northwood deserved a little crap for his behavior. When she interviewed for an entry-level assistant position at Mahogany and Moon Creative Agency right out of high school, he'd barged into the hiring manager's office, and within two minutes, joked she should call him "King" or "Captain" and asked her, with her shaved head and all, if she ever "caught pneumonia."

Whatever that meant.

Six years later, besides the company growing to five hundred employees and now occupying four floors of a Seattle high-rise, not much had changed with George. So yeah, office bingo was just fine, in her humble opinion.

She focused on the screen, reviewing the remaining tactics needed for her latest campaign—frozen meatballs. Sure, it wasn't a sexy product like what the other project managers had, like coffee, sodas, or technical gadgets. Someone even did an ad for a twelve-speed, purple unicorn vibrator that she was still envious over. Yet, even with the sub-par campaigns her manager assigned her to, this job was her dream.

After spending the last six years in this office doing every-thing from coffee runs to faxing (*like, seriously, who faxes anymore?*) to answering emails, she'd applied every scrap of energy into landing her dream job—creative project manager. The heartbeat of the campaign, diligently executing against timelines, evaluating risks, and communicating between teams. For so many years, she wondered what it would feel like to walk into a room and have people snap to attention. And finally, it happened. The validation was borderline addictive.

She yawned and tossed back the final few droplets of coffee. Today was only Wednesday, but she'd put in over thirty hours already, with no end in sight. The project management plat-form pinged with a new notification. She reviewed the most recently uploaded creative—a social post with a steamy Crock-Pot of meatballs. *What a crock of... deliciousness! Enjoy Jorge's mouthwatering salted meatballs with BBQ or teriyaki.*

Suppressing the twelve-year-old level of maturity to giggle at "mouthwatering salted meatballs," she messaged the creative lead that they needed to review the copy—and crossed her fingers they changed it up at least a little, so people like her would not crack up over the words. She bit back the overwhelming urge to provide feedback, as the creative team never took kindly to those nudges.

The heavy, dark wood office doors slammed. Sophie strained her neck to look past the swinging, flaming-magenta hammock chair that no one ever used to confirm King George had indeed entered the room. The sun reflecting off his multiple gold stacked rings, rope necklace, and overly whitened teeth nearly blinded her.

"All right!" His baritone voice bounced against the walls. "Who's ready to take it to the next level, Northwood-style?"

"Bingo," a voice muttered in the corner.

Dammit. She'd have to clear her card and lose the ten-dollar ante. She sighed and refocused on her computer screen.

An instant message popped up from her manager, Malcolm.

Can you come to my office?

Thankful for solid Malcolm-relief, she rushed to the end of the room, and knocked on his open door. No amount of bamboo plants, paperwork, multiple monitors, and scattered coffee mugs could hide Malcolm's smile while looking at his phone. No doubt she was about to be bombarded with images of his infant.

Malcolm waved her in and shoved the phone under her nose. "Wifey just sent these. I mean, for real! Look at that face."

Sophie slunk into his beautiful, yet dreadfully uncomfortable, overstuffed white sitting chair. "Isn't there some sort of HR code that says you shall not force your staff to look at pictures of your baby?" Scrolling, she smiled at what seemed the same twenty images of a drooling, bald baby. "God, she looks like Amanda." She handed the phone back. "Let's hope she inherits your wife's personality, too."

"Hey!" His full black beard jerked as he twisted his mouth.

Man, she'd missed this—sitting with her mentor, getting the shot of serotonin needed to get back to the grind. The twelve weeks he had been gone were some of the longest of her life. "You adjusting from being back from paternity leave?"

"Truthfully? No." He tossed the phone to the edge of the desk. "It's been what... seven, eight days? I'm ridiculously jealous that Amanda gets another three months with Gracie. Might be time to invest in some obscure cryptocurrency so I can retire."

She huffed and peeked out the window. A rare stream of sunlight elbowed its way through the dense spring Seattle clouds. She crossed her fingers that she could take a ten-minute walk over lunch to suck up some vitamin D before her bones crumbled. "Well, you don't look terrible for staying up late with an infant. New haircut?"

"You like my new fade?" He brushed his hand over the top of his tight black curls with a grin. "Once I get rid of my dad bod, I'm gonna look just like Michael B. Jordan."

"We all have dreams. Maybe if I grow out my hair, I'll look like Paris Hilton." She grinned. "Did you call me in here to force me to look at your baby, who won the genetic pool lottery from your wife? Or were you saving me from Captain Dillweed."

"Sophie." He wagged his finger. "Be nice."

Malcolm never blatantly said that George Northwood made him want to gouge his eyeballs out with a silver-plated fountain pen. But he never *didn't* say that, either. George was relatively harmless, mostly clueless, and the clients loved him. But she'd bet good money that did he not hand out the best bonuses in the business, half the staff would've fled by now.

Malcolm drummed his fingers on the desk, his wedding band clinking against the wood. "Do you know what today is?"

"Hmmm." She crossed her legs, her fishnet stockings

scratching her thighs. "The day I keel over dead from the most drawn-out conversation of my life?"

"*Nooo.*" He pushed up his sleeves, the black ink tattoo of his wife's birthdate on dark skin peeking out of the fabric. "Today's your official six-month anniversary since your promotion. I just had a morning meeting cancel. Want to have your review now or wait until our scheduled time on Friday?"

All lightness vanished. Sophie sucked in her bottom lip, her tongue circling the metal lip ring. Her arm lifted to rub her head, but she forced it back into her lap. *Let's get this over with.* "Um, now's totally fine."

"Great." Malcolm cleared his smile. "You've been killing it. Really. Every campaign you've executed on time, if not early. I get continuous feedback from the creative partners that you are diligent, organized, and prepared. Not that I expected anything less. But... I did an audit on your platform entries, task completions, and logins. What do you think I found on your computer?"

She chipped at her black fingernail polish with a thumbnail and tiny flecks fluttered into her lap. Nerves shouldn't be consuming her as much as they were. She was pretty damn amazing at her job—here before everyone, stayed late every night, was Superwoman-lightning-speed responsive. Being scrappy, she had an edge, a street smart that most of her co-workers lacked. She knew the real world, had picked it up by riding along with her dad on his classic Harley and working odd jobs since she could remember.

But, the vast majority of her co-workers had college degrees, and over half had either MBAs or MFAs. She had the finest high school diploma from a South Seattle public school with overcapacity classrooms and burned-out teachers.

So, what did Malcolm find on her computer? A laundry list of terms she scribbled down during meetings to google later when she didn't know what the hell they were talking about.

YouTube instructional videos. A hundred bookmarked online courses that she desperately wanted to take but had no time. She forced a grin. "Um, funny cat videos? Which I will not be ashamed of. It breaks up the day."

Malcolm cracked a grin, then flatlined. "Trust me, I didn't have IT dig into your internet searches. I was scared it would say *how to poison your annoying manager and get away with it,* and honestly, I don't have the energy to fire you and look for a replacement." He sipped from his bedazzled *Best Dad Ever* mug. "No, I saw your access times. Sophie."

His voice took a decidedly dad-tone turn, and her cheeks flushed warm.

"You're burning on both ends, averaging close to sixty hours a week. There was only one day in the last six months where you didn't log on for a little bit."

He paused like she was supposed to say something, but what could she say? These were facts. The dark circles under her eyes weren't to rock a Seattle-emo look. She was damn tired.

"I feel awful." His leather chair squeaked under him as he rocked. "When I was on paternity leave, I just assumed you'd take some vacation time."

Vacation? The word sounded both terrible and incredible. She needed some downtime, for sure. Her parents, her best friend, even her apartment neighbor had called out that she looked fried. But if she took time off, and they managed without her... then what did that say about her skills? "It's all good. I want to nail this job." She softened her face and prayed it didn't convey her real thoughts.

"You're gonna burn out. This is not sustainable."

Her neck tightened.

"At the same time, your campaign execution is flawless." He tapped off his buzzing smartwatch. "Less than a year of being a PM and you're operating at a senior level. I gotta say, you must've had one hell of a manager leading you."

She rolled her eyes. "Yes, Malcolm. I owe everything to you. Shall I call you the king, too?"

He sucked in his lips. "I'm not taking that bait." He rolled the chair up to the desk and propped his elbows on the cherry-wood. "I have a proposition for you."

She tugged on the collar of her cropped leather jacket, the tiny lapel spikes digging into her fingertips. "I don't babysit."

"Thank God, 'cause Gracie is too young for an eyebrow piercing and too small for a leather coat." He twisted his wedding band. "George finally landed the huge account for the Latoure cruise line."

No way. Latoure was the new luxury cruise ship out of Seattle. A floating city, oasis, *heaven on water*, at least according to the *Times*. She remembered reading an article—and by article, probably a TikTok or Reel—about this new ship set to bring in tens of millions of tourist dollars while melting the guests' worries as they sailed the Pacific to Alaska. Cruising used to be a dream for her until life got in the way. But the moment she saw the promotional materials the team gathered for George's pitch, it catapulted back to the top of her vacation mood board.

"It'll take a fully dedicated team to execute. We're even bringing on some consultants to help. Anyway, Latoure is sending five employees of our choosing on an Alaskan cruise to inspire us to create the best ads."

Sophie tilted her chin. "So, what's the proposition?"

"George wants a rep from each team to go. One designer, copy, lead, manager, and... *one project manager*."

He landed the last two words with a heavy tongue, and her spine straightened in response. She was only six months into the role and had the lowest seniority of all the PMs. No way would they let her go on this trip. She snapped her fishnet stockings at the knee. "What are you saying?"

He breathed out, hard, through his nose. "You need a break.

You might be new to this particular position, but you've outlived half the company by now."

He wasn't wrong. Shelf life at an agency usually topped three years.

"And you've earned this," he continued. "But so did your teammates. However, I have full discretion, and I want to offer the ticket to you."

She did not hear him right. She couldn't have. All the moisture in her mouth zapped away, and she eyed his water bottle. She'd only been on a plane once in her life when the company sent her to Vegas for a conference. A cruise? On the actual ocean? "Malcolm—are you saying I get to go on a cruise?"

"Before you get too excited, there's a couple of stipulations." He took another sip from the mug. "One, a new assignment came in for you today, with an expedited timeline. A series of social, web, and digital ads for Devil's Doughnuts."

Her chest lifted. "What? *Sweeeet.* No pun intended." Devil's Doughnuts was one of the hippest bakeries in Seattle, boasting everything from a twelve-inch, truffle-butter, sugar-dusted doughnut to pickled-lemon mini-cakes, which sounded disgusting but she could vouch for their salty-sweet deliciousness. "For real, I love that place."

He jiggled the computer mouse and scanned the monitor. "We're gonna have to hand off your current campaign to another PM, because the Devil's Doughnuts campaign needs to launch before you all leave."

Okay, okay. She could do this. She'd been under tight timelines before... The nightmare of a reactionary ad during last year's Cyber Monday shuddered to mind. "When does the cruise leave?"

His dark brown eyes softened. "Eight weeks."

Eight weeks? Her throat jerked with a hard swallow. "The entire campaign needs to be done by then? All of it?"

"All of it." His mouth dipped into a frown. "And we haven't even started building the messaging strategy."

The math didn't math. Marketing strategy took a minimum of two weeks. Project workback schedules, kickoff, and handoff one week. Creative and copy developed, for a full social, web, and digital campaign, was three weeks minimum—with a solid A-team assigned. Then creative rounds with leaders, operations, execution... No chance in a fiery hell they could execute this in eight weeks.

She squinted, as if that would give her the clarification needed. "I don't get it... why the push?"

He slid the mouse to the side. "Quick version. Sounds like some shady stuff happened to one of the main Pride Parade sponsors and the association dropped them. Devil's swooped in and nabbed that spot, but they want to capitalize on it fully with the limited time. George guaranteed this turnaround time."

Of course he did. The dude was damn near clueless about what it took to run a full campaign.

"And we can't let all the top performers leave on a seven-day cruise if this is still in flux."

Logically, it made sense. Obviously. If the top creatives were basking in the immaculate view of marine-blue glaciers and northern lights, the execution of the campaign—arguably the most important part of the entire campaign—would be left to the replacement team. A logistical nightmare and surefire way to fail a campaign launch.

But just because it made sense, didn't mean it felt good.

"Give this to me straight." She shook out her tense fingers. "Are you saying I need to project manage all of this, *alone*, to go on the cruise?"

"We'll have a senior program manager overseeing the entire scope, but you'll be the main PM on all the channels."

So... web, social, and digital. *Combined.* She coughed on the nervous saliva pooling in her throat. The deadline was not only on her—the entire team would have to work double time to get this out. Part, sometimes a large part, of Sophie's job was keeping up morale. The ones going on a cruise had an incentive to work long hours. The others didn't. And she didn't foresee a world where the overlooked teammates would jump at the long days to help ensure the others made voyage time. "I... I honestly don't know if I can do it."

"Good news, though." Malcolm's grin returned. "We brought in relief. A last-minute PM. Just heard about it this morning, actually. She's getting introduced to folks today and starts tomorrow. You'll be training her and she can partner with you on this project."

The heat trapped in her chest released. They trusted her to train someone? Hell yes! For the past two years, training was a personal goal. Probably living out some childhood fantasy like when her parents left her alone and she passed the time pretending to be a teacher to her raggedy dolls. If they brought in a new PM, that person might have more project-management experience than her, which meant, together, they could knock it out of the park.

Maybe the cruise could be a reality. And if she were on a cruise, maybe there would be another woman who was traveling alone. And their eyes would meet across the deck, a whisper of wind fluttering through her hair, and they'd be drawn together, her true soulmate, while waves crashed in the background—

Malcolm's fingers slapping the desk jolted her out of her thoughts.

"What do you think?" he asked.

About the fact that she'd been single for almost six years, and the idea of meeting someone was basically the only other thing that occupied her mind besides work? But that she didn't want just anyone, she wanted that *someone*, the one that flipped her stomach and zinged her to Jupiter and back and curled her toes, and if *only* she would have a tiny bit of time off work, she was convinced she could find the woman of her dreams?

He probably meant what did she think about the work situation. "Do I have a choice in all of this?"

"Sure you do." He crossed his arms over his chest. "Pink Flamingo is hiring, I heard."

She groaned. She'd never work for the competitor. When Pink Flamingo moved into the same high-rise as Mahogany and Moon's building, occupying the second and third floor, friendly banter and threats of a field day competition with tug-of-war and tire races flung between the agencies. But soon, rumors of client meddling and sabotage filled the space, and all friendly banter ceased. It was them or us. And Sophie chose her alliance. Besides King George, and a couple of less-than-desirable co-workers, she loved this place.

"The cruise leaves May 15th out of California. I'll send you the info."

She glanced at the calendar hanging on his wall and quickly counted the weeks with her fingertips. "That's *exactly* eight weeks from yesterday."

He tugged on his beard. "I know. Sorry, Soph. I really want you to have this opportunity, but you have to wrap up by then in order to go. Believe me, I'd love nothing more than to know you're hanging out with retired folks playing bingo, eating at the chocolate buffet, and reading romance novels while watching the waves."

She scowled. "Um. I'm twenty-four, not sixty-four. Why wouldn't you assume I wanted to go to the nightclub and bars?"

"Because I've worked with you for six years and know your type."

"What's my type?" She lifted a brow.

"You're a baby boomer wrapped in a Gen Z body. Pretty sure you'd rather knit than go on a pub crawl."

She popped a hand to her hip. "I'll have you know that

methodical stitching is incredibly therapeutic and a good way to release tension."

"While watching *Wheel of Fortune*." He grinned into his mug.

"Best game show ever, and I'll never let you tell me otherwise."

He laughed and stretched his neck, looking behind her. "Looks like George is making his way here with the new hire."

"Poor thing," she muttered, and ignored Malcolm's fatherly glare. She looked down at the pile of black chipped nail polish in her lap, unaware she'd scraped off nearly everything from her fingers. *Oops.* She brushed it into her hands and clapped it into the wastebasket.

George walked in, his massive frame hiding whoever was behind him.

She could smell his deep, musky scent that was probably some super-expensive brand, but it overpowered the small room. Did he bathe in it? Running out of time to eat breakfast this morning was doing her no favors, as the combo of the sickly-sweet smell and her empty stomach made her want to gag.

"Sophie! Did you get a new haircut?"

Do not roll eyes. She'd been buzzing her hair since she was fifteen, and once a month he asked her the same question.

"Ha ha." He smacked his palms together. "I'm just messing around."

You don't say...

His thunderous voice banged against the walls. "You need to smile more."

Dammit. That was on my bingo card! She pushed out a grin.

Stepping aside, he waved his arm at the woman behind him. "I'd like to introduce you to our new project manager. Meet my daughter—"

"Ella," Sophie choked out. The air vanished from the room.

Sophie's hand flew to the back of her neck and slid up and down the prickles.

Ella looked different from when Sophie last saw her six years ago. Black bangs so straight they looked like a titanium sharp-edged razor sliced them. Tortoiseshell, chunky frames covered deep brown eyes. Ruby-red, flatlined lips. Perfectly matched, freshly manicured, blood-red nails. The same pretentious, narrowed eyes that made Sophie cry her first week on the job.

Ella tugged once on the edge of her crisp, tailored, navy power suit that absolutely cost more than Sophie's monthly rent. Who the hell did she think this was, anyway? No one wore suits. She was joining a Seattle *creative* agency—home of purple hair, sleeve tattoos, and ripped jeans. Not a stuffy financial institution.

Standing beside George, Ella wasn't subtle as her gaze trailed over Sophie. And for the first time in forever, Sophie's insides flared with heat. She wiggled her toes inside her heavy combat boots and wondered why the hell she'd chosen today to wear her ripped purple-and-black fishnet stockings.

The black-haired demon shook Sophie's hand, absent of any emotion, except for a hint of a smirk when she looked at Sophie's chipped nails. "Hi, Sophie. Good to see you again."

TWO

ELLA

The door slammed against the single-stall, gender-neutral bathroom wall on the ninth floor of the Mahogany and Moon Creative Agency. Ella locked it behind her and flailed her hand under the paper towel dispenser's sensor. "Come on, come on." She balled the towels in her hand, doused them with cold water, and held the sodden lump against her neck. The tiled wall was cool against her forehead as she rested against it until her blazing internal temperature lowered. How in the hell did she let her mother convince her to wear this goddamn suit? She looked like a kid trying to play dress-up, and everyone here knew it.

A few hours ago, she was in mom jeans, low heels, and a knitted sweater, going through her breathing exercises before her mother barged into her room. "Oh, honey. No. Not for your orientation day. You want them to respect you, right? Wear the suit we bought last weekend. You don't want to embarrass your father or have anyone think you're not serious about this job." She'd turned to shut the door, but paused. "Put your lips on, dear. You look so pale."

And Ella listened to her, of course. She always fucking

listened to her, but that would change. Soon, she wouldn't *have* to listen to her at all. She flipped the paper towel for a coolness jolt and counted in reps of four. She tried to shake the image of the most awkward five minutes of her life when she'd stood in Malcolm's office, and stared at the woman who was so rude, who shot so many death glares at her when she visited years ago, that she'd avoided her on every visit to her father's office since then.

Her father had told her a project manager would train her in, but Malcolm was just coming off paternity leave and needed to check schedules. Why in the hell hadn't she asked more questions? She'd just blindly nodded and followed his lead, like always.

But enough was enough. She was a college graduate, *finally*, and ready to be an actual, working adult. And although she had no real sense of finances, the starting salary seemed pretty decent. If she saved, she'd only have to work here a few months to earn enough for a security deposit and down payment. *Freedom.*

Did it suck having to take a job at her father's office? Sure. But it was a necessary evil. And, admittedly, after the twentieth application auto-rejection, she realized how lucky she was to have this level of connection. Not that she blamed the other companies for rejecting her. Right now, her resume was hardly a thrilling read. Experience—none. First job—nope. Hard skills—zip. Technical skills—logging into her social media account. Budget experience—does having an Amex at twelve years old count? Probably not.

But she wouldn't be here for long. She simply needed to learn the trade tricks and move on.

She lifted herself from the wall and looked in the mirror. *Ugh.* Her mother was right. She was too pale. She dug in her purse, pushed her emergency nasal spray medication to the side, and pulled out red lipstick. After she reapplied, she checked her teeth, once, twice, then three times to confirm no lipstick stained. She'd never forget the time she'd had lipstick on her teeth at a party and her mother had chastised her on the way home on the importance of having a purse mirror to avoid such embarrassing situations.

Pulling her shoulders back, she exited the bathroom and walked back to the office where Sophie was smiling and comfortable and just... *so flipping cool. All 5'2", shaved head, pierced lip and nose, leather jacket, combat boots* cool. Ella unbuttoned her suit jacket, but quickly fastened it again as she approached.

"Why don't we go grab a coffee in the breakroom." Sophie ran her palm across the top of her head, then pointed the way.

"Sounds great." Ella firmed her voice, matching the icy tone in Sophie's. *Don't fidget. Look straight ahead. Keep lips steady and serious.*

The office had changed over the last fifteen years since her father started his agency. Back then, the entire agency filled only one floor. But now they were spread out between multiple floors. Even with her memory issues that were particularly bad before her medication adjustment and stint at the Children's Hospital, she recalled the space was stuffy and had cubicles like the show *The Office*. Now this area was reminiscent of a nightclub, or ultra-trendy coffee shop. They swapped the carpet-padded half-wall cubicles in the middle with massive, long white desks, almost cafeteria-style, but with monitors and chrome barstools. Teal lights glowed from under the tables, and wicker-back swinging chairs hung from the ceiling.

She definitely would've remembered the breakroom, so they must've updated it. The espresso machine looked like they lifted and shifted it from Starbucks itself, a row of syrups lined the counter, and a plethora of mugs with R-rated phrases lay across the shelf.

Sophie stuffed ground beans into a portafilter. "How do you take your coffee?"

"Black." *Lies.* Caffeine was on a long list of things Ella was forced to avoid. The very few times Ella drank coffee—and only after months without an incident—was normally some variation of double chocolate with extra whip.

"Cool. I'm a *double the cream, double the sugar* kind of woman myself." Sophie grabbed two mugs from the floating shelf and put them under the spout. "Want me to show you how to use the espresso machine?"

"No." Ella grabbed a napkin from the holder. "I don't think I'll be making these for myself."

Sophie's neck flashed pink. "Ah. You have people for that, I suppose."

Ella's throat tightened. That was not what she meant at all, but hell if she was going to explain to Sophie the potential adverse effects of caffeine on her brain. She might not have remembered everything from their first meeting, but she distinctly remembered Sophie's same tone from all those years ago. The *you think you're too good, don't you?* tone. The *no matter how hard you try, you'll never be as cool as me* tone. The one that made her feel like a spoiled kid that knew jack shit, made her fighting spirit burn and the need to prove herself jolt to the forefront.

Ella accepted the coffee Sophie handed her and followed her to the high-top table in the corner. She plunked on the barstool across from Sophie, sipped on the espresso, and nearly choked on the deep, dark hues. *Gross.* How did people drink this on the daily? The sludgy remnants settled on her tongue, and she discreetly tried to scrape it off with her teeth.

The abstract sloped steel light fixture cast a ray and illuminated Sophie like a halo. Her eyes were a spectacular mix of greens, and Ella shifted her gaze. She'd tried colored contacts once, hating the overly *bleh* brown shade of her own eyes.

Everything about her was boring, dull, and basic. She knew this to her core. And sitting with city-hip Sophie, Ella had the urge to up her game.

Sophie checked her watch. "I have a meeting in ten minutes, so we'll dive into actual training tomorrow."

"Excellent." Ella lifted the mug to her mouth and pretended to sip. "I can come in early if needed."

"Sure, if you want." Sophie tapped the outside of the cup. "We have a ton to do and a high-profile campaign with an expedited timeline. Not sure if your dad gave you any information?"

Ella swore Sophie added an irritated enunciation on the word "dad."

"All of this came up sort of... quickly." She would never let Sophie, or anyone else, know the circumstances of how she'd landed this job.

Sophie twirled the drink, took a hefty sip, and swiped the corner of her lip with her thumb. Ella wondered if the chipped nail polish was part of her whole rocker-edge look. For a quick moment, Sophie's lips, which were fuller, smoother, rounder than she'd remembered, caught Ella's attention.

"Anyway," Sophie continued, "I have multiple briefing meetings today and hopefully we'll align quickly on strategy and messaging."

Ella nodded. *Strategy and messaging.* What the higher-up people wanted for a campaign, right? Who they target—millennials, people with cats, kids. Her brain worked overtime recalling the details of a Marketing 305 course in a major forced on her by her parents. Why didn't she pay more attention during class, instead of counting down the minutes until she could rush out to paint at the art studio?

"The messaging hierarchy is pretty standard for social, especially..." Sophie rattled off more details.

Ella's ears grew warm. Hierarchy? Like a pyramid? Or maybe that was what an ad looked like online.

Sophie sipped. "Is this how they worked at your other company?"

The heat sprung to Ella's cheeks. "I, uh, there was no other company."

The words seemed to sink in as Sophie's eyes grew wide and whatever softness that existed dropped. "You didn't work anywhere before? Like ever?"

Ella wanted to dive into the ice machine. Did she have to say it like that? Like it was the most incredulous, asinine thing Sophie had ever heard of. Ella dug her nails into her palm to steady herself. "No. I was... I was in school." And now she probably had to explain why it took her six years to complete a four-year degree.

"Did you intern?"

"No."

Sophie's eyes narrowed, widened, and narrowed again. "Wait. Are you saying you've never worked a job *in your life?*"

Those words were an industrial-size paper cutter that sliced Ella in half. Sophie didn't have to say any more—Ella knew exactly what she was thinking.

"How the hell did you land a job like this *without ever working?*" Sophie paused for several long moments, then her lips twitched into a smirk. "Oh, wait... of course..."

Dammit. Sophie just slapped Ella with her greatest fear: She wasn't worthy, she was incompetent, and she got the job handed to her because of her dad. She stiffened her spine. "I went to the University of Washington for my undergrad, graduated with honors, and took extension courses from Stanford."

"And that qualifies you to *start* as a creative project manager?"

Enough of this. Ella had every right to be here, too, and didn't need to explain herself. "I don't think I ever got the name of the school where you graduated." *Shit.* She sounded just like her mom, and a metallic taste grew in her mouth. She knew good and goddamn well that Sophie didn't go to college, because her dad made multiple comments with an impressed voice—which he rarely used—about how Sophie grinded every day without an education.

Sophie's cheeks reddened. Her soft green eyes narrowed into a steely gaze. "Tomorrow we'll start early. Seven thirty is ideal. With your *vast* education, I'm assuming you will dive right in. The brief will come post-strategy, and you'll want to vet prior to handing off to the creative team. Messaging hierarchy should be firmed. Of course, you'll know the pixel size, images, and video playback speeds needed for tablet, mobile, and desktop versions, and it's always a good idea to QA the content prior. The workback schedule needs to be created ASAP. I'm sure you got this."

Ella's head spun. She didn't remember any of this from her classes and was mentally notating everything she could. God, why didn't she record this conversation? The second she left she needed to write down what Sophie said to research later.

The chair squeaked against the floor as Ella pushed herself from the table. She grabbed her nearly full cup of coffee to toss once Sophie left. "I know you have a meeting, and I need to see HR for some paperwork."

Sophie jerked her head once in a nod and stuffed her cell phone in her leather cropped jacket.

Screw her. Just because Sophie looked like she just stepped off a stage as a lead singer in a punk band, and was the epitome of everything Ella wasn't, did *not* mean she was better than her. "Quick question. Do you all use agile or waterfall?"

Sophie's pause and scrunched forehead was everything Ella needed.

"What?" Sophie asked.

"Project methodologies." Ella lifted her chin, a delicious warmth spreading. "I mean, since you have *so much* experience, I assume you've already locked if it's sprint based or not."

Sophie sucked in a side of a cheek.

Ella could barely contain her smile. "I'd love to get your thoughts around scrum methodologies, too." Oh God, this felt good. This moment was exactly what she needed after the brutal last few months, the terrible morning, and the even worse last hour. She'd show Sophie she was not incompetent. "What about a RACI? It's crucial to establish that from the project's start, right?"

Ella's pulse quickened. Shit. Why did she choose RACI? Responsible, Accountable, Consulted, Informed. Right? *Wait!* No. Was it Reasoning, Accountability, Consultation, and Inclusions? No, that didn't make sense. *Crap.*

"I—" Sophie's cell rang, and her face screamed "Oh, thank God." "I need to take this." Her clunky boots pounded against the floor as she scooted away.

Ella tossed the remaining coffee down the drain and slammed back water. Even though it'd been years since an incident, the heightened stressful situation and caffeine could trigger her.

Thudding footsteps rounded the corner, and she could hear her dad's heavy, former pack-a-day smoker breathing outside the door. "Hey, kid, how did it go?"

"You cannot call me kid when I'm working. Or ever, honestly," she snapped. "Really, Dad, I'll be twenty-four in a few months."

He tossed up his hands. "Whoa. Is it that time of the month or something?"

Her blazer constricted her chest. The coffee grounds branded her tongue, and her armpits were a dam about to break. "*Don't* ask me that. I need to go to HR and fill out paperwork."

"Good." He held his arm out to escort her. "You and Sophie will do great."

She ignored his outstretched hands and marched ahead.

"Remember, it's my reputation on the line, along with

yours. Don't ruin the good Northwood name," he said in a lowered tone. "I'm still not sure this was the right idea."

Her dad could not pull her out now. She needed this to land before her parents realized what she was doing. Softening her stance, she leaned into him. "I'll make you proud." Making him proud was on the list of course, but down low. Championship-limbo-bar-style low.

Top of the list: proving to everyone, especially that snarky-ass Sophie, that she deserved a spot.

THREE

SOPHIE

Cool. So you went to school. UW? You want a purple cookie or something?

Perhaps Sophie's internal dialogue was not the most mature. Who did Ella think she was, anyway? How hadn't she changed —at all—from the snotty girl Sophie met when she first started?

She'd seen Ella a smattering of rare times over the years. A holiday party a few years back when she wore an actual gown like some Southern debutante. Once when she rounded the corner at work and Ella was talking with her dad. Last year, as a passenger of George's chauffeured car. Ella's face always held a sour smile that didn't reach her eyes, a slightly scrunched nose like she just smelled something rank but was trying to be polite, and a trailing gaze like she measured the person next to her and declared they weren't as good. Having received that look many times had sadly not made Sophie immune to it.

The coconut-scented steam filled her small shower space, and the moisture clung to the gray-blue tiles. She scrubbed her skin within an inch of its life with an organic loofah as the irritation from yesterday bubbled up and spilled over. *Must be nice to have a daddy who gives you everything. What do dinner conversations around their custom-made, knotty-wood banquet table sound like? "Hey, honey, need a new car? Let's go to the Mercedes dealership. An education? Here's my wallet. You need a job? Of course!"*

Nepotism at its finest.

And she absolutely refused to acknowledge the soft mouth and sultry dark eyes that she'd forgotten about over the years. Finishing the shower, she toweled off, threw on a tank and underwear, and grabbed her phone.

She needed some best friend relief, stat. Her fingers flew across the screen, and she prayed Maya would respond.

SOPHIE:

You up?

FaceTime rang within a minute, with her bestie Maya's tired face and floppy blond ponytail splashed across the screen.

"Why you up so early?" Sophie propped the phone on the edge of the dresser.

"You're the one who texted me," Maya whispered as she walked down the hall. "Remi's still sleeping. But Ben got home at 5:oo a.m. from his hospital shift and I've been up since."

"Ah." It had been close to a year since Maya found the love of her life, Remi, and a new family member in Remi's roommate, Ben. But sometimes, Sophie still struggled with the change. She'd never tell Maya, but part of her, buried somewhere deep and low that she didn't like to acknowledge, was envious. Not *of* Maya and Remi's relationship.

Sophie wanted her *own* Remi.

So many things had shifted over the years. When Sophie met Maya as kids, they'd quickly become as close as twins. Being an only child, with two parents that worked double shifts to pay for their home, she spent more time with Maya's family than her own.

Everything was fun back then. Easy. Sophie egged Maya on

to ditch school, or run barefoot in Lake Sammamish at night, or shove as many grape-flavored pixie sticks in their mouths as possible until the sugar buzzed their brains and limbs. Fits of giggles, popcorn fights, and sidewalk chalk filled their days.

But when Maya's dad died when they were teenagers, part of Sophie died along with him. Maya's dad was a sitcom dad— goofy, drove her mom crazy, and loved his kids to his core. He even loved Sophie. He'd ask her about school, marvel at how many books she could read in a month, eat her terrible snack concoctions (*sugar and cinnamon on onion chips, anyone?*).

Sophie's heart had broken for her friend, and for herself. It seemed so selfish, so ridiculous, for her to mourn a dad the way she did that wasn't hers—like she was stealing from her friend and simultaneously betraying her own dad.

"What time is class?" Sophie dug into her closet and yanked out a shirt.

"Not till ten."

Maya started her master's in nursing at UW last semester, and the morsels of time they previously had together vanished. Sophie liked to blame Maya's graduate schooling for the fact they never hung out anymore, but in reality, Sophie's work sucked up almost every free second.

Maya yawned and dug into the refrigerator. "I'm gonna swing by Mom's house before Harper goes to school and terrorize her a little."

Sophie tugged a shirt over her head. "Tell them I said hi."

"Tell them yourself." Maya raised an eyebrow.

Fine, Sophie deserved that. When Maya left for college in Minnesota after high school, Sophie picked up the sister slack, as Maya called it. And Sophie loved bonding with Harper and Laney. Since she was little, there had always been a hole inside her, and being around them filled it. She loved her parents, of course, but when she was a kid, they worked so many hours and couldn't always find babysitters, and she spent too much time alone. But with all the hours she'd been putting in these last six months, this last year, these last few years, her second family slipped away.

Sophie dug in her drawer, looking for one of her favorite black skirts with pink gemmed bones and skulls. "How's Remi?"

"Cranky." Maya huffed with a grin and poured a glass of juice. "She doesn't think the new bartender they hired is up to speed."

"It's been a week."

"I know!"

Sophie shimmied the skirt up her legs. "Maybe you'll go back to slinging drinks."

"I miss it a lot, actually." Maya gulped the juice and wiped her lip with the back of her hand. "But nope. Nursing has my full attention. Oh, did I tell you…"

Maya plopped down on the kitchen stool and proceeded to talk about research on some blood-borne something or other, and Sophie tried, she really did, to focus on the foreign words. Her face probably mirrored Ella's lost expression in the café yesterday. As Maya droned on, Sophie stood in front of the mirror. The shirt looked ridiculous. She ripped it off and tossed it in the corner. She grabbed another. Tossed another.

"So, I asked the professor about apple cider vinegar being an insulin aid, and I read an article—wait. What are you doing?" Maya pulled the phone so close to her face that Sophie could count her eyelashes. "That shirt looked great. Why did you toss it?"

"Not the look I'm going for today." *I'm so full of shit.* For the first time in forever, she was self-conscious about the funky thrift-store finds stuffed in her closet. She finally settled on a cropped, off the shoulder sweater and neon pink tank. "So, big news time. Guess what? Malcolm offered for me to go on a cruise."

Maya bolted upright. "What? How did you not lead with this? Are you serious? Tell me everything."

Sophie made her way to the kitchen and propped the phone on the counter. "We landed this new account for Latoure—you know the new Alaska cruise line porting in Seattle? Anyway, they want to immerse the creative team in the cruising experience, so we can create the campaign."

"Soph, this is huge! A freaking cruise. Are you kidding? You always wanted to go on one." Maya slammed her hand against her mouth and muffled a screech. "Remember in high school when you signed your parents up for one of those timeshare demos with a promise of a free cruise?"

"Oh God, they were so mad." She popped bread into the toaster. "They were held hostage in some crappy hotel conference room all afternoon."

"I remember that! Didn't we run around the lobby talking in fake accents and try to pretend we were European or something ridiculous?"

"Right!" Sophie giggled at the memory of a very irritated front desk agent who repeatedly asked them where their parents were. "Who knows, maybe I'll find my soulmate off the coast of the Caribbean during the midnight chocolate buffet."

Maya rolled her eyes. "Seattle is like the land of lesbian opportunity. Why don't you try dating here?"

So many reasons. "Seattle might be filled with gays, but right now I feel like I'm only surrounded by dry-erase markers and laptops." She'd gone on a few dates over the years, but by the time she worked late, logged off, and rushed to meet the person, she was tired and mentally preparing the next day's agenda. By the first drink, her heartbeat would kick up a notch, worried about after-hours emails, and she'd sneak off to the bathroom to check her phone.

Maya's lips turned into a frown. "I think you're working too much."

"I know." Sophie's voice turned soft. "But I have to."

Maya nodded.

What Sophie loved the most about Maya was that she just inherently *got it*. Sophie didn't need to explain her obsession to prove she was right for this job, prove to everyone they didn't make a mistake, prove she could excel like her co-workers, even without a fancy degree. No need for her to justify the fear of winding up like her parents, who'd have to work until they were eighty just to stay in their run-down, two-bedroom home.

Sophie scraped butter across the toast and crunched into a bite. "Honestly, the cruise is probably not gonna happen."

"Why not?"

"'Cause I have to project manage and execute a whole new campaign beforehand. You know Devil's Doughnuts in Fremont and Capitol Hill? It's for them." She dusted off the crumbs from her fingers. "But me and the team have to get out social, web, and digital in eight weeks."

Maya set the phone on the counter and propped her elbows onto the table. "I'm not even going to pretend I understand the difference. They all sound like the internet to me."

"Well, social is social, like Instagram, Facebook, whatever," Sophie said. "Web is landing pages and banners on their website, and digital... you know, never mind. The details aren't important. But it's nearly impossible to do. The entire team will have to work triple time."

"I can't believe they're making you do this on your own."

Right now, Sophie actually wished she were doing this on her own. Then she could avoid the chocolate-eyed demon for one more second. "I'm training in a newbie."

"That's amazing! You've always wanted a trainee." Maya's eyes brightened. "You should make them get your coffee and tell them to rub your feet. Bark orders like a boss."

Sophie grinned but followed it with a groan. "Never gonna happen. It's George's daughter."

Maya's lip twitched in a grimace. "Oh God, don't you hate that guy?"

"I don't hate him as much as, I don't know... He's kind of a goober. Sometimes I see snippets that make me think he's human. And he signed off on my promotion, so... But it's total crap his daughter is my trainee. Not only is she a rookie, but she only got the job because she's his daughter." Sophie stuffed her laptop in her bag and zipped. "It's going to be like training an infant. She's a rookie, and they put her in the big leagues, and she is one hundred percent gonna eff up my shit."

Maya's head snapped back. "Jesus, whoa. This doesn't even sound like you. The last time I heard you this heated was when you waited all night to see Dave Matthews and they sold out."

Sophie exhaled through her nose. Maya was probably right. This ball inside her gut, fiery and icky and gross, wasn't her. On her way to work, she needed to listen to a podcast of Brené Brown, Simon Sinek, or some meditation guru. "Do you remember me talking about her? Years ago, when I first started?"

"She was kind of a shit, right? Didn't she sneer at your combat boots? Clearly, she has terrible taste."

"It wasn't just my combat boots! It was everything... what I was wearing, how I looked, the fact that I never went to college. You should have seen her face when I broke that devasting news. She didn't even look me in the eye." Sophie kneaded a knuckle into the corner of her eye and flashed back to that day. She'd only been at Mahogany and Moon for a week and was desperate to make a good impression. Since she was fourteen, she'd always worked—sweeping at her dad's mechanic shop, bussing tables at her mom's diner, summers at the pier cleaning fish guts from the Market. But this was different. This was a *real* job. A *respectable* job. And she even had a title!

Then what started as forced conversation took a dark turn, and flew downhill from there. A few snarky comments tossed, glares flung, and the burning pit in Sophie's stomach accelerating to an inferno degree. When Ella finally left, Sophie ran to the bathroom and cried.

Sophie looked at her watch. *Crap.* If she didn't bolt now, she'd miss the metro and hell if she'd let Ella beat her there on day one. "I've gotta run. Tell Remi I want a do-over, double or nothing, on our pool match last week."

"Are you still mad you lost your ten bucks?"

"Yes, yes I am." Sophie grinned. "Luvs."

She hung up the phone and zipped up her boots. Day one.

Ella better buckle up. She had no idea what it was like to work in the real world.

FOUR

ELLA

Cashmere sweaters tickle. And not in the good way. The microscopic pieces imbedded into Ella's skin. But the top looked cute, so the tradeoff was acceptable. Ella smoothed the neckline and clasped on a simple pearl strand. Pink was her color, her mother had told her on more than one occasion. And sure, it was risky to wear white pants in the spring, but there wasn't supposed to be rain today.

Maybe cashmere was too much. The suit yesterday had definitely been too much. But she'd been so focused on learning all the tasks that she wasn't sure what everyone else wore. Her father was old-school and wore a suit and tie almost every day. Surely cashmere was acceptable in the office? She bit her lip and swapped her pearls for a simple gold clasp.

She probably should've visited more over the years and gotten a feel for the office culture. But besides the fact she had a complicated relationship with her father, she rarely had time in between school and appointments. And after meeting snarky-ass Sophie all those years back, her desire to visit turned to nil.

Stepping past her easel with her latest work in progress, an ocean-at-dusk scene, she made a mental note to order more crimson, aquamarine, and yellow #5. She'd been too nervous this last week to work on the canvas, focusing instead on rereading old textbooks and conducting project-management internet searches. But hopefully this weekend she could buckle down for some serious self-soothing painting time.

The natural light bulbs on her chrome vanity illuminated her face and she stared. "Ugh." She could just imagine what her mom would say. Reflected in the mirror was her lack of sleep, plagued by dreams of wandering an empty parking garage, frantically seeking an unlocked door. She dabbed extra concealer under her eyes and heated her iron.

Thirty minutes later, Ella spritzed on heat oil spray and flat ironed her bangs one last time, *finally* achieving optimal smoothness. After years of having long, bang-free hair, it took some getting used to this new shoulder-length blunt bob. She pushed her chunky frames up with her forefinger and made her way through hallway one, then hallway two. The only sounds around were the quiet buzz of the housekeepers starting their daily routine. The place was eerily quiet. She refused to look at any of the six-foot-tall paintings of Italian women that lined the burgundy walls. She swore their gaze followed her, judging her behind the frames. She loved art and painting, but these ones had freaked her out since she was little. Sometimes she had this tingling sensation that they, or something, were following her. She'd bolt down the hall, or run up the stairs, and slam her door shut.

The kitchen had a fresh bouquet in the middle of the marble center island. Her mother was a stickler for the arrangements, usually requiring a mix of colors and sizes. This arrangement was all pink Stargazer lilies. Beautiful, but hopefully none of the staff were on the receiving end of her mom's disapproving frown and a passive-aggressive statement like, "It's okay. You must not have been given the right instructions."

"Umph." Ella's breath released as she opened the massive

stainless-steel double-door fridge to grab a quick breakfast. Facing her was a lunch bag with a note.

Good luck on your first day! So proud of you.

Mom

Despite herself, she grinned. Although her mom most definitely had someone make whatever was inside, it really was thoughtful. Needing to bolt out of here before her mom returned from Pilates, Ella double-checked that her emergency nasal spray was in her purse, and that her smartwatch with the medical alert had a full charge.

Let's do this. She texted Thomas, her driver, that she was ready to go.

Among a household of revolving-door staff where Ella long ago stopped trying to learn names, Thomas had been with her family since she could remember. He drove her family to doctor appointments, dinners, and random events. When she went to college, every day he dropped her off, then waited on a bench at the University of Washington's Red Square, or a "within jogging distance" coffee shop. She hated it... until she didn't. Especially after a particularly turbulent period during her sophomore year when she'd blink open her eyes to a sea of concerned bystanders, disorientated with a bloodied lip or nasty head bump. His face provided the comfort she needed to cut through a confusing blacking out.

When she was little, he seemed *so old*, like her parents. His blondish hair turned white in the summer, his cheeks were red like he carried a permanent sunburn. But over the last few years, she noticed the gray fanning his temples, the lines across his forehead deepening, the crinkling of his crow's feet spreading.

"Good morning, Ella." He held the door open, long ago

swapping the "Ms. Northwood" for "Ella" after she told him it felt weird for him to address her that way. He'd smiled that day and said that was his way of showing respect. She remembered thinking it was a funny statement since she was only thirteen.

She slid into the back and set her bags on the floor. "Morning."

That would be the extent of their conversation. Where her parents suffocated her daily with a blanket of questions, Thomas seemed to know during solo drives she needed time to rejuvenate in silence. She was never comfortable with small talk. Most any talk, really. During a high school junior year homeschooling class, she studied nature vs. nurture, and went to bed that entire week wondering if her aversion to eye contact and conversation was because she was born that way or was a product of her parents' forced isolation.

The massive black SUV bumped over the gaping down-town Seattle potholes like the dips were pesky puddles. Each jerk made her want to lurch, and she exhaled through her nose, breathing in sets of four. She closed her eyes. *I can do this. I can do this.*

Social media. That will help. As Thomas weaved through rush-hour traffic, with coffee shops, pho restaurants, and tourist T-shirt shops selling cheap, yet expensive, souvenirs zooming by, she scrolled. A blur of images and faces and reels overtook her space when her breath hitched. *Was that... No...* Ella's finger flew back until she confirmed what she saw. *Jasmine.* In a lip-locked, posed selfie with a mutual, the sun setting in the background creating the absolute perfect shadowed profiles.

Bet it took her an hour to pose. Whatever.

Ella enhanced the image. Was her ex really dating a former college-mate of Ella's? Or did Jasmine snap this photo knowing Ella was linked with this woman on social media? *Probably.* The level of mind-fuckery that took place during their yearlong rela-tionship could fill a book.

She shoved the phone back in her purse and stared out the window. Jasmine was the one who decided to bring someone else home that night, disregard her commitment to Ella, throw their relationship out the window like trash, like Ella was meaningless. The heartbreak was more than Ella ever thought possible. Her stomach knotted thinking of the night she discovered what Jasmine had done.

Gray clouds hovered, blanketing her in murkiness. Even with the windows closed, the damp, briny Puget Sound air filled the vehicle. She shivered against the luxury leather seat and snugged her jacket lapel. Seeing her ex was not the way she wanted to start her first day of work. She had to focus. Starting now, she would bring her A game every day until she could land a different job on her own.

The car eased into its double-parked position. She'd long ago accepted the fact that her family had a driver. But was it necessary to have a twelve-mile-a-gallon giant that was the least subtle car known to exist? She didn't love the fact that five times out of ten when she stepped out, bystanders tossed disappointed glances. People probably hoped she was a celebrity. Or maybe they scowled because she was contributing to the ozone layer deterioration.

Thomas opened the door. "Happy first day." He inched closer. "You're going to do amazing."

Those hushed words and the genuine tone delivering them was the boost she needed. She thanked him and pulled in a deep breath.

A hint of cherry blossom scent wafted to her nose from a budding tree. She stepped onto the sidewalk, careful not to slip with her low heels on cracked pavement. The last thing she needed was a nosedive on the sidewalk.

She tugged the strap of the luxury cross-body laptop bag her mother bought her and glanced up at the skyscraper that would be her home for the next few months. The career self-help book she read last week repeated in her mind. *Look people in the eye, smile, firm handshake. I can do this.* Her first real day of work, earning money that was *actually* hers. Her parents were staunch regurgitators of the phrase *Just because we're rich doesn't mean you are.* They aligned to the philosophy that they would never give her enough money to live on her own, otherwise she wouldn't properly understand the value of a dollar. Which she called bullshit on as her mom handed out this lecture over the years while drinking from her heirloom teapot that cost more than most people's weekly income. And she called double bullshit as her mother never worked a day in her life, after being handed down money from grandparents to parents to her. Ella knew in her core that withholding finances wasn't only to teach ethics or fiscal responsibility. It was another way to tighten her golden handcuffs, which may have worked for a while. But she'd be damned to let them hold her hostage much longer.

A metro's electric wires banged against its metal roof and the bus screeched to a high-pitched stop. And out popped Sophie, headphones wrapped around her buzzed head, rocking a retro '80s punk-singer outfit with a skull-patterned skirt, backpack, and off-the-shoulder black shirt. *Ugh.* If Ella even attempted to pull off an outfit like that, she'd look ridiculous. Cool was never a word one would use to describe her. Not that she hadn't tried. Two years ago, she made a nose-piercing appointment and freaked out when the guy approached her with forceps and a giant needle. And here, Sophie had her lip, nose, ear cartilage, probably even nipples pierced. Ella tapped her fingers on her neck and thanked herself for at least having the foresight to swap her strand of pearls this morning for the gold clasp.

A couple of cars honked behind Thomas and swerved, and the heat of a stare bored into her. She peeked at Sophie, who held an unreadable expression. Sophie's gaze flicked between

Ella and the monster SUV, her mouth twisted in an odd half smirk, half frown. Ella may not have decoded the expression, but her body did, and a sickly bubble rose in her chest.

Whatever. A lot of people had drivers, right? Okay, that wasn't entirely true. Growing up, she hadn't even questioned it. Only when she turned ten or eleven did she start to notice how different she looked from other kids tripping out of cars at the mall. The hot second she spent in a certain prep school in the greater Seattle area (yes, *that* one), she distinctly remembered a fleet of black SUV and sedans. Not all were parents dropping off kids. Right?

Sophie stomped over, thigh-high, thick black boots with buckles running down the side.

Cursing herself for forgetting to do one final lipstick-to-teeth mirror check, Ella ran her tongue over the ridges.

"Morning." Sophie removed her headphones and hung them from her neck. "First day. You ready?"

Not even for a second. "Yes." Ella held back a smile until she could verify MAC Ruby Woo lipstick hadn't seeped onto her pearly whites.

The SUV pulled into traffic, and Sophie's gaze followed it down the street. "Funny how vehicles like that think rules don't apply to them and can double-park and hold up traffic."

Vehicles like that. Ella's face heated. It didn't take a genius to catch what Sophie was throwing. Ella bristled and walked toward the large glass doors. "I've seen plenty of Uber and Lyft drivers doing the same."

Sophie glared, and Ella felt a surge of satisfaction in seeing defeat.

Sophie stepped ahead and looped her backpack behind both arms. A large button pinned to the top featured a feminine flying superhero with a rainbow cape and the words *Have no fear; I'm here and queer.*

It wasn't any of Ella's business if Sophie was queer. And she didn't appreciate the tiny tingle that manifested in her belly from knowing that information.

"After you." Sophie held the door open.

Ella wondered if Sophie was being polite, or digging at her perceived princess-nature. Ella couldn't help but sense it was a dig.

The building was too quiet, with only a few folks trickling through the lobby, sipping coffee with AirPods glued to their ears and faces buried in cells. Ella squared her shoulders and tried to ignore the amplified clacking of her heels against the waxed floor as she moved toward the elevator. She cleared her throat, part to mask the sound, part to rid herself of whatever tacky monstrosity was happening in the back of her throat, part to cut the thick tension lingering in the air.

Was Sophie nervous? Even a little? Ella shot a quick side-glance at her and... *nope*. Thumbs looped through the backpack straps. A foot tapping against the floor to whatever was still streaming through her headphones. Blinking up at the flashing floor numbers. She had no idea what a monumental moment this was.

In all fairness, Sophie couldn't possibly know. That Ella being here, now, meant Ella was on the cusp of changing her life. That what happened that night with her parents might be worth it... The threats... the words she screamed... She shook her head. She refused to revisit that moment.

Her phone buzzed, and she swiped it open.

Reminder: *Appointment at UW Med.* 11:00 *a.m.*

Crap. How had she forgotten to cancel? She shoved the phone into her bag. No chance in hell she'd leave early on her first day and let Sophie think she was getting another favor.

"The facilities person should've set up your desk by mine." Sophie stared ahead.

Was Sophie avoiding eye contact? Hard to tell. Maybe she wasn't a morning person. Or maybe Ella should apologize for being a total shit yesterday.

The elevator door opened, and Ella followed Sophie. Tables with dangling cords and monitors sprawled before her. They rounded a corner to the "Creative Hub" space, with long working tables, empty rolling chairs, funky lamps, and strange bobbleheads strewn on the desks. Ella breathed through the belly knots at seeing her home for the next few months.

"You'll be sitting right next to me until we get through this." Sophie jerked her finger towards a vacant space next to Sophie's with nothing but a monitor and docking station.

Sophie's space wasn't messy, per se. It felt more lived in. Seasoned, almost. The half wall had an oversized Sasquatch mug stuffed with pens and highlighters shoved up against it. A faded rainbow mouse pad held the mouse. Stacks of Post-it notepaper and several notepads scattered the desk. In the corner, a tiny-framed photo of Sophie, a pretty blond woman, and a kid.

Ella glanced at her own space. The area felt too sanitized, even a little sad. "Where will I sit after training?"

"No idea. Not up to me."

Je-sus. It was not like she asked Sophie for her blood type. The snark was at skyscraper level, and it wasn't even 7:30 yet.

"Gonna grab coffee." Sophie walked away without an invitation for Ella to join. Not that she needed one. Ella was just fine sitting here in the creepy open space, with strange radiator sounds and the jarring electric buzz of fluorescent lighting, thank you very much. The second Sophie rounded the corner, Ella grabbed her purse mirror and checked her teeth.

Opening her laptop, she logged into the software she'd be using, and tried hard to remember all the passwords. Yesterday, the IT guy had put the fear of the technology god into her that she had to memorize her passwords, but she had multiple different logins on several platforms. She'd finally settled on "IcanDoThis#90days." She wouldn't forget that one.

"You getting all set up?" Sophie stirred the coffee, then chucked the stir stick into the wastebasket a good ten feet away.

"Impressive."

Sophie's lip bounced as she lifted the corner of her mouth. Oh boy. That mouth. How had Ella forgotten how pretty it was? Sophie had a pair of lips that people don't normally forget. Maybe it was the ring accentuating the Cupid's bow shape, the small gap in between her front teeth, the plump, nearly symmetrical top and bottom. Or maybe it was because Sophie was wearing gloss and the moisture drew Ella in. Or maybe Ella needed more than a yearly hookup and her body was making her very aware that her last hookup was almost twelve months ago.

"Today, we'll develop a solid workback schedule." Sophie flipped open the laptop and patted the space next to her.

Ella gave one firm nod. Exhale, inhale. *I belong here as much as anyone else.* She vowed to keep saying that to herself until the words sank in. Slipping into the chair near Sophie, Ella couldn't help but indulge in the surprising scent drifting from Sophie's skin. She thought Sophie would smell like leather and bourbon, but instead, coconut and vanilla wafted to her nose.

Thank God Ella remembered building several mock workback schedules during her final year in college. But just because she knew how to build a project plan backwards in school didn't mean she had any idea how to do it in the real world.

"You want to take that one?" The keyboard clicked like gunfire under Sophie's fingers.

Ella's cheeks burned. "Oh, um..." This project management software looked totally different than the one she'd used in college, which was like a spreadsheet. As she frantically clicked the mouse, fancy colors, headings, and different navigation, fields blurred in front of her. She barely knew how to log into this platform, much less navigate to the right places.

Sophie glanced at Ella with a tilted head. "Don't worry about it. I got it."

Whew. The tightness in Ella's chest released at the surprising kind words. Maybe Sophie wasn't completely horrible.

"Sorry. I keep forgetting you've never worked before."

And now her chest turned cold.

The next two hours muddled with content documentation, terminology, and training videos when Sophie's phone rang, interrupting the tornado of information. She grabbed it on the second ring. "What's up, kiddo? You good?"

Ella's ears perked up at the gentleness. She tried to busy herself with reading asset-approval documentation, but the curiosity nipped.

"I mean, you called without texting first, so clearly I assumed that a demon crawled out from that sketchy-ass cellar in the basement and was dragging you by the ponytail down the hall, and this was my time to lecture you that if you'd just shave your head like me, then you could avoid these types of mishaps." Sophie grinned, and several moments passed. "Okay, yes, for sure. I promise. I'll be there." She hung up and faced Ella. "Sorry about that."

"Sister?" Ella asked, curious about what would soften Sophie like that in a snap.

Sophie exhaled. "Sort of? She's my best friend's younger sister, Harper. But we're tight. I don't have any siblings, so I kind of adopted her as my own." She turned back to her laptop. "And by adopt, I mean I basically forced Harper to pretend she was my sister when we were growing up."

A tenderness filled Ella with Sophie's light chuckle.

Sophie peeked at Ella with the corner of her eye. "You have any siblings?"

I wish. For so many years Ella wished for a sibling. When she was younger, she tried everything to will it to happen—squinting as hard as she could at the stars and crossing her fingers while begging, throwing coins into each one of their four Greek god stone water fountains on their property, rubbing a crystal rock her aunt gave her. Friends were minimal, she had no close cousins, and she just knew if she had a sibling, she wouldn't always feel like *this.* Lost, or wondering if the thoughts in her head were healthy, or wondering if her parents were terrible or good. She'd have someone to play with besides a nanny or her mom.

Ella rolled her lips into her mouth. "No," she finally said.

A slight tilt of the head, and Sophie cleared her throat. "All right, launch date is May 15th. That's exactly..." She counted on the calendar on her computer. "... thirty-eight business days from now. Although we'll probably end up working some weekends, so let's say forty."

If Ella didn't know any better, she'd swear Sophie's tone softened.

Ella poised her fingers above the keyboard, clicking at a furious rate as Sophie rattled off information about buffering in a week in case leaders went off in a different creative direction, talking about aligning on the vision, and building strategy. "And we always, *always* need to do a final handoff to the legal department, no matter what."

"Got it." *Don't got it. Don't got it.*

The room spun as Sophie kept talking. Ella's fingers couldn't keep up. Her mouth grew dry, her lower back beaded with sweat. "Wait. I thought the leadership approvals had to be done before creative approvals."

Sophie returned a deadpan stare.

Stupid, stupid, stupid. Ella swallowed. "No, sorry. I just misspoke."

The screen popped up an error message and Ella froze. Did

she press a wrong button? As Sophie continued talking, Ella pounded on the delete button. Nothing. *Come on!* Why wasn't it working? Sophie's going to think she was an idiot. Multiple mouse clicks and hitting escape like a lunatic did nothing. Her pulse thumped in her throat. She hooked a finger in her collar, pulling away the fibers sticking to her neck.

Her arm flung out to grab the reusable water bottle, but instead knocked it over, the metal clanking with a shriek against the desk. "Shit! Sorry." She swiped it up, fumbled her grip, and breathed out a prayer of thanks she had kept the top covered.

A gentle hand rested on hers. "Breathe, okay?" Sophie's eyes softened as she stared at the red error message of death on Ella's computer. She sighed and leaned forward. Her sweater dipped, exposing a rounded, creamy shoulder with a constellation of freckles on the upper arm, and a hint of a racerback lace bra.

Ella averted her gaze.

"This program can be super finicky," Sophie said. "It's not your fault. Go back to the home screen."

Ella slunk back into her chair, the thudding pulse lowering. "Thank you."

Sophie returned to slapping at the keyboard. "Once we get set up, we'll set a kickoff meeting..."

Soon, people began funneling through the office doors. Chatter and key taps thundered in the air. Ella took notes and updated a timeline using Sophie's guidelines on time buffering when the large corner doors swung open, ricocheting into the wall with a thud.

"Teamwork makes the dream work!" Her dad's booming voice filled the space how only it could.

Ella rolled her eyes.

His slicked-back, pomaded, thinning black hair bounced with each heavy stomp. Pulling his lips back for a wide, toothy grin, he patted a guy on the back, tipped a phantom hat at a woman in the corner, and smacked his palms together with a piercing pop. "How's it going, you two?"

God, he's loud.

Ella bristled and avoided Sophie's gaze. It was inevitable, of course. She worked at her father's company. Everyone here surely knew this was her dad, but they didn't need a constant reminder. She may not have landed this job on her own, but she was damn grateful for the opportunity and determined to bust her butt to prove she earned her place. A terrible memory of her in a dance troupe class when she was ten flashed into her mind. She'd thought she was a good ballerina, great even. Her mom had told her a million times and cheered the loudest at rehearsals. But behind the backstage velvet curtains, she'd heard the dance instructor say, "We know Ella's not gifted like the other students, but her parents are huge donors, so..."

Fourteen years later, the words still scarred.

"Sophie, this isn't high school, you know. Hazing is totally legal and encouraged for new hires." Her dad laughed with a sharp crack, and nudged Sophie with an elbow. "You can take it. Right, El?"

Ella wanted to crawl in a hole. No, a crater. No, she wanted to catapult to the deepest, darkest part of the solar system. She needed to hide from whatever the hell look was on Sophie's face, with her lips pulled tight into her mouth. She was either trying not to laugh or seriously annoyed, and neither one was great for Ella.

"Sure can." Ella smoothed out the top of her sleeves. Like it or not, her dad was her boss. She had to play the subservient employee-daughter game for just a few months. Then she could break free. Run like she was being chased, strip off the shackles that had been on her since birth.

"So, we are, um, just locking things down here, Da—" She was *this close* to saying *Dad*, but sucked back the words. "Did you need something?"

Her dad smiled. "Nope, just making sure you're putting your best foot forward. Don't try to boil the ocean on day one." He pivoted on his freshly shined loafers.

Someone she didn't recognize muttered, "*Bingo.*"

Sophie coughed through a grin and turned back to her computer screen.

An hour shy of lunchtime, Sophie rose from her chair and rolled it under her desk. "Follow me."

Oh, thank God. As invigorating as it was being in the trenches, Ella needed a brain break. She trailed Sophie, pulling back her shoulders as Sophie led her past several glass-encased rooms. They stepped into a large, stark-white conference room where a smattering of folks huddled around a table. Besides a whiteboard wall and an impressive array of markers, the room was totally barren.

"Hey, everyone." Sophie's smile turned warm and genuine, and Ella wasn't sure why that bothered her. "Thanks so much for being here. Super-quick pre-kickoff meeting to let you know what's ahead. We all got the timing for the new project. It's okay, let it out, we can collectively groan now."

A couple people did actually groan, and Sophie chuckled. "Now that we have that out of the way..."

Sophie was 5'2" at very most. But in this moment, as she rattled off the project's needs, timelines and expectations, she seemed a million feet tall. All eyes focused on her, furrowed brows and wicked fingers transcribing her words. Ella studied her, absorbed by what made this team respond to Sophie this way, made them lean forward in silence like they were afraid of missing anything she may utter. She was confident, yes, but her shoulders weren't tight the way Ella's mom told her to show self-assuredness. Sophie looked comfortable, at ease, even, like she was rattling off a menu at a pub.

Would anyone ever see Ella that way? Or was she destined

to live a purgatorial life, always looked at as someone who received without earning?

"And... as I'm sure you all know we have a newbie in the house." Sophie motioned toward Ella. "Everyone welcome Ella Northwood to the team."

A half wave was all Ella could muster at the sea of faces. She stared directly above everyone's heads to avoid collapsing on the spot from the invasive stares.

"Northwood like George?" some guy in a hoodie, who looked like he smelled like a gamer in a basement, called out from the back. Nearly everyone in the room threw him a distinct *duh* look. Either he missed the memo, or he was an ass for pointing it out.

"Yep, boss's daughter, so everyone be nice," Sophie said, her tone flat.

Ella's chest burned. At this agency, she'd never be anything other than her father's daughter. To the rest of the world, she'd never be more than her mother's daughter, reaping the benefits of generational wealth. She had no merit. Her only clout was her last name. All eyes focused on her, measuring her, probably staggering through a laundry list of reasons why they had to accommodate her.

Maybe Sophie meant to call out the elephant in the room. Or maybe she'd meant to humiliate her. Ella ignored her dampening pits and forced her lips to twitch into a grin.

"Okay, that's it." Sophie wrapped up the meeting half an hour later. "Get your manis, pedis, and Reiki sessions in now while you still have a chance. It's going to be a crunch once strategy comes in."

The team scattered as quickly as they arrived, and Ella followed Sophie back to the desk. An anxious pit developed in Ella's stomach, and no matter how much she tried to force it, her head refused to hold high.

Instant messaging, a trip to the IT department, and

reviewing archived creative filled the next couple of hours. Ella's stomach bellowed with a fury, and she peeked to see if Sophie noticed. Sophie's eyes remained focused on her screen, minus the few smiles she directed at everyone but Ella.

Seriously, what was Sophie's problem, anyway? *She* was the rude one. Ella had only ever acted in defense. Never the aggressor.

Sophie snapped her laptop shut and rolled her chair away from the desk. "I'm starving. Gonna grab some lunch."

Ella checked her watch. "How long do we get for lunch?"

Sophie's irritated stare was like Ella asked her how much she weighed. "We're adults and treated as such. Take whatever you need."

Seriously? Did every single word she muttered need to be done with such annoyance? Sophie spun on her chunky boots and speed-walked across the room.

Ella beelined it for the bathroom to fan her face and remove sticky cashmere threads from her chest and Sophie's coconut vanilla scent from her mind.

That was it. Tomorrow, cotton only.

FIVE
SOPHIE

The soggy ground squished beneath Sophie's feet, the moss and mud feeling like pebble-filled putty under her heels. Damp, green air filled the surrounding space. Her lungs were heavy, her airway cut off, the breath constricted in her throat. "I... can't... breathe."

A slap on the arm met those words. "Dude. We've been hiking for like ten minutes." Maya rolled her eyes. "You are the most dramatic human alive."

Sophie grunted and followed Maya up the trail. Easy for Maya to say. She was an avid runner, ate like a nutritionist, and always got a proper eight hours of sleep. Sophie ate Goldfish crackers, if anything, for breakfast, hadn't worked out for months, and often fell asleep with a laptop on her chest.

It wasn't always this way. Sophie loved hiking. The burning lungs, dry mouth, and sweat mixing with mist were a small price for the elation of reaching the top. For years, she'd done this on the weekends—Cougar Mountain, Tiger Mountain, Mount Si, Snoqualmie Falls, even Mount Rainier. Okay, fine, not the *entire* mountain as that was reserved for the hard-core, uber-fit, and ultra-prepared, but she had done a Paradise trail multiple times, reaching high enough to touch snow in June.

But since the promotion to project manager, physical activity had taken a nosedive. Walking to the bus stop or forcing herself to take the stairs at work was about the gist of her weekly cardio.

Ten more minutes and the burn subsided. The fern-filled air turned refreshing, even rejuvenating. She concentrated on stepping over the rocks and fallen tree trunks lining the path, inhaling the cedar and Douglas fir scent, her backpack slapping against her body with each stride. The mist cooled her face, and she tugged off her knit hat to let the moisture touch her buzzed scalp.

No words were spoken, per their rule going up, unless it was "passing on your left" or "excuse me" as slower hikers shifted to the side. This was meditation time, and Sophie took that as seriously as Maya. While ascending, she didn't need to think about work or project plans or deadlines. Nor would she noodle on the fact that she was wasting her prime mate-finding years by marrying herself to Mahogany and Moon. Right now, her work was her love, her life, her mistress. She couldn't tear herself away.

Just because she didn't *need* to think about work, didn't mean her mind listened. Her thoughts drifted to Ella and the first week they'd completed. Was it as terrible as Sophie had expected? No. Was it still terrible? Yes. Much to her surprise, and a bit of annoyance, Ella worked hard. She drafted memos, took detailed notes, hung on every word. She'd tuck her dark hair behind her ear, revealing a cute, petite earlobe with a small hoop earring, and lean forward to bang against her laptop.

But Sophie hated that when she finally got the chance to train someone, be a real mentor, even a leader, Ella was the trainee. When Sophie looked at Ella, the humiliation of their first meeting boomed front and center and smacked the patience from her. The look she got that first day was the same from the popular girls in school, the ones who ganged up outside of Sophie's bathroom stall, snickering at her clothes, saying no matter how often she washed it, the secondhand store smell was imbedded into the fabric.

Her foot skidded on a rock and she'd never been more grateful for her well-worn Timberlands than right now.

"You good?" Maya asked.

"Yep." Sophie rolled her ankle and kept moving.

Higher and higher, the air turned thinner, the light fog like a smoke machine. The top was within sight. Hundred feet, fifty... twenty.

"My God. Look at that." Maya threw her hands on her hips and stared out.

Sophie unzipped her nylon raincoat, flopped down on the earth, and guzzled one of two water bottles. Her heartbeat pounded so hard she could feel her neck skin stretch against the vein. She pulled her knees to her chest and wrapped her arms around her shins.

From up here, she could see the world. She swore if she could stretch just the tiniest bit, she could touch the clouds. Mountains surrounded her, evergreen trees touched the sky. The lake below was an oasis, so peaceful it looked as if it wasn't moving.

Sophie had never been a believer. Agnostic, maybe, but she never put too much thought into spirituality. But up here was God's country.

"Here." Maya passed over a protein shake. "Got to keep those blood sugars regulated."

Sophie downed the chalky chocolate, feeling the mucky substance slide down her throat. *Ick.* "Your obsession with blood sugars is truly remarkable." Maya would know she was kidding. Maya's younger sister, Harper, was a type 1 diabetic, and Maya was almost a year into her master's focusing on diabetes. Besides her family, friends, and Remi, Sophie swore Maya's true love was plasma and platelets. "Well, catch me up on the latest. How are things with you and Remi? Ben? I feel like I'm so behind on everything."

"You are." Maya wiped off her mouth with the back of her hand. She leaned back against her palms and her gaze followed the outline of the trees. "Remi. God, I love that woman. So much. I know we U-Hauled pretty quick—"

"It wasn't *that* quick. I mean, you were together, what, like, six months before you all officially moved in together."

Maya crossed her legs and leaned on her elbows. "I'm going to ask her to marry me—"

"What! Maya, that's amazing. I'm so—"

"Whoa. Slow down, tiger. *Someday. Someday* I'm going to ask her to marry me." Maya laughed. "She's my everything."

Her voice turned soft, and sincere, and Sophie's heart pinched. Yes, of course she was happy for her friend. Maya deserved love and companionship more than any other human on earth. But a tiny part of Sophie couldn't help but wonder... *Will that ever be me?*

"And this is super on the DL right now, but Ben is talking more and more about settling down with someone or a couple. Remi said she's never seen him like this before."

"Oh yeah?" She'd gotten to know Ben over the last year a bit, and had liked him immediately. Quick with his bright smile, funny, loyal to his core. But admittedly, the stories he told made it seem like he loved living in single-land.

"Yep. We're keeping our fingers crossed for him that he just finds some happiness, whatever that looks like." Maya readjusted her ponytail. "So... how's it going training the newbie?"

Sophie flicked her tongue against her lip ring. "Shitty."

Maya lifted a brow. "Really? Have you still not let go whatever it is you have to let go?"

No. "I'm over it." Of course that was a lie, and yes, Sophie knew she needed to move on. But feeling disrespected was a poison that burrowed deep and infected everything. Once you knew someone didn't respect you, the urge to change their mind felt all-consuming. "I really hate that the boss's daughter got a shot that took me four million years to get, just because she's the boss's daughter, you know? It's not fair. I've given up so much. Time with you and Harper, friends, relationships..."

"Sex." Maya released a puff through her nose.

She wasn't wrong.

"When was the last time you got laid?" Maya asked.

"You already know." Sophie picked up a stick and drew circles into the ground. "You love to grind my dry spell into me, huh?"

"Well, I do like grinding."

Sophie rolled her eyes. "Sorry, I don't have the time like you to get tongue blasted every day by my hot girlfriend."

"Oooh, Remi will love that you said that." Maya unwrapped a peanut butter sandwich and bit into a chunk. "And you're not wrong. The stamina with that one. Last night—"

"Nope." Sophie shuddered. She loved her bestie. But she had absolutely no desire to know her bedroom details. "Not another word."

Sophie's gaze followed a bald eagle soaring through the clouds, its wings flapping so effortlessly, yet with so much power, moving the majestic creature through the air. Deep breaths pulled through, and the silence of nature allowed her mind to drift. Maya might have been teasing, but Sophie knew she needed to make some changes.

Maybe after they landed the campaign, and after the cruise, she'd start dating. Her last serious relationship was in her teens. Her *teens*. Very few, one-to-two-month scattered relationships followed—which amounted into nothing more than the standard handful of dates, every-other-day texting, and both realizing it would never go further. And even that was at least two years ago. A onetime hookup last year with a woman she met around the block during happy hour was the last physical contact she'd had that was more than a hug.

The crisp air pulled through Sophie's nose and filled her lungs, and she exhaled slowly. She had already exceeded her first five-year plan, and was full swing into her second. If she kept going, kept this pace, kept showing up and killing it every day, she could move to senior PM and then manager within three years. Then senior manager, director, then vice president —her North Star. They'd feature her in "40 Under 40" articles, people would ask how she became so successful so young, how she rose through the ranks without a degree, how she managed to become vice president by *hustle alone*. The *Times* might pick up the article, *Forbes* would get in on the action, maybe KING 5 would request an exclusive. She could go on a speaking tour, or write a book on how to break into the corporate world with nothing but grit and resilience.

She deserved this. And it wasn't fair that Ella got the chance of a lifetime that Sophie busted her ass for. It wasn't fair that some kids wore designer clothes and vacationed in Hawaii, where the most she ever did was pop a tent at Deception Pass. She felt like she was losing the control, the power she gained, and wasted the shit sandwich she ate that first year in laughing at dumb old white man jokes, and running to get dry cleaning even though that was never on the job description.

"You ready?" Maya asked, cutting through her thoughts. "Might be time to head back."

Sophie shook out a breath, not nearly as relaxed as she hoped. "I think I need another minute."

6:30 a.m. was for punks. But yet, here Sophie was, seeking out caffeine to drag her through week two with Ella. *Ugh.* Yes, she was being ridiculous. But she couldn't help it. Her deep dislike for rich people had imbedded into her at a young age. It was irrational—*of course* it was irrational—but she swore rich people didn't feel. They *couldn't* feel, at least not to the depths that working-class or food-insecure people felt. If they were sad, they could just go buy something. A handbag, a Lambo, a designer-bred dog, to pull them out of their funk.

Rich people didn't need to prove their worth. Simply by status, they had the luxury to demand respect wherever they went. They could just get things. They never needed to work for things.

But *beautiful* rich people? *Pfffft*. People like Ella, with her apple cheekbones and thick, straight hair, and full, round hips that swayed when she walked. Not that Sophie was looking. She just noticed it once, maybe twice. This odd, probably indecent fascination in watching Ella move was simply Sophie's hormones acting haywire that fresh feminine energy had invaded her space.

Sophie loved women, of course, but she *really* loved women. Wanted to lift, validate, and support women, always. Matriarchy was next to godliness. But did Ella deserve her admiration? The way she made Sophie squirm, and not in the good way, indicated Sophie shouldn't be admiring her looks at all.

The special smells of body odor, perfume, and someone eating an egg sandwich engulfed the metro to downtown. Sophie breathed through her mouth as she scrolled through her podcast backlog and started an episode on brand messaging. Closing her eyes, she pushed away thoughts of Ella, and tried to absorb the content.

It was useless. All the way to her stop, Sophie's mind flashed images of Ella, with her irritating heart-shaped face, and those deep, warm brown eyes that reminded Sophie of fall, with leaves changing colors, burning wood scent, the feel of pulling on your favorite hoodie when the air turned crisp.

Gripping a coffee cup in hand, Sophie strolled the sidewalk.

Traffic, honks, and the zip of cyclists passing on the bike lane surrounded her. She flicked at the mist on her face. The brassy scent of moist pavement and brick reached her nose, and she leaned into the smell. She loved spring, the mist turning warmer than the winter mist, the sweetness of the cherry blossoms, the promise of needed sunshine.

She had so much work to do and tonight looked to be another late night. A pile of meetings, emails, and reviews sat heavy on her chest. She ran her palm against the prickles in her hair and inhaled. She could do this. She *would* do this. That cruise was hers, and nothing would stop her. She'd sleep at the office if needed to execute this campaign.

Growing up, she never went anywhere that wasn't within driving distance. Sure, she'd seen the ocean. Ocean Shores was only a few hours away. Oregon a few more hours. But this cruise meant she'd *be* with the ocean. Whale watching, saltwater, and coffee on the balcony.

Sophie stepped into the nearly vacant building. Five days until another Ella-free weekend. She rolled her shoulders like a fighter stepping into the ring and mentally prepared for her first meeting. Soon, a grin reached her lips. Ella may have been handed this job on a platter, but she'd never have Sophie's edge.

Being scrappy her entire life, she picked up on things that others may miss. Details mattered. The VP liked her coffee with sugar-free vanilla, and her love language was fancy, fine-point gel pens. The creative director had two kids, nine and eleven, who were obsessed with the Hunger Games. The senior director of accounting was an avid Seahawks fan, and never got over Russell Wilson leaving the team for the Broncos. Even with Ella unfairly getting this job, it would take years to learn these things. Sophie would inherently be better. She exhaled. Maybe she should cut Ella some slack.

Cut Ella and her perfect mouth some slack.

Dammit. Not again.

The elevator dinged and Sophie crossed onto the floor. Joan Jett blasted through her headphones, and she tried to pull the energy into her soul. She rounded the corner and saw Ella at the desk, with King George hovering over her. It was barely after 7:00 a.m., but they looked like they'd been here all day.

She lowered her headphones and inched forward but halted at their expressions. George's normal pompous-y, arrogant-y, salesman-y face carried a look that could only be described as fatherly—a frown, knotted eyebrows, a gentle hand on a shoulder. One that she'd seen many times over the years from her own dad accompanied with some variation of "I'm worried about you."

"Shh." Ella snapped the word quick and harsh, like a whip.

George stopped mid-sentence and morphed his face into a toothy grin. "Sophie Black. Just checking in to see if my daughter shared any embarrassing family stories."

Ella's nostrils flared, and she pulled her lips into a straight line.

Sophie unraveled her backpack from her shoulders as she approached. "Nope, not yet. Looking forward to them, though."

George stepped back and waved Sophie to her desk. "Sophie, did I ever tell you how I got my start? Delivering newspapers..."

Rain or shine. Snow or hail. Then worked his way up to answering phones in the classified section. Then moved to cutting and taping the ads, old-school-style, to see how they'd fit on the 12 x 22 page, to working in a small agency.

She waited for him to finish telling the story she heard at least once a year during the annual summer picnic. But at the end, she grinned—she always did. She could respect someone who started at the bottom and worked their way up.

"Point is," George said, "I see the good work you're doing, and it reminds me of me."

A bit of Sophie swelled with pride. She glanced at Ella to

see if she caught what he said about her. Goober or not, getting a compliment from the boss always felt good. And it felt doubly good that Ella heard it.

Ella cleared her throat. "Thanks for stopping by. I, uh, think we're good now."

George glanced between Ella and Sophie. Sophie swore she could see his wheels spinning, probably in the common father-adult daughter dance, weighing what he should and should not say. "Well, a guy can take a hint, am I right?"

Ella remained silent and thumbed her frames back up to the top of her nose, a low blush sweeping her neck. She tugged on her fitted button-down shirt, a surprising change from last week. Although the moment itself was tense, Ella looked more relaxed. Skinny jeans and a long cream-colored shirt that somehow made her skin look, well, creamier.

Sophie set up her station and vowed to keep her eyes on the prize. They were inching towards thirty working days left to complete the Devil's Doughnuts campaign, then... the cruise. A vacation. Saltwater. She, they, could do this.

"Ready to get back at it?" She had absolutely zero time to waste, and like it or not, she needed Ella's help to execute on time.

Ella nodded, flashed a fiery, quick side-glance. "You have no idea how ready I am."

SIX

ELLA

Ella slept hard. So hard that the banging on her door jolted her awake so quickly that she almost hit her head on her Victorian oak headboard. Her mom burst into her room and Ella tugged the comforter to her chest.

"Jesus Christ. Privacy much?" She seriously needed a place of her own. *Three months.* In three months, she'd have enough money. She would trade in her 15 x 20 walk-in closet, two sitting chairs, wraparound desk, and wrought-iron coffee table for a studio any day of the week. All she needed was a bed, her paint and easel, and her favorite lipstick. She was so close, she could almost taste freedom.

"Sorry, honey." Her mother's hand flew to her chest, gripping the top of her rose-gold silk robe. "You're normally up by now, and I was worried."

Worried. If ever a word existed that her mother muttered the most, this would be it.

Her mom tucked a frosted blond lock behind her ear. "It's not a good look for your father if you show up late to work."

Disappointment. That would be next on the list.

Ella snatched her glasses off the counter and squinted at the clock. 5:37 a.m. Her mom had a point. But the reason she'd been up at four every morning was from nightmares about lost emails or missed meetings—not because she needed the time to get ready.

And besides, how did her mom know she was up at four every morning? Actually, it didn't matter. Her mom had a freakish ability to know everything. Ella had even checked for nanny cams a few years back in her room, until she realized her mom wasn't really that terrible.

Ella cleared her throat. "Out. Please." She pointed to the door. Her mom pinched her lips, then pivoted on slippered feet and closed the door.

Ella flopped back onto the king-size bed and wrapped the cushy linen around her head. *Wednesday*. Hump day. Halfway-there day. By noon, the weekend would be closer than farther, and then she could take a couple days off from the Sophie firing squad, badgering her about timelines and experience and how many project schedules she'd built.

Part of her wished she could call Jasmine. Not actually *Jasmine*, but a someone. Their relationship may have ended in a disaster, but they had clicked and it had been so nice having someone to share things with. Ella had fallen, *hard*—until she had discovered who Jasmine really was.

Ella shook her head. Nope, today she would not go there. The lingering effects of getting hurt, losing trust, being *betrayed*, was a nasty, chronic disease. Sometimes, if she thought too hard about when she discovered Jasmine had cheated, and the way it tore her insides to shreds, she'd lose hope about finding a rela-tionship.

Today, she couldn't afford to be less than perfect. She shot out of bed and stumbled into the bathroom.

The shower eased some tension. After taking her medica-tion and finishing hair and makeup, she fastened on her smart-watch, threw on jeans and a soft sweater—not cashmere, never making that mistake again—and thudded down the winding stairs. The savory scent of fried pork filled the air, and she followed the salt-cloud to the kitchen.

Her mother was sitting at the breakfast table in the corner overlooking Lake Washington. She was leaning forward with her new bifocals perched on top of her nose, staring at the laptop screen. Papaya and cantaloupe sat on the side. She bit into an avocado toast with crumbled prosciutto and glanced up. "Is it casual week? You've been dressing awfully... down."

Ella shifted in her clothes and moved to the fridge. "I work at a marketing firm. Everyone dresses down."

Her mom lifted a coffee mug to her lips. "Not your father."

Solid point. Why *was* he always dressed up? He clearly didn't make the staff dress like that, and he was the boss. Maybe she'd ask him later today, but she was still heated from how he'd cornered her on Monday morning. He'd droned on about the pressures of work and how she might feel more comfortable in a part-time capacity. Thank God Sophie appeared to not hear any of their conversation, or Ella would have officially lost it on him.

"Are you hungry?" her mom asked. "I sent Lydia away, but could call her back and have her prepare something. Maybe poached eggs? Brioche toast with jam?"

Ella grabbed a green juice and shook her head. She was perfectly capable of making her own food and did not need a staff member to cook it. Besides, when she lived on her own, she'd need to do these things herself. She rummaged through the massive pantry and pulled out a croissant and butter. "What are you working on?"

Her mom stuck a fork into a piece of cantaloupe. "Reading through a few emails for the Seattle Cocktail Wars."

The narrative in Ella's head that her mother never worked wasn't fair. Granted, she didn't *need* to work, and she'd never had a formal 9-to-5, but she threw herself into a couple of key philanthropist events throughout the year. Seattle Cocktail Wars—where the top greater-Seattle service industry professionals competed against each other in field-day-style competitions—was her favorite.

Ella spread the butter on the croissant and tore off a chunk. "Did Dad leave for work?"

"Yes, but Thomas will be back any second to take you."

"I'm going to Uber today." Ella popped a bite in her mouth and gathered lunch items.

Her mom's head tilted. "Why would you take an Uber?"

"Trying something different. Consider this my act of rebellion for the week."

Her mom lifted a brow. "I thought your act of rebellion was wearing those pants with those shoes."

Of course, her mom wouldn't understand giving up the luxury and convenience of having a driver, for the chance that Sophie, or any other co-worker, would see her dropped off by a town car. And maybe a week ago, she wouldn't have fully understood herself, either. In the U District, with so much car and foot traffic, people shuffling from class to class, or barreling down The Ave to get pad thai, no one paid attention. A certain anonymity existed in campus life.

But now, being around working people, feeling the same crunch herself of earning dollars for independence, she was hyper-aware of the perception.

It's not like she hadn't asked her parents for the money to move out. Her mom had lamented about how when they had over ten thousand square feet of living space, there was no reason for her to get her own place. Here, she had a staff to attend to needs, her art studio, Thomas... She didn't even have to do her own laundry. Her mom tackled this ask with a kind voice, talked about how difficult it would be for Ella to wash dishes and learn how to clean clothes and mop floors. And she should realize how blessed she was, and why would she want anything else? "It's like slapping the less fortunate in the face," her mom had said.

That statement had made zero sense to Ella.

When Ella had shifted into begging, her mom snapped and said if she moved out, she'd refuse to support her at all. Credit cards gone. Cash allowance gone. Sure, she had a modest trust fund, but that was wrapped up in more lawyers than a celebrity sex-scandal case, and she couldn't access it until she was thirty-five. Which at this point may as well be a hundred.

Her mom added a dash of creamer to her coffee and stirred. "Did you reschedule the doctor appointment you missed last week?"

Ella opened the Uber app. "Ah, no. Not yet."

"What? Why not?"

She avoided what was surely her mother's heated gaze and hand pressed against her heart like she was warding off a heart attack. Why hadn't Ella gone? Because the very last thing she needed was to leave work early and have Sophie shoot dagger eyes all day for Ella getting more special treatment.

"Ella. Jean. Northwood."

Great. The full name. Ella was twenty-four and still cringed at the tone.

"When are you going to reschedule? I can do it for you."

She glanced up at her mom's fierce gaze and swallowed. "I've got it."

Her mother pressed her slim hands on the table and sucked in a breath through her teeth. "Epilepsy is nothing to take lightly. You always want control and to not listen to a word we say, but this is serious. I don't think you understand the implications—"

"You don't think you've pounded this into my head since I was nine? I *don't* take it lightly. My whole fucking world revolves around making sure I am doing everything right, avoiding things, not avoiding things, med schedule, nasal spray, my alarm, everything." She exhaled fire. "I just need to reschedule. Christ."

Her mom barely flinched at the tone, or the cursing, and Ella's stomach turned. She hated that any time she was frustrated, her mom took the brunt of her outbursts. Deep down, she knew it wasn't right or fair.

"We're just worried." Her mother crossed her arms. "With this new medication, we just don't know when something may trigger a seizure."

"Enough! Okay? Jesus Christ, I get it."

Her mom's gritted teeth made it look like she was on the verge of smacking something or tears, and at this point, Ella couldn't handle either one.

Ella softened her stance, stuffed the rest of the lunch in a bag, tossed in an ice pack, and zipped. "I appreciate you looking out for me. I really do. Just—"

"Just what?" her mom demanded.

Just... I can't breathe. Ella couldn't stomach looking at her parent's face like she was a fragile doll that would splinter if the wind hit hard enough. Sometimes it felt like salt and ash soaked the air, and no matter how much she pulled in, she couldn't fill her lungs.

And how could she explain that it felt as if she lived in a prison? Sure, the prison was luxurious and huge and filled with everything she needed—except freedom. She ached to swap her luxury Egyptian cotton sheets and bathroom suite and Victorian dressers for something that was only hers. "Nothing, Mom. I'm really sorry I worried you. I got this, I promise."

The fruit plate was pushed aside, and her mother rested her head into her hands. "I can't have anything happen to you. I just... I'd never forgive myself." The tiniest crack left her mom's normally stoic voice.

And there it was—that pained look, followed by a crushing guilt that consumed Ella and made her want to bolt.

Ella could never fathom what her parents felt when they went from chatting over banana pancakes to having your child seize on the kitchen floor. Apparently, there was no warning. No genetics, no head trauma, no prenatal trauma, nothing. For years, they visited every doctor, every specialist, flew all over the country, to find out when, how, and why these occurred. The doctors put Ella on different medications, ones that hurt her stomach, or made her sleep for half a day, or made her head scream in pain. She had terrifying electrodes attached to her hair, and she cried at night trying to remove the glue. Her mother, panicked that Ella would seize in her sleep, kicked her dad into one of the guest rooms, and had Ella sleep next to her for years.

Short, quick visions emerged of her un-showered mom lying in her bed, exhausted and crying. She remembered one night hearing horrifying sounds coming from her dad's office, and was sure that an injured animal had snuck through the window. But instead of seeing a cow or horse, she saw his shoulders crumpled and shaking, his hearty laughter swapped for a hollowed sob.

But then her mother channeled all her fear into suffocating Ella. She seemed to believe if she controlled everything, she could protect Ella. No matter how strong, how emotionless her mom appeared, Ella saw it in her face. She was fifty-five, but looked older. All the forehead Botox and fancy skin cream in the world couldn't hide the worry bags around her eyes.

Ella's phone beeped that the Uber had arrived. *Thank God.* "Gotta go. I promise, I'll call the doctor later today." As she went to toss the phone in her purse, an email notification popped up from Sophie. Her gaze flew across the screen.

Her mother called out something, but Ella ignored her. Right now, Ella had more pressing items to attend to.

SEVEN
SOPHIE

Sophie pulled open the door to her favorite coffee shop, Sugar Mugs. A quaint shop plunked in the middle of a residential neighborhood, where the owner, Charlie, had converted the house's downstairs living space into the shop. The deep hues of freshly brewed espresso hit Sophie's nose, and soon she was in a sea of rainbows, plants, and Macklemore. She had to smile... Charlie had an obvious fascination with the Seattle rapper.

The line moved swiftly, as two baristas built drinks while Charlie charmed the customers at the till. Sophie reached the counter and grinned at Charlie, who pushed her long, curly red braid away from her face. "Sophie, hey! Haven't seen you for a minute."

Sophie dug out her wallet. "I know, I've been stupid busy at work."

"Isn't that the theme of your life? Or so Maya says." Charlie grabbed an empty cup and a marker. "What can I get you?"

"Something salty and sugary and super terrible for me."

"I have the perfect one." Charlie waved the Sharpie in the air. "Loving your outfit."

Sophie flashed her hand across her Guns N' Roses T-shirt,

ripped cropped mom jeans, and flannel. "This old thing?" She laughed, hating that it took her longer than normal to pick out a *I don't care* (*but I actually really care*) outfit. "When did you chat with Maya?" A small ache in Sophie's heart grew that besides the recent hiking trip, everyone else saw her best friend more than her.

"We had movie night with her, Remi, and Ben a couple days ago." Charlie scribbled on a cup and set it behind her. "I hope you can make it one of these times."

Work sucked every ounce of Sophie's free time. It wasn't lost on her that she stopped receiving invites for most things. Maya still let her know about movie nights, but it was clear no one expected her to show.

But soon, work would calm down, and she could live a more balanced life. Once she finished this Devil's Doughnuts campaign, things would change. Her inner voice whispered snidely that she'd been saying this line to herself for the last six years.

She shushed it.

She crossed over to the order pickup line and swiped through work emails on her phone.

"Have you ever thought we are in one of those strange, universal swirls, like *The Matrix* or something?" Charlie asked while frothing milk. "Maybe more like queer *Days of Our Lives*?"

Sophie lowered her cell. "What do you mean?"

"Your bestie is stupidly in love with my bestie's roommate."

A very small queer world indeed. Charlie's best friend, Ben, had been roommates with Maya's girlfriend, Remi, since they were teens. "And now your bestie sees my bestie more than me."

"That's a lot of besties happening. I'm already confused." Charlie handed her the drink. "Maybe we should dump them, and you and I can become besties."

"I kind of love that idea." Sophie blew into the cup and took a small sip, the salted caramel and chocolate flavor hitting her taste buds. *Yum.* She glanced around the filled coffee shop for Charlie's girlfriend. "Is Mack around?"

Charlie wiped a minor spill in front of Sophie. "No, she's with her dad. They had a super early tee time."

"Golfing?" Sophie asked. "I can't even picture that."

"I know. She was all paranoid about getting grass stains." Charlie tossed the rag behind her. "This is good for her." A group of customers entered the shop, and Sophie moved to a table.

Sophie breathed a sigh of relief that Mack wasn't here. Mack was a talented author and Sophie, much like most of the country, had devoured her debut thriller a few years back. Sophie tried not to flush at the memory of when she'd attended Mack's book signing in Seattle and shamelessly flirted with the woman. *So embarrassing.* Of course, she'd had no idea Mack was with Charlie at the time. The few times she'd seen Mack since then, Mack never said anything, and Sophie never said anything. Instead, she prayed to the lesbian gods that Mack forgot about the interaction.

As mortifying as that situation was, it also highlighted a dejecting truth—the interaction with Mack was one of a few times in recent memories that Sophie hit on anyone. Her dry spell was a legit famine-level, shriveled-up, dehydrated state of being, and she really needed to get laid by something that didn't require a USB cable. She pulled out a dating app and her belly sank. Not that dating apps were wrong, but because she had zero free time, she usually looked at the hookup-only statuses. And after a few swipes, she felt cheap. Hookups were fine, great, even—for people who only wanted hookups.

She knew she wanted more. She wanted a damn soulmate. A woman to come home to, to sit with in front of the red-brick fireplace on a Sunday morning with endless sugared Colombian coffee and an afghan they'd crocheted together. She wanted to hike at Snoqualmie Falls, and take selfies at one of the rainbow intersections in Capitol Hill, and eat dim sum in the International District. She wanted to lie under the cherry blossoms at the University of Washington and marvel at how the quad turned into a sea of cotton candy. She wanted to watch the salmon swim at the Ballard Locks and watch the cruise ships leave the port and snuggle with a fat rescue cat while binge-watching rom-coms.

She wanted love. Even if she had no idea how to make space in her life for it.

From the corner, a woman peeked up and gave her a look. A definite, *definite* look. Sophie clicked from the app to emails, but the words muddied. She glanced back up, her eyes skimming the dark pixie cut highlighting a sloped neck. The woman's outlined ruby lips looked a bit like Ella's. Yesterday, Sophie noticed Ella's lips curved up in the corner in a rare smile, and the tiniest dimple appeared. A flutter started in her gut.

Wait, nope. *What the hell am I doing?* Why compare this stranger to Ella? See, she needed to get laid. Now she was having warm thoughts about her highly annoying, yet beautiful, co-worker.

The woman tossed another look, with her lashes fluttering beneath her downcast eyes. Sophie set her phone upside down on the table—the universal sign for "I'm open for conversation."

I'm doing this. She might be rusty, but Sophie could absolutely do this. Her outfit was cute, her makeup on point, her loins were rising from hibernation. She tugged on her jeans, took a quick sip of her coffee, and stood.

"Hey," the woman said.

"Hey." A deep voice behind Sophie responded and a man passed her to approach the woman at the table.

Sophie froze. Her cheeks, chest, even her ass turned red.

I'm dying. Seriously, just bury me. As the man approached, Sophie slunk back into her chair, and focused hard on her phone. Flipping back open the dating app, she scrolled through pictures until she could unbury herself from the six-feet-deep embarrassment coffin.

Face after face, she swiped and swiped. Choosing a hookup based on a profile picture alone, not on the million other things that were more important to her, made her feel grosser by the second. But she needed someone messy right now, to scratch an itch, so she could focus on—

No fucking way. Sophie brought the phone closer to her face. Was that... No. Yep. Definitely, yep. Ella's face in a muted, black-and-white photo, a thin black strap draping off the shoulder, a shy, bit-lip pose, the hint of some glorious, full, *robust* even, cleavage that Sophie hadn't noticed under the suits and sweaters. Right there, right in front of her, on a queer hookup site. The picture could almost be passed off as someone else. *Almost.* The hair was longer, softer with beach waves, no blunt black bangs. But those signature lips, and the smattering of freckles above her nose, sometimes hidden when her glasses dipped, and that heart-shaped face confirmed Ella's identity.

Relationships suck. Queer Seattle woman looking for one-night-only friendship. No strings attached, no gushy love match, no need to exchange anything more than an astrological sign. A few hours, some stress relief, maybe some good chocolate.

Ella was queer? Jesus, Sophie was off her game. Her belly tingled, her toes tingled. Even her freaking scalp tingled.

Ugh.

She stood and threw her backpack over her shoulders.

"Sophie!" Charlie called out, and motioned her forward. "Mack and I are going to see if everyone wants to go for dinner next weekend. Can you join?"

She needed a night with friends like people needed air. "I'd love to, but not sure I can swing it. Can I let you know later? Work, you know?" She rolled her eyes and checked her watch. "Speaking of, I'm going to head out. Say hi to everyone for me. Even Remi." She grinned and skip-jogged to catch the metro.

Maya's girlfriend was a tough case to crack. Sophie wore her emotions on her sleeve, but Remi... did not. Months passed before she really got to know the woman. She tried not to take it personally at first, which was an utter failure, because how else would she take someone giving her the cold shoulder? Sophie even complained once to Maya, about six months back or so, that she thought Remi hated her. Maya explained how sometimes when kids grow up in the system, their ability to open up takes a long time. Once Sophie let that go, and it seemed Remi accepted Sophie was a permanent, although sporadic, fixture in their lives, things shifted. A few pool nights, mocktail hours, and a random shared love of HGTV shifted Sophie and Remi into buddies.

As the bus trudged through the city, Sophie reviewed a half dozen emails and messages that had come in since logging off last night. The creative team was ready for the pre-strategy meeting, but the passive-aggressive email string indicated that the social and web teams were having a vast difference of opinion. This meant that in addition to being an organizer and cheerleader, Sophie would have to be a mediator. Maintaining a Zen-like state within the office, especially during crunch time, while dealing with fragile egos, was one of the toughest parts of her job.

An image of crying from the dock as the cruise ship left the port among hollers and whistles from passengers filled Sophie's mind. What if they couldn't get it done? Training in Ella took more time than what it was worth, and the irritation grew at the loss of productivity. George hovered more these last two weeks than the last six years, and as "approachable" as he may be (*I'm just like you guys*, he'd say in his five-piece tailored suit), he was still the CEO and it wracked her nerves. In the past week, she'd sent out an email with a typo, failed to book a large-enough space for a strategy overview, and showed up late to an integrated marketing all-hands meeting.

She was frustrated with the chaos Ella brought into her workspace. Unfairly, for sure. *Maybe*.

The bus pulled to a stop, and she checked the time. *Perfect*. She had a few extra minutes and needed to hear the voice of reason. She grabbed her cell and dialed.

"Hey, honey!" Her mom's voice rang through Sophie's headphones. "What's going on?"

So many things. She was tired. She wanted this cruise so bad. And she hated working with Ella. Even more, she was irritated with herself that when Ella concentrated really hard, her glasses would slip down her nose and she pushed them up with a charming, doe-eyed look. "I don't think I'm going to get to go on the cruise."

"Oh no! Why not?"

Sophie stepped into the bare building lobby and took a seat on a bench. "There's just no way we'll finish in time. The deadline's too aggressive."

A pause followed. "Do you know your dad last week said he wanted to read every book in the library before he died, going A to Z. That was his goal."

Her mom—queen of the random responses. "Lofty goal." But not a surprising one. Her dad had a target to read two hundred books a year, and he almost always exceeded it.

"Yeah, and then as we were talking about it, he quickly realized that they have a constant rotation. Even if he finished, he will never *actually* finish because of the new ones coming in, and the old ones they remove. He got pretty down for a few minutes, you know, until he perked up at the idea that he'll never run out of books to read."

Made sense. But also, Sophie had no idea what this meant in terms of her not going on the cruise.

"The ride is what he likes. If he actually read all of them, then what? He'd be lost," her mom continued. "Point is, sometimes it's about the journey. You love what you do. And you deserve to go on a cruise, if that's what you want to do. But stressing about the result is not doing you any favors."

Ah. Okay, maybe she had a point. Sophie dropped her bag at her feet and stared at the front doors to make sure no one she knew was entering. "So, I have a new co-worker, Ella, that I've been training in the last couple weeks."

"Couple weeks? I can't believe you didn't tell me this earlier. Wasn't that one of your big goals? They're so lucky to have someone as sweet and patient as you to be their trainer."

Sophie's throat bobbed with a hard swallow. "Not sure she'd feel like that."

"Really? Why not?"

Divulging the crappy way she'd been treating Ella made her stomach curl. "I could be better, you know? I haven't, um, been the nicest."

The sound of her mom sipping echoed through the phone. "This isn't like you. You're nice to everyone."

"Not her." Well, she said it, and facing the truth was definitely on the top-ten ick factor list.

"Well, if you don't like her, I don't like her, and she must've done something to deserve it."

Did she, though? Sophie pushed a thumb into her temple. Sure, it was hugely unfair how she landed the job and got special treatment. But did anyone really deserve being treated less kindly? "No, she's actually pretty cool. Really smart. She went to UW, and even took some grad classes at Stanford."

"Ah. She's one of those."

Sophie winced at the remark. What would her mom say if

she found out that Ella was the CEO's daughter? "I mean, she's a super hard worker."

"No one is a harder worker than you." Her mom's tone had a defiant snap. "You get that work ethic from your dad, you know."

"He'd say I got it from you." She grinned through the words, engaging in the familiar bragging-rights ritual of who passed along the long lineage of working yourself to the bone. It was always a compliment—her parents acknowledging her hustle.

The door swung open, and she jutted her head at a woman who worked in a different office.

"Hey, Mom, gotta run. Love you."

"Love you, kiddo! Come see us soon, we miss you."

The office was quiet. All week she'd arrived early to monitor the demonic thirst trap, but today she was looking for some time to herself. After tossing back the rest of the Sugar Mugs coffee, she needed a second cup. The motion sensor lights kicked on in the breakroom, the leftover lemon and bleach scent of the night cleaning crew lingered. Her shoulders softened. She enjoyed the quiet, with nothing but the hum of the refrigerator and the faint murmur of the city street twenty floors below.

She tapped the espresso into the filter and clicked it, the screech of pressurized water pushing over the beans. Two pumps vanilla, a bucket of cream, an extra packet of raw sugar, and she moved to the large window. The city bloomed alive below. Bike riders zigzagged on the bike lane, cars filled the road back-to-back, commuters speed-walked to their respective builds. All she needed was five minutes of silent bliss and she could—

"Good morning." The brisk, smile-less voice accompanied a brisker, heels-against-hardwood walk as Ella made her way to the refrigerator.

Sophie's neck grew tight. Peaceful moment—gone. "Morning."

Ella looked softer today somehow, wearing black jeans, flats, and a deep purple puff sweater. Purple was definitely a good color on her, showcasing the soft pink that highlighted her cheekbones. *The fact that she's looking for a hookup.* Sophie shook her head. Her face burned. She needed to stop, focus, and slow these swirling thoughts. Ella was fresh blood. That was all. Sophie didn't even *like* her.

Try and be nice. It was Thursday, after all. Only one more day before a weekend of sleeping, streaming, and sapphic-novel reading.

Ella bent over and Sophie just so happened to catch the curve of a particularly juicy ass perked up in the air as she wiggled to dig out a sparkling water from the drawer. Who knew? *Stop!* She snapped her gaze to the ceiling, then her cup, then decided it'd be safer to turn around completely. Dear God. She needed to shake that sultry image from the dating app. Sophie knew this personal secret about Ella, but she and Ella were colleagues. Knowing Ella was looking for a hookup didn't feel right.

And it shouldn't feel this good, either.

EIGHT

ELLA

Come on! For everything that is holy and good in this world, please, please give me a win. Ella focused on the instant message screen with so much intensity she was sure her eyeballs were going to split in half. The bubbles appeared, and she stopped breathing.

TM:

Sure. I can make 2:30 work.

"Yes!" She pulled her fists in for a pump, fully Napoleon Dynamite-style.

A hand gripped her forearm. "She said yes?" Sophie's eyes were wide and expectant.

"She said yes!" Ella had no idea the rush she would get from a single person saying she could meet. A moment passed as Ella glanced at Sophie's delicate, multi-ringed fingers wrapped around her arm. Sophie whipped her hand back, but not before a small heat imprint seeped into her skin.

"Awesome." Sophie smiled. "Good job."

Whoa. Did Ella have a praise kink? Those words sparked something deep, and she wanted to hear it again.

All morning, Ella had scrambled with Sophie's instructions: Set a one-hour concepting call for today with the lead creatives. The task seemed easy enough—there were only four leads total, plus Sophie and Ella. How hard could it be to get everyone in a room?

Turned out, super freaking hard. The kaleidoscope of calendars showing *busy, out of office,* or *green, but only for thirty minutes* had swirled and swirled until Ella caught a break.

"Feels like you need a smoke after that one, huh?" Sophie wiggled a brow and rubbed the back of her head with a palm.

Was that a... was she flirting?

Something felt different with Sophie today. She hadn't said one snarky comment, she'd smiled, she just said *good job.* Whatever the shift was, it was both amazing and put Ella on edge. She'd had the rug pulled out from under her before, thinking people were her friend. She was older now, wiser. She'd never let that happen again.

"A smoke?" Ella tipped back a sip of water. "I wouldn't know. Never tried it."

Sophie stopped typing. "You've never smoked? Like... anything?"

Ella shook her head. Sure, Seattle was one of the first states to legalize weed. And half the teen population had tried a cigarette at least once. But Ella had never tried, well, anything. She'd had some wine on her twenty-first birthday, but wasn't sure if it'd trigger a seizure, so she didn't risk more than a small glass. Same with marijuana. Cigarettes smelled disgusting, so even if she thought it was completely safe, she still wouldn't try. Hell, she didn't even have a tattoo. Her full-on devious act of anything self-indulgent was being a proud owner of a variety of shaped and sized vibrators.

"So, what happens at a concepting meeting here?" Ella added the *here* part just in case it was something super obvious. She could play it off and say she learned different types of concepting at school. Which was not true, but Sophie didn't need to know that.

"Come on, let's grab some coffee." Sophie pushed out her chair and took off toward the breakroom.

Ella locked her computer and followed Sophie into the room. "Don't you ever get dehydrated?" she asked as Sophie filled a cup from the communal coffee pot and added in a truck-load of sugar.

"Probably."

Sophie smiled—again. Twice in a day, and Ella hated that the motion made her insides flip-flop.

Sophie stirred the contents and took a hesitant sip. "So, the pre-strategy meeting is really level-setting. Making sure we heard the client, their needs, the timeline." She tapped in more sugar and tasted again. "But the concepting is where fun begins. The creatives bring forth the high-level concept of the campaign based on the strategy, and they start building the creative brief."

Clear as a foggy Seattle day.

Sophie pointed to the high-top table in the corner, and Ella grabbed a seat.

"I watched a speech one time, and it finally made sense." Sophie slid into a chair across from Ella. "When building strategy, it's so much more than 'put two products next to each other and say buy one get one free, and make it sparkly.'"

Ella's brows scrunched. Seriously, she should have paid more attention in school. They must have talked about this stuff in her marketing classes, but Ella's brain blanked.

"Here's another way to explain." Sophie tapped the cup. "What's your favorite movie?"

"*The Shawshank Redemption*," Ella replied with zero hesitation. When she saw that movie ten years ago, she knew she'd never see a better one.

Sophie's breath sounded like it hitched. "That's, um, wow. Super random. That's mine, too."

Interesting. Ella would have pegged Sophie as a Marvel movie lover, or maybe something old-school like *The Shining*, or *A Clockwork Orange*. Ella filed away this little nugget for later.

"Why do you like it so much?" Sophie asked.

Ella fiddled with her fingertips under the table. "I've seen it probably thirty times, and even though I know what will happen, it still gets me directly in the heart, you know? The friendship, having someone's back, the whole found-family concept... it strikes a chord." Probably more personal than Sophie needed to hear, but it was true. Ella studied her cuticles and hoped her face hid her embarrassment for oversharing.

"I get that." Sophie's voice was uncharacteristically quiet. "Let's break this down. The story is about two guys in prison and how they both handle incarceration. If the creative brief only listed that as the concept, it would be a different film. Now, let's say the producers requested a sweeping story of redemption, triumph, and a beautiful friendship. And add in an underdog story that shows the human spirit and leaves the viewers motivated to find joy in this world, and it's a totally different prison story, right? *That's* what a creative brief does."

Sophie's eyes sparkled under the fluorescent lights as she spoke, and it was clear she loved her job. Ella couldn't imagine feeling this way about marketing, but she could relate the dreaminess Sophie projected to how she felt when she painted.

"So, before we hand this off to the team, it's our job to make sure it captures the right story," Sophie continued. "Not just 'sell doughnuts to millennials.' But 'make doughnuts sexy and fun.' Make people want to eat at Devil's Doughnuts and leave with merch because the place is super cool."

A slow grin crept over Ella. "So, the essence of the ad."

"Exactly." Sophie twisted her wrist and checked her watch. "Better get back at it. We have a ton to do before two thirty."

Sophie's chair squeaked against the floor, and she stood. "Hey, what do you think about running this meeting on your own?"

Ella's heartbeat kicked up. Sophie trusted her to run a meeting, solo? Already? "On my own?" She hated that her voice cracked and hinted at anything less than un-faltered self-assurance.

"Yep." Sophie tossed the empty cup into the garbage and leaned toward Ella. "Don't worry. I got you. If you stumble at all, I'll step in."

Warmth filled Ella's chest and she bit back the urge to hug Sophie.

The next few hours were packed with creating what seemed a thousand project plans. Each major deliverable, Sophie had explained, needed their own project. Web landing page, one project. Instagram post, one project. Facebook ad, one project. But that was for one single message. They were juggling multiple ads, multiple messages, and more than just two social platforms. One team member was gathering a short-list of influencers for TikTok. One was looking at paid search and SEO options. Another was determining banner ads. The firehouse of information was fast and furious, and Ella's head spun.

"I've gotta eat something." Sophie scooted back from the desk, locked eyes with a woman in the corner, and pointed to the breakroom. She walked away without another word, without an invitation, and Ella shook it off. She and Sophie weren't friends. But they'd been working together for two weeks now, and not once had Sophie invited Ella to anything more than grab a coffee.

Ella had typed out a rough agenda for this afternoon when her stomach growled. She continued typing until her stomach roared. She grabbed her lunch bag under the desk and unzipped. "You've got to be shitting me."

The ice pack surrounding sashimi and sushi rolls must've

had a hole, and water had seeped over the fish. Soggy, room-temperature raw fish could create some sort of mortifying explosiveness. *No thank you.*

Keeping fingers crossed the breakroom had snacks shoved in drawers, she walked past clusters of tables, monitors, and conversation, and turned the corner to the open space. Like when a drunk stumbled into a speaker at a party, the laughter from Sophie zipped to a stop when she caught Ella's gaze. *Cool.* Just her presence alone proved she was a fun sucker. Wouldn't be the first time she'd been accused of dulling the life of the party. Her gut turned over, recalling a cafeteria situation at her new school in the sixth grade, when she held the tray with shaky hands and froze because she had no one to sit with.

She jutted her chin once in acknowledgement to a woman giving her a sympathy wave, and marched over to the sparkling water. The bubbles burned her throat, but she finished the drink. She tossed the cup, raced back to the desk to snag her wallet, and bolted to the elevator.

"Ella!"

Not now. She didn't want to talk to her dad, but here he was, speed-walking toward her with his open suit jacket flapping against him.

Breathless, he caught up to her. "Where are you headed?"

She pounded on the elevator button and checked her watch. 1:10. Wherever she was going, she had a maximum of forty-five minutes. She needed to get back and collect herself before the 2:30 meeting. "I've got to grab some lunch."

"Excellent." His palms smacked together and echoed in the hall. "I was just stepping out myself. Let's grab some grub together."

"No one says the word *grub* anymore." She glanced behind her shoulder to see if anyone was watching. All she needed was for more people to see her talking with her dad, mumbling about nepotism and unfair advantage. "I don't think I have time. I really need to get something quick."

Her father shook his head and stepped into the elevator with her. "Stop. Thomas is already waiting."

"Dad, I—"

"Come on, it's your favorite." He nudged his elbow into her shoulder.

Her ears perked up. "Cuban sandwiches?"

"Sure is."

The line wrapped around the corner. The hearty scent of fried onions and pork cut through the gray, foggy air. Locals surrounded her, everyone knowing about the neighborhood's worst-kept secret, a small, red bungalow in Fremont with minimal signage, a few picnic tables, and the best Cuban sandwiches in existence. Her mouth watered, waiting for the salted goodness. She flicked her wrist to check her watch. Traffic was slow, even in an off-tourist season, and it had taken almost twenty minutes to arrive. "I think we need to go back."

Her dad crossed his arms in front of his broad chest. "Are you worried you'll get in trouble? You know I am the boss, right?"

Everyone knew he was the boss. She loved her dad, but he wasn't exactly quiet about his position. "I just want to make a good impression. No special favors."

He raised his eyebrow and closed his lips into a thin line, no doubt swallowing the comment burning on his tongue. With his limited filter, that had to have been hard. She knew damn well getting this job was a major special favor—it normally took years in the business to work up to this position. She wasn't proud of her behavior the night her dad reluctantly agreed to hire her. In fact, it was the lowest point she'd ever been. But years of suffocating took its toll and had forced her to do something drastic.

And, well, it worked.

She clicked her heels against the pavement and shuffled forward. Finally, less than two people in front of them.

"You getting dunked in the toilet like the old initiation days for being my daughter?"

"Seriously, what hellhole fraternity did you belong to?" She tore her gaze from the man sautéing a mound of onions. "No, everyone's been good."

Her dad removed his money clip, ordered, and motioned to a picnic table. She stood on the side and tugged her coat tighter. No chance was she coming back to the office with dirty butt marks.

"I bet Sophie's a great trainer. Reminds me a bit of me, you know?"

Ella breathed out through her nose, not understanding why out of all his employees, Sophie stood out to him so much. She'd heard this comparison more than once over the years. Rumblings of meager beginnings, and how her dad respected anyone who "had the stones" to work their way up like him, how he started a company MacGyver-style with two effing markers, a half-used notebook, and a dream.

Mist gathered on her glasses. She yanked them off, rubbed the lenses with her sweater, and peeked at her watch. 1:52 p.m. Her neck heated. They needed to leave now. She should be prepping for her first solo meeting, not waiting for food.

"She treating you well?" He stepped to the side as a group passed him.

Not really. Sophie wasn't doing anything inherently wrong, and today was the first time Ella saw the chip on her shoulder crack, but she certainly wasn't part of the cheer committee. "Yes, everyone's been really nice." A notification buzzed, and she grabbed her phone. A wait-listed doctor appointment opened. She made a mental note to check her schedule to see if she could snag it.

"You have to get that?"

"No. It's UW Medical. I'll call back." She shoved the phone in her purse. She took her health seriously, she really did. Limited caffeine, lots of sleep, medications ritual perfected, avoided blinking lights. But right now, work came first. She needed this to land more than she needed her doctor's laundry list of restrictions, harping on the same message she received since her first seizure fifteen years ago.

Her dad shoved his hands in his slack pockets. "Seems like the new meds are working."

She stretched her neck and looked behind him, verifying that none of her co-workers had followed them here and overheard her dad blab about her personal business. "Dad." The words pushed through gritted teeth. "You promised."

"We promised we wouldn't tell your new co-workers about your condition, and we're outside of the office." He flailed his hands. "I don't see any of them here."

Perhaps she should have been clearer with her threats that during working hours, he was never, ever, allowed to ask about medical things.

"And I want it stated, for the record, I think it's ridiculous your co-workers don't know," her father said. "They should all be trained on the nasal spray, and the doctors have repeatedly—"

"I know, I know." She put her hand up, not wanting another word. Of course, having the ones surrounding you know about your condition in case of an emergency was best practice. She knew that. The entire world probably knew that. And she would tell them, eventually. But right now, she didn't want any more attention.

"I told Mom I'd keep an eye on you at work. You know how cranky she gets if I fail. Especially when it comes to you." He chuckled at his decidedly unfunny remark. Tapping his fingers against each other, his chest expanded in a large inhale.

"We're exploring the possibility of getting a therapy dog for you."

A blaze tore through her chest. A therapy dog? *A therapy dog!* Yes, they were wonderful and amazing and gifted creatures for *other* people. *Not* for her.

Never once had Ella been ashamed of having epilepsy. Sometimes even, the disorder was a badge of honor. She wanted to hug herself for the way she powered through EEGs as a kid with technicians attaching electrodes to her head, glue sticking in her hair, taking meds, therapy, doctors, everything. She wanted to high-five her thirteen-year-old self who missed a year of school because the memory loss that year was pretty substantial, and studying was impossible.

So, no. She was not ashamed. But the reaction in others gutted her. A sliding scale from "oh, you poor thing" to people terrified she'd drop and shake like a priest dumped holy water on her to rid the demons from her soul. It was her mom damn near having a panic attack when she was younger and left her alone, practically announcing her condition via a bullhorn, while reminding everyone not to stick a metal spoon in her mouth. Or her parents homeschooling her for most of her life, then sending Thomas with her to her college classes like she was on parole. It was having a nanny/nurse/prison guard be on staff at the house, and baby monitors in her room until she was fifteen when she broke down about how invasive it was.

She clocked the time and her stomach burned. 2:08. She was barely going to make it back for the 2:30 meeting. How in the hell had she let her dad talk her into coming here? She should have stood her ground and grabbed a granola bar from a vending machine. Her heartbeat thudded in her chest. Her first meeting, and she was going to come in reeking of onions and sweating. What the hell was she thinking?

The cashier yelled their names and she rushed to the

counter. She pushed the bag into her dad's chest and grabbed his arm. "We need to go. Please, hurry."

In the vehicle, sinking her teeth into the salted pork and onion sandwich brought a moment of temporary reprieve. She basked in the flavors of the chewy fresh baked bread and warm goodness. Her belly filled, the nauseating hunger bubbles slowing as she checked her watch. It would be tight, but as long as they kept going at this pace, she'd have five minutes to spare.

The SUV slowed to a stop. Ella stretched her neck. "Thomas? What's going on?"

"Looks like a minor fender bender. Down to one lane."

No. No, no, no! Her heart thudded against her chest wall and her stomach rolled into a ball and threatened to spill over. "Dad, I can't do... I'm supposed to be running a meeting in like ten minutes."

He looked up from his phone and glanced up at the traffic. "Not much you can do about it. Just text Sophie and let her know you're running late."

"I don't have her number!" This was such a rookie mistake. Heat was everywhere. She unzipped her jacket and fanned her face.

"Kid, it's good. I'll message Malcolm and have him send it to you." He set the phone on his lap and gripped her on the shoulder. "I know it's not ideal, but things like this happen. Don't worry, Sophie's great. I'm sure she can handle it."

Of course Sophie could handle the meeting on her own. That wasn't the point. Ella wanted to show Sophie that *she* could handle it.

When she arrived back at the building, she didn't even wait for her dad. She sprinted into the lobby and slipped into an open elevator. She pulled out her phone and double-checked the room number. G-75A.

What the hell kind of number was that? She bolted to her

desk, grabbed her laptop, and glanced at a man with a hoodie and headphones. "Do you know where G-75A is?"

He shrugged with an uninterested gaze. "Not offhand."

Her pulse kicked up another notch as she raced down the hall, through the maze of conference rooms, private rooms, and sitting spaces, and finally found a room buried in the corner. The large windows showed Sophie seated at the table, chatting. Ella peeked at her watch. 3:07. Almost forty minutes late to her own damn meeting.

Go in? Wait? Nothing?

She pulled in a sharp breath and reached for the handle. The heavy metal fire door screeched like a cat, and all gazes zoomed toward her. She glanced at Sophie, who gave a small, disappointed shake of her head. The heat to her chest was immediate and the Cuban sandwich threatened her belly. She scanned the room, debating where to sit, debating what to say, when Sophie's words cut through the silence. "So, it sounds like we're close to alignment..."

Sophie finished the meeting without a single acknowledgement toward Ella, as Ella fought hard to blink back tears. As they wrapped up, Sophie flicked a narrowed gaze to Ella, then back to the room. "Thanks to all who made this meeting a priority."

Gulp.

Ella's gaze cast downward. She swore when she looked up everyone would stare at her with disappointed eyes. But something worse happened.

No one even acknowledged her at all.

NINE

SOPHIE

Whoever invented the phrase TGIF needed to be handed a bucket of THC-filled cherry gummies and a cream soda as a thank-you, because nothing had ever quite described the feeling Sophie had getting a break from Ella after spending the last two weeks together.

And after that little stint yesterday, when Ella took a long, leisurely lunch—leaving Sophie scrambling to cover a meeting she thought Ella was running—she needed some serious space. Ella had seemed excited, stoked even, to lead her first meeting. Sophie might be type B or C in her private life, but at work she was a proud type A-er. It had taken a lot for her to relinquish the reins for an hour. And of course she was prepared, because she wanted to support Ella if she fell, but she wasn't *prepared*, prepared, at least not the way she would've been if she owned the meeting. And when 2:25 p.m. had rolled round and she had not heard a word from Ella, she stumbled with creating an agenda and she. Was. Furious.

Sophie stepped into the office. It wasn't quite 7:30 yet, and Ella was reading her laptop screen with a half bottle of water and a last bite of a breakfast sandwich littering her desk. Sophie walked up behind her, ignoring the way the blunt black hair grazed the back of her neck, not looking at her long, smooth fingers tapping against the keyboard, definitely not noticing how the dark and citrusy scent hit her nose.

"Morning," Ella said, seemingly avoiding eye contact as usual, as she looked at her monitor and nothing else.

"Morning." Sophie's tone was flat by intention. She tried to logically think about this situation. If it were a different trainee, would she have kindly taken them aside and explained when they set a meeting, they were expected to be there? Would she have given a butt-chewing about if they weren't five minutes early, they were five minutes late? Would she have had a heart-to-heart and talked about how to make it in the corporate world?

Sophie shushed the guilt knowing even though she told Ella to take whatever time she needed for lunch, no one exceeded twenty-five minutes for a lunch unless it was a required team-bonding event. But why did Ella scooting out of there like this job wasn't her life, her love, her freaking wife like it was for Sophie make her so irate?

Bottom line, Ella wasn't just any trainee. She had privileges that no one else did. She was *un-fireable*. Promotable without merit. The CEO's goddamn kid, who could do what she wanted, when she wanted. And that tied Sophie's hands. Was she really supposed to scold Ella for having lunch with the CEO? What if that got back to George? It'd be Sophie's job on the line, not Ella's.

"Hey, um, I'm really sorry about yesterday and the lunch and everything." Ella's cheeks pinked. "My dad wanted to take me out."

Must be nice to get extra perks. Ella completely effed up Sophie's dream of being a trainer. The one shot Malcolm gave her to test out her managerial chops, and Ella made it impossible. Should Sophie even give Ella any assignments? Just assume she was unreliable, but would probably rise in the ranks and be her boss one day? Whatever it was, Sophie was completely and totally over it. "Understood."

Ella pulled in her lips. She opened her mouth, then closed it, and released a sigh through her nose. "Won't happen again."

The next few hours the only words spoken were work-related. Gentle banter, gone. Smiles, gone. Sophie kept her tone even, professional, and shelled out the minimal information needed to get her point across.

Sophie had to give some credit to Ella. Since this morning, Sophie wasn't sure if Ella so much as left to use the bathroom. During moments of downtime, Ella's screen filled with training videos, she scoured the digital asset repository for old creative, or she reviewed retired project plans.

Why did people like Ella always win? Why was the rich girl in high school always chosen as prom queen, why did the woman with the Gucci bag get seated first at a restaurant, why did the pretty woman get away with murder? It wasn't fair. Over the years, her mom had told her stories of the prep school kids who went into her diner, hassled the waitresses, made a mess, and left. Or how businessmen with chunky gold Rolexes used to pinch her butt. Or how the suburban moms would come in with their custom-embroidered canvas bags fresh from the market dripping with flowers and make comments like "This place is just so... *cute*. They must use special freshener here—I can hardly smell the grease like last time."

But really, what Sophie hated most was the monster festering inside that wasn't who she was. If Harper were watching, Sophie would be mortified. How would she justify treating someone like this? Just because she wasn't outwardly awful, or screaming at Ella like the grocery store manager where Sophie worked when she was fifteen, didn't mean she was being kind.

Sophie clicked her fingers against the underside of the

chair. *Enough*. Like it or not, they had to work together. And, besides Ella leaving for lunch, she'd been kicking ass since day one. Olive-coffee-branch time. "I'm going to grab an espresso. Want me to make you one?"

"No, I had plenty at home." Ella sipped from the water bottle and swiped her lip with a thumb. "I wanted to let you know I'll be leaving for a few hours this afternoon."

Are. You. Kidding. Me! Sophie handed her a branch, and Ella just took that stick and shoved it up her... *Whatever*. Less than three weeks in, and Ella took an extended lunch yesterday and *then* leaves early on a Friday? You earned that right after paying dues. And as far as Sophie was concerned, Ella was in her overdraft.

Ella was an amateur. And a bit of this made Sophie smile. Everyone knew that you didn't leave early on your first few weeks of work. Hell, on your first year of work. You arrived first, left last. You picked up the crap work that your manager didn't want to do. You rolled up your sleeves and helped co-workers build a PowerPoint presentation. You did boring content QA. You fucking hustled—you didn't *leave early*.

"Did you hear me?" Ella asked, her fingers suspended over the keyboard.

"I heard you."

Ella exhaled through her nose. "I couldn't tell because you didn't say anything."

Sophie's face flamed. "What do you want me to say? I'm not your boss. I don't need to give you permission. For a newbie, I'd normally tell you to check with the manager, but since your dad is the CEO, I sincerely doubt the same rules apply to you."

Ella's bottom lip clamped between her teeth. She pounded her keyboard with such ferocity that the letters were likely to crack off and pop across the room.

The cursor froze on Sophie's computer. She clicked and shook the mouse. And clicked again. *Really?* Tossing Post-its, notepads, and too many pens aside, she dug around the desk drawer for replacement batteries. She slammed the drawer and rummaged through a different one.

Stupid low batteries. She didn't have time for this. Her heavy combat boots thudded against the floor as she crossed over to the storage room.

Malcolm was inside, digging through a cabinet. "Morning, sunshine." He tossed a quick glance behind his shoulder. "What are you doing?"

She banged one cabinet, then another. *Where are the goddamn batteries?* "Is our admin out or something? How am I supposed to work if I can't even get batteries for my freaking mouse?"

"Whoa, whoa." He held up his hands. "It's way too close to the weekend for this much aggression." He opened the cabinet to the left of him and pointed. "The admin sent out an email that they reorganized the supplies. You must not have seen it?"

She ripped a package from the shelf and looked up as Malcolm dipped his head. "What are you looking at?"

He lifted his dad eyebrow that could deflect anything, and she softened. "Sorry." She exhaled. "I sound like a jerk."

He brought his index finger and thumb an inch apart. "Just a tad." He tugged on his black beard and leaned against the counter. "This is what burnout looks like, Sophie. You're a classic, textbook case. You need to slow down."

She vise-gripped the package, but finally admitted defeat and handed it over. "No, I need to hustle now, so I can slow down later."

He tore the wrapping and dropped the batteries in her hand. "I really hate that I'm contributing to your pressure so you can go on the cruise."

"I'm glad you are." The last thing she needed was for him to change his mind and say she couldn't go anymore. The cruise was the only thing keeping her afloat. "I want this so bad. I just... Ugh." She scraped at her thumbnail paint with her other thumb.

Malcolm stood silently for several long moments, then tossed the packaging into recycling, and rested against the wall. "Talk to me."

Malcolm had a new baby. And a wife, diaper duty, a lawn to mow, and dishes to clean. He had multiple employees, juggled reports, expenses, client meetings, and God knew what else. Fresh dark circles lined under his eyes, and yawns replaced his normal laughter. The very last thing he needed was her complaining.

"Sophie."

"I hate working with Ella." She glanced up at him, praying she didn't see disappointed eyes. "When you told me I was training someone, I had no idea it would be King George's freaking daughter—who's never had a job in her life."

Malcolm crossed his arms in front of his chest. "Hmmm. Lack of experience is tough, but she's educated, smart, and dedicated, right? Or is she slacking?"

Sophie might have been pissed about Ella leaving early on a Friday night to swing by Tiffany's for a two-week charm bracelet, but it wasn't her style to tattle. "Nah. I mean, she's here early, stays late, and pays attention."

"You always wanted to be a trainer, right? You realize not every trainee will be perfect."

The words sunk low and heavy. He was right. Part of proving she could handle this mentor role meant she needed to choke back the irritation. The last thing she needed was Malcolm thinking she couldn't make it as a leader. She rolled the batteries in her palms and exhaled, relaxing her stomach.

She leaned forward, squinting at a white stain on his shoulder. "Dude, what's up with your shoulder?"

He pinched the fabric and peeked. "Ugh. Baby spit."

She grinned. "How's the lack of sleep going for you?"

"Amazing, as you can see." He swiped at his shoulder. "I'm going to clean up. Be easy on her. She's new."

Sophie left the room as Malcolm's words sunk in. She jutted her head to a copywriter who dragged themselves with what looked like a gnarly hangover. After rounding the corner, she sucked in a breath as she approached the desk.

"I think the creative brief came in." Ella's words were sharp. "At least that's what the email said. I scanned it but wasn't sure if you wanted to review it together."

The brief? Did she not have her alerts on? She would've jumped on that immediately, mid-conversation with Malcolm or not. "When did it come in?"

"About ten minutes ago, when you stormed out of here."

"I did *not* storm." Okay, fine, she might have stormed.

"Sure," Ella muttered.

Maybe she deserved a little pushback.

Ella thumbed her glasses. "It was lighter than expected. Not sure if this is a standard objective statement or not."

Sophie hated that Ella had seen it first. *Hated.* Sophie should be the one coming to Ella—the trainee—breaking down what they needed, teaching her about objectives and statements and spotting when a team would need clarification.

"What did they teach you in your classes about the brief?" Sophie didn't mean it to come out as harsh as it did. She genuinely meant the question to gauge Ella's baseline understanding, but her subconscious slipped through her tone.

"They, ah." She squared her shoulders. "At UW..."

U-dub. If Ella muttered those words one more time, Sophie might toss a docking station through the skyrise window.

"We reviewed templates and wrote mock ones with the, ah..." She looked at the wall and chewed on her cheek. "...with the demographics and requirements and things."

Demographic, requirements, and *things*? She hated the voice in her head, hated the way she felt a bubbling dam inside her about to break. She wanted to pull it in, stop it from rising, but she couldn't. But she was tired... so freaking tired. And Ella was leaving early, Ella went to college, Ella got everything. It was so deeply unfair how people just got things depending upon where they were born—a fancy home, an education, even health insurance, for God's sake.

She was done.

"*Things*, huh? So, if someone says they are targeting an eighteen-to-thirty-year-old demographic, then that's good? Hey all, create an entire marketing campaign based on the require-ment that it's not a heaping pile of shit, and *things*."

The words were unfair, but so was this entire situation. She was already further behind than had she just run this entire campaign by herself, but she couldn't give up now. Letting Malcolm down or showing her co-workers that she couldn't hack it as a project manager, was not an option.

Ella's fingers spread across her desk, her knuckles turning white. "Why are you such a—"

"Such a what?"

Ella crossed her arms. She turned to Sophie, not only making eye contact, but hard eye contact. *Fiery* eye contact. "A bully."

"A bully?" Was she *kidding*? Bullies were the girls who ganged up on Sophie in the seventh grade. Bullies were the men she worked with at the pier who said, "Good thing you're cute, 'cause you'd never make it otherwise." A bully was how Ella treated her the first time they met, degrading her and making her sob in the bathroom. "You cannot be serious. *You* are the one who is a bully."

"Me? Me?" Ella's hands smacked against her thighs. "I have done nothing but eat your shit with a spoon these last two weeks. Seriously, what have I ever done to you?"

"I can't believe you," Sophie hissed. "When we first met..."

"When I first met you? What? I barely even *remember* you."

Ella's head snapped back, and her darkening gaze flickered between Sophie's eyes. "Clearly you don't make the impression you think you do."

She barely even remembers meeting me? How Ella made her feel that day gutted her, enough to leave a six-year lasting impression.

Ella exhaled through her teeth. "You have not given me a chance to prove myself."

Enough! A chance? Everything Ella had gotten since the second she walked in here was a chance. "You are trying to pay your dues with the currency of your father's legacy. You've probably done that your whole life, and it's not going to work with me. CEO or not, you haven't proven shit. In fact, the only thing you've proved thus far is your incompetence."

Sophie winced at her own words, not recognizing them as they flew from her mouth. This was too far, totally unlike her, unfair, and her stomach sank. Jesus Christ. Maybe she *was* a bully.

Come on, yell. Please. Puff your shoulders, flare your nose, something. Ella sat for a moment, stiff and silent. Then, like an emotional domino, Ella's shoulders slouched, then her head dipped, then her chin trembled. Behind the tortoiseshell glasses, Ella's eyes filled with tears.

Shit. Oh no. No, no, no. She went too far, and the regret was instant, hot, and gross. "Ella, I'm so—"

Ella sprung from her chair, pivoted like a dancer, and speed-walked out of the room.

And Sophie almost threw up.

TEN

ELLA

Tugging on red rubber boots, going makeup free, and not straightening her hair within an inch of its life was a bit of a ritual for Ella. It was like her body knew what to expect when she left the house like this, and the lumps in her shoulders started melting. She pushed up a headband to keep her newly acquired bangs out of her face, grabbed a rain jacket, and jumped in the back of the SUV for the hourlong drive to Snoqualmie.

"Quiet time today?" Thomas asked from the front as he pulled out of the winding driveway.

"Yes, please." She leaned against the seat and stared out the window.

Hopefully today she could forget about her atrocious few weeks with Sophie. Yesterday would haunt her for months, and she couldn't get over that she nearly broke down crying at their desks. What a childish move to make at work. She'd snapped again later that afternoon, crying in front of her longtime doctor. But Sophie shined a spotlight on her insecurities and illuminated every terrible thought she'd ever had about herself. Her eyes filled again, but she bit down on her cheek to stop them.

But Ella shouldn't have said what she said—that Sophie didn't make an impression. It was a bald-faced lie. Ella may not have remembered *exactly* what happened the day they first met. But she certainly remembered Sophie, and the way she felt after their first meeting. And, if memory served, it was Sophie who was awful, not her.

Sophie left an impression anywhere she went. With her soft-butch look, her edgy outfits, and eyes that caught the light, everyone knew who she was. And she was *smart*. So freaking smart. She whipped through concepts, statements, and time-lines like she could recite them in her sleep. She pointed at bits of creative and why the leads rejected them. "See the lines that match up here to make a T? That's the opposite of what we are going for when creating an ad of openness," Sophie had said earlier in the week. "You may not have noticed it, but your subconscious did."

Trees whipped by, evergreens and weeping willows, filling the foggy air. Snow-topped mountains surrounded her, and after a while, the traffic reduced. Her heart rate lowered with each mile closer to her sanctuary.

Thomas navigated the vehicle up the hill. The weeklong knots in her stomach released, and her softened belly pouched against the seatbelt. She cracked the window and inhaled. Seattle air was pretty decent, especially for city air. Salt and seaweed mingled with misted pavestone. But the air in Snoqualmie, with its gushing waterfalls and meadows, smelled crisp and clean.

The SUV bumped up the gravel drive. A white horse fence enclosed the property and greenery surrounded the space. They passed the massive red barn with its chipped-paint door and continued bumping up the road. Chickens, seemingly unimpressed by the vehicle, casually strutted out of the way.

Thomas pulled to a stop in front of the early 1900s brick home with sunken windows, a stained-glass front door, and wraparound cedar-fenced porch with scattered and mismatched rocking chairs. Ella glanced at the influx of potted plants lining the pathway. "Did she get more plants than last time?"

"How can one even tell?"

Ella stepped out of the car. "You heading to get a cinnamon roll the size of your head?"

Thomas patted his belly. "You know me. Don't worry, I'll save you some."

"You said that the last three times and failed miserably on your promise." She couldn't blame him. The town had a local breakfast joint that had been there since the '60s, boasting items like the Dungeness crab omelette, freshly squeezed juices, and the thickest, heartiest oatmeal with whole milk and brown sugar. But the cinnamon rolls were the unofficial star. The owner made them fresh every day, and Ella swore she could smell the buttered dough and cinnamon sugar for a mile.

She waved goodbye, knowing he'd actually sit and wait until she was inside the house. A cock-a-doodle-doo and horses neighing echoed across the valley as she trudged through the mud up to the house. She breathed in, hard, for the first time since she was here a month ago.

After kicking off her boots at the door, she rang the doorbell and cracked it open. A hearty, sweet sage fog pummeled her. "Jesus. I think all the demons are gone." She fanned away the cloud and navigated to the kitchen, where her aunt stood in her signature peacock-colored muumuu, smudging like her life depended on it.

"Ella girl. I'm on my final room." Colleen twirled the bundle of sticks, murmuring something under her breath that Ella couldn't make out.

Tears sprung to Ella's eyes to combat the smoke. She lifted her shirt to cover her mouth and nose. "Oof. Why so much sage?"

Colleen circled the wand, the sleeves of the muumuu fanning the air with each movement. "Spring is in the air, my love. Time to cleanse, rejuvenate, and make space for the body and mind to heal."

Ella was not much for naturopathy, spiritual healing, or eating live sprouts to keep the doctor away. By the time she'd leave today, she'd probably have some combination of frankincense, lavender, and bergamot oil mixed in a bottle for her with a reminder to do chakra breathing and pay attention to which moon they were in. But maybe her aunt was on to something. Colleen's soft smile lines in her cheeks and around her eyes showed happiness, not fatigue.

Colleen snuffed out the burning embers. "Come here, sweet girl."

Ella melted into the hug and absorbed the multiple kisses against her forehead. This place was the only spot where Ella was both loved like a child and given the respect she deserved as a woman.

Colleen pulled back. Her gaze scanned Ella's face and her brows knitted in concern. "Want some tea? Or are you just here to brush the horses?"

"How did you know?" Brush horses, run away, bury herself under a stack of hay, did it really matter? Maybe Ella didn't need a job, maybe she could just live in Colleen's guesthouse next to the goats. She could earn her keep by feeding the chickens and scooping poop. *Oh, wait... that's right.* When Ella begged her aunt last year to move in, that was part of the deal. As much as Ella loved the animals, she drew the line at poop duty.

Colleen guided her into the kitchen. She pulled down two mason jars from the cabinet and filled them with water from the tap. "When you texted last night to see if I was around, I knew it wasn't a social call. You were just here a few weeks ago."

Colleen sliced two hefty chunks of lemon and tossed one in each jar. "Want to talk about it?"

Ella shook her head and remained silent. Colleen gave her a quick squeeze on the shoulder, then grabbed her work gloves and straw hat and headed to the front door.

The earth crunched beneath Ella's feet, massaging her toes through her boots as she walked to the barn. At home, everything was pristine. Perfectly manicured hedges surrounded the circular driveway. Rose bushes, cherry blossoms, and a mixture of annuals and perennials the primary gardener maintained lined the border. The lawn was mowed in an intricate diamond-design. One would be hard-pressed to find a blade of grass out of place. But here, Colleen didn't even have a paved driveway. Sticks and debris littered the gravel path, and overgrown plants and trees filled the yard.

Several goats scattered the area and filled the space with their happy chomping sounds. "Goats are the most natural land-scaper. My blackberry bushes would've taken over by now without them," Colleen said at least once a year.

That Colleen and her mother were raised by the same parents blew Ella's mind.

"Grab the apples." Colleen pointed at the bucket in the stall's corner.

Ella went to the stall to retrieve them, running her fingers across the wooden sign with the burned inscription *Who Rescued Who* hanging from the barn wall.

The sound of galloping horses grew louder, and Ella's heart swelled. It was like the animals knew she was here, knew she needed love, and ran to give it to her.

Mocha-Tina, one of three rescue horses, and the one that Ella designated as "hers" when she was around ten, trotted towards her.

"Hey, girl," Ella whispered. She rubbed the side of the rich, chocolate brown mare, who dipped her head. The horse was an anxiety med that, with every pat and glide, made Ella's tension evaporate. She held the apple in her palm and swore Mocha-Tina flashed a gummy, toothy grin before consuming it in one bite.

They worked in silence as the sun broke through the clouds. Colleen grabbed the pitchfork and separated the hay. Ella doused Mocha-Tina with detangling spray and began methodical brushes. Strand by strand and with long strokes, Mocha-Tina stood proudly as Ella worked the tangles and groomed the coat until it turned nearly reflective.

"Not a great week," Ella said, shaking out her forearm muscle.

Colleen tossed a chunk of hay to the side. "Work?"

"Work. My mom. My dad. My life." She spritzed the mane and continued brushing. Her mother's overbearingness catapulted to the Space Needle-level this week. Text messages at work, harping on her about appointments, making sure she took her meds—which she absolutely never forgot to do. "People treat me different because of my dad and it really sucks."

Colleen kicked away a rock. "Is that true? Or is that your perception?"

Maybe it was perception? Besides the dipshit in the conference room, who called out that she was George's daughter, only one person brought her lineage to her attention. "There's this woman, Sophie." She tugged out a strand of horsehair from the brush and flicked it into the breeze. "And she makes comments all the time."

"All the time, huh?"

Okay, maybe that was a stretch. She'd only brought it up twice, maybe three times. But Ella saw the thoughts and judgements behind those green eyes. "And she thinks she's super cool, you know, and can get away with everything because of... like who she is."

Colleen lifted her gaze from the hay. "Who is she?"

"She's like this, ugh, I don't know." Ella waved the brush in the air. "Like this shaved-head rocker chick. And beautiful. But I don't think she knows she's beautiful, which is somehow more annoying than just owning it. And she thinks she's really smart and everyone else is an idiot."

Colleen shoved the prongs and twisted, concentrating on moving the straw. "Beautiful, huh?"

Of course Sophie was beautiful. The sweetest face, a full mouth, and eyes that were green, but not just any old green. A green with speckles, that, when the sun hit, adjusted into the type of jade that belonged on a canvas. Ella returned to brushing. "I mean, if you're into her type."

Colleen stuck the prongs into the ground and rested her flattened forearm on the wooden handle. "Tell me about your mom and dad."

Ella set the brush down and took a sip from the mason jar. "They're up my ass constantly. I need my own space."

"I remember a similar conversation when you wanted to go to college in person instead of online."

Being homeschooled for most of her life, when Ella strolled into her mother's den six years ago and demanded to go to college on the University of Washington campus—not online— her mother nearly fell into the ten-foot-high bookshelf. Two hundred million conversations about "danger" and "unsuper- vised" and "how special" she was followed, until Ella screamed like a toddler, threatened to run away (she wouldn't have actu- ally run away), and sobbed until her parents let up. She hated that this was still the only successful way she was able to retain some control of her life. "This feels different. I mean, yes, I wanted to go to school, but I didn't actually want to leave home. But now... I'm an adult and I want my own place."

Colleen tipped a bucket upside down and sat. "A lot of people live with their parents."

True. But that didn't mean Ella wanted to.

She knew what it looked like from the outside. She had *everything*. At the same time, she felt like she had nothing—at least nothing that truly mattered. Mocha-Tina nickered at Ella's side, and she scratched just beside the horse's ears. She finally took a seat on the ground next to Colleen, and rested her head against her aunt's hip.

Colleen didn't push or pry. After a bit, she used the pitchfork to help her stand up and walked to the barn. She returned with a bucket of chicken feed and handed it to Ella. "Come on. One more hour of chores, then we can move to the studio."

Swiping a fresh canvas with creamy acrylic paint was akin to heaven. Ella dipped the round brush into magenta, citrus orange, and a touch of white, and swiped. She tilted her head... *Pretty*. At home, she painted with a full sketch outline, exclusively in watercolor, and an end date in mind. Devices were always turned off, and her parents had strict instructions not to interrupt. At Colleen's, the only rule was no rules. She used this time to experiment with the abstract technique and mixing hues.

Colleen returned with two PB&Js, cookies, and homemade lemonade, and set it all on the rickety TV tray between them. Ella eyed the distance from the canvas in case the tray collapsed and a lemonade-spray disaster occurred.

"Thanks." Ella wiped her hands and dug for a cookie when she got a text from her mom.

MOM:

Just checking in. Colleen keeping an eye on you?

LOL.

There was no *lol* about it. Ella huffed and closed the screen.

Colleen lifted a brow and brought the sandwich to her lips. "Your mom?"

Ella nodded. "It's too much." She bit into the bread, the chunky peanut butter sticking to her mouth's roof. She chewed slowly and swallowed. Her mom's overbearingness was all she'd ever known. And when she was younger, it felt incredible. She was always the most important person in the room. But when she pulled away, her mother gripped harder. "Why is she such a control freak?"

As soon as the words slipped from her mouth, she wanted to take it back. She absolutely knew why her mom was the way she was. Deep in her core, she wanted to hug her mom and tell her that she was okay, that she would be fine, and that she needed to stop worrying.

Colleen stuffed the chocolate chip cookie in between the sandwich. "Hmm. That's the stuff right there, Ella girl. Try on your next bite." She nudged the plate toward Ella. Several moments passed and she sighed. "After your first seizure, your mom changed."

Of course she did. Ella wasn't so dense that she couldn't understand that when a parent discovers their kid has a major medical issue, it rewires their brain. But at some point... shouldn't they get over it? Learn to cope?

"When you had your first seizure, I thought your mom was going to lose it." Colleen clapped the crumbs from her hands and dipped a brush into emerald green. "Until you have kids, you'll never understand. I'll probably never fully understand. Your mom handles you... this... the situation, the best way she knows how."

Ella knew this, but she still hated it.

"You know, it's not like your mother and I were raised in an empathetic family and taught how to nurture strong daughters. Our consistent message was to be seen and not heard. And when seen, your hair better be done, your clothes wrinkle free, and your smile wide."

Growing up, Ella remembered monthly visits to her grandparents' mansion in Bellevue. Her grandpa had passed when she was very young and she barely remembered him, but she remembered her grandma. She had been nice enough. But Ella remembered a playmate talking about her grandma who wore an apron and made homemade brownies and sticky slime in the kitchen, and Ella couldn't reconcile that image with her own. Visits with Grandma were about wearing dresses, drinking tea, and never, ever doing anything to embarrass her mom.

Ella squeezed a dollop more of crimson and gold, and swiped the canvas. The picture—whatever it was—came alive. "You didn't change when Dottie got sick."

Colleen held her brush in midair. "Part of me did."

Her words were soft, and Ella immediately regretted bringing up Colleen's wife. When Dottie died almost ten years ago, Ella didn't remember Colleen stopping her sage-waving, or hiding all her crystals, or becoming an overbearing aunt who monitored everything Ella did when she visited.

"I remember having terrible thoughts. Terrible." Colleen's brush clanked against the side of the glass water jar, and she wiped it with a towel. "I kept thinking your mom and dad were *lucky* that the only thing they had to worry about with you was epilepsy. And that it was unfair that your dad was healthy, and my sister wouldn't understand what I was going through." She huffed through her nose. "Who thinks that way? I'm embarrassed even to say it. But watching the cancer eat Dottie's bones for more than a year... I wouldn't wish that on anyone."

A sadness filled the air. What would it be like to lose your wife, your soulmate, your person, in your forties? Ella couldn't even imagine having a person. She'd thought a while ago Jasmine might be it. She was *so* in love. Or so she thought. She dreamed about her at night, thought about her during the day, the flutters shook her for the first months. At first, Jasmine represented everything Ella craved—fresh air, a confidante, laughter. God, she could make Ella laugh. That was one of the hardest things to let go of post-breakup. When she discovered Jasmine cheated, that she held such little regard for her, Ella thought she'd never laugh again.

But a small part of Ella always knew they weren't going to last. A few weeks before Jasmine broke Ella's heart, Ella brought her here to meet Colleen. Jasmine spent half the time complaining about the smells, how her shoes got dirty, and how scary the horses were.

"How are you and my mom so different? You were raised by the same people."

Colleen leaned back and eyed her canvas. "It was probably easier for me. Being the older sister, she had way more pressure than I did. And I was lucky. The earth soothed me. I'm not sure your mother ever found something that provided her the same comfort." The brush swiped back and forth until she smiled. "Your mom's not a bad person. You know that, right?"

Ella knew that, but sometimes it was easier to think she was terrible. Her mom was quick with the guilt trip and slow with the sympathy. And even though Ella thought leaving home was no big deal, it would be hard for her mom to become an empty-nester.

"You need to give her some grace, okay?" Colleen tapped Ella on the knee. "And maybe apply some of that grace to your new co-worker. My guess is she's working through something, too."

Ella's stomach fell. It never really occurred to her that Sophie might have her own issues. She always seemed so self-assured, so confident, so totally in charge. Maybe tomorrow, Ella would make some changes.

ELEVEN
SOPHIE

The headphones blared an old school Melissa Etheridge song, but Sophie couldn't focus on the lesbian power anthem. She hung the device from her neck and pushed the elevator button. Even after sharing a brunch with Maya and Harper on Saturday morning and falling asleep early after finishing Casey McQuiston's newest release, she couldn't shake the regret she felt about Friday.

She hated the way she acted towards Ella. *Hated. It.* The conversation with Malcolm had knocked her on her ass. Not only did she fail to show solid leadership qualities, but she had also been straight-up childish, allowing pre-conceived notions to cloud her judgement. And purely for the sake of self-preservation, if she ever wanted to have a trainee again, she needed to put aside her irritation at the situation.

Because really, her issue was the situation. And she took it out on the human.

The office was quiet as usual at this time of morning. Ella was at her desk, the soft light from the lamp creating an angelic effect around her as her fingers tapped the keyboard. For years, Sophie was always one of the first to arrive, desperate to get a leg up on her colleagues. She knew the signs of a chase well, and Ella was definitely chasing.

"Morning." Sophie dropped her bag on the floor under her desk. Why did Ella always have to smell so good? It was distracting. And it was always different, like she wanted to keep people guessing. Sophie leaned in, subtly, of course, as sniffing your co-workers was probably not approved in the HR handbook. A warm, deep cedar and rose tone filled her nose.

She stayed a moment longer.

"Morning." Ella's normally straight shoulders shifted like she was bracing herself, and Sophie's stomach knotted. Was that what Sophie had become? The person who caused someone to flinch? It made her think of Mr. Docks, her dickhead eighth-grade science teacher who read the worst test scores out loud, lamenting on "how embarrassing" the student was and how they were "not meeting *the barest of minimum* state standards." She remembered walking into his classroom and shrinking, keeping her fingers crossed she wouldn't be seen.

And that was what she did to Ella—Sophie had become the dickhead.

Ella reached for the large paper coffee cup to her right and handed it to Sophie.

Sophie wrapped her fingers around the cup and lowered herself to the chair. "What's this?" *Probably poison.* And honestly, Sophie wouldn't blame her.

"I got you a burnt orange mocha." Ella tugged at her sleeves, her eyes focused on the cuffs. "They claim it has the most sugar of all the drinks at the shop."

Whoa. Sophie absolutely didn't deserve the thoughtful gesture after how terrible she'd been. Maybe Ella laced it with ghost peppers or laxatives as a payback. She took a tentative sample and moaned into the sip. "Dear God, it's delicious. Was this from Red Lava?"

"Yep." Ella twirled off the top to her water. "They started

serving crepes, too, with honey butter and nuts. I got you one, well, I got each of us one."

"Yeah?" Sophie took a hefty sip this time and the orange sugar trailed her throat. She peeked behind Ella. "Where is it?"

"I ate it." Ella shrugged with a small giggle.

A giggle. She'd never heard Ella giggle before. She wasn't even sure she'd seen Ella smile, except for a couple of polite grins during co-worker introduction time. Sophie never thought about what Ella's giggle would sound like, but if she had, it probably would have been high-pitched and squeaky. Instead, it was deep and husky, and Sophie wanted to say something to hear the sound again. She looked at the water bottle next to Ella. "You didn't get yourself anything?"

Ella shook her head. Her frames slipped, and she pushed them back up her nose. "I have a confession to make."

Sophie's ears perked. "Oh yeah? What's that?"

"I hate coffee." The corner of her lip twitched. "Like I *really* hate it. It feels like I'm drinking hot, muddy water that eats away at my stomach lining."

"No. Way." Why was this little factoid so amusing? Besides knowing Ella's dad was George, she went to UW, and that she was an only child, Sophie realized she knew absolutely nothing about her co-worker. "Well, here's my confession. I hate pancakes. And crepes are pretty close, so I'm not sure I would've eaten them except to be polite."

Ella cocked her head. "Pancakes? You mean the sugary fried dough that you top with butter and syrup? No one hates pancakes."

"I do."

Ella pushed back from the desk and crossed her legs and *holy shit.* She tugged her skirt lower beneath the knee, but not before Sophie caught a peek of a smooth thigh. Sophie snapped her gaze to anywhere but there, ignoring the warmth spreading inside her. It was just surprising, that was all. Ella had worn nothing but suit pants or jeans since starting. A bare thigh was simply... unexpected.

"I'm so curious about the hatred of pancakes. Is there a backstory here?"

So much backstory. A childhood filled with a tired mom smelling of day-old fryer grease and Biofreeze. Of late nights eating the diner leftovers on the couch with her parents, as her dad rubbed her mom's feet and Sophie begged to go to McDonald's. Of upset stomachs from eating peanut butter sandwiches every day because her parents made a touch over the limit to get free lunches at school but couldn't afford to pay for actual school lunches every day. "My mom works at a diner, and she used to bring home leftovers all the time."

"Oh really?" Ella asked. "Which one?"

"J & J, over by Green Lake. You've probably never heard of it." For once, Sophie didn't mean it to sound the way it came out. The place was small, and even though it'd been around since the '60s, she couldn't imagine anyone who lived on Lake Washington had visited. It wasn't like the other Seattle local joints who boasted the famous twelve-egg omelette, or the ones that made the crab-cake benedict. J & J had nothing special except for large malts and homemade jam.

Even though Sophie didn't mean the words to sound rude or condescending, Ella's smile disappeared, and she dropped her gaze to her hands.

"God. I'm sorry. I really didn't mean it the way it came out." Sophie dug at the polish on her cuticle to pry up a fleck. After the tension-filled last few weeks, this exchange gave Sophie the bit of spark needed to think they could work together—at least until she boarded her cruise, or Ella was reassigned to a different project. But the words she spewed last week—they had to be addressed.

Sophie dropped her nail polish hunt. "Look." She cleared her throat. "I really owe you an apology for Friday."

Ella straightened. "Yes. You do."

Damnnnn. Sophie rubbed the back of her head, the buzzed hair prickling against her hand. Now was not the time to dive into her feelings on socioeconomics, unfair privilege, how it felt to be food insecure in America, and how the 1 percent—which Ella's family belonged to—was responsible for poor folks staying poor. Ultimately, Ella had as much choice in the family she was born into as Sophie. "Truth is, I hold really stupid grudges. Like *really* stupid. And, well, what happened when we first met... I just need to let it go. It clouded my judgement and I'm sorry, again, for the way I've been treating you."

The words tasted like sand. How did she let this resentment build and grow for years? Her chest grew hot, the shame sticky and unforgiving.

Ella squinted. She paused for several long moments, lightly tapping the desk. "You held a grudge? Like, against me?"

Obviously. "Yeah. From the first time we met." This moment had been nice. Sweet, even. Sophie really didn't want to ruin it by rehashing the event six years ago.

Ella's eyes filled with confusion.

Did Ella really not remember? Sure, she'd alluded to that on Friday, when things were heated. But they'd been having a nice morning, so far. She was really sticking with that story, huh?

"What happened that day?" Ella finally asked.

Sophie's chest pinched. "You really don't remember?"

Ella's gaze cast down and she fiddled with the water bottle. "I really don't. The details are... fuzzy."

For weeks, Sophie had thought about that moment. The first year of working, she used Ella's words and looks as justification for her self-doubt talk, knowing she didn't belong here. Then she used it for motivation. But the feeling she got when someone acted as though they were above her, that she was not good enough, never faded.

Sophie needed to prevent herself from spiraling anymore.

"You know what? Fresh slate? What's done is done, and we both probably said some things that day that we regret."

Ella nodded and scooted her chair back under the desk. Her breathing picked up so much that Sophie wasn't sure if she was fighting off a sneeze or suppressing a yawn.

"I, ah." Ella's voice was hesitant. "I have epilepsy."

Epilepsy? That was the very last thing Sophie thought Ella would say in this moment. How was Sophie supposed to react to that statement? Say sorry? That didn't seem like the right word. Especially since Ella didn't look like she'd revealed something negative, just something private.

"Wow," Sophie said, because what else could she offer? Her chatterbox mouth rendered shut. But... she had so many questions. What was it like? What should she do if Ella had a seizure? How long had she been epileptic? What did it feel like? "I had no idea. That must be... hard."

So dumb. She sounded unsympathetic at best, an idiot at worst. But she wasn't sure if Ella wanted to explain any further. It wasn't like they were friends. They weren't even *friendly* until this morning.

"I'd really appreciate if you didn't tell anyone." Ella stiffened.

Sophie appreciated that Ella had to say this, but the one thing Sophie didn't do was spill secrets. But shouldn't people know in case they needed to help her? She certainly didn't know what to do if Ella had a seizure.

"Do you have any experience with epilepsy?" Ella asked.

Sophie remembered hearing never to shove anything in their mouth, and make sure the person's surroundings were safe. She vaguely recalled hearing about different types of seizures, and what they showed in the movies was not always accurate. Beyond that, she had nothing. "No, not at all."

Ella dropped her hand into her lap. Her cheek sucked into her mouth, and she paused. "Listen, it's not an excuse. Like, at all. But after a seizure, even up to a few weeks after, they make me super irritable. And, well, they mess with short-term memory."

I am the most supreme asshole in the world. Maybe even universe.

"For a few years, especially during my teens, they just couldn't get my meds under control. I had more seizures than the doctors wanted. If I did, or said, something terrible to you, and I don't remember, it's not because I don't care. It's because... I don't remember."

It felt like one of those archaic computers from the 1980s had just fallen onto Sophie's chest. All these years holding a grudge, knowing so clearly what someone thought of you, knowing to your core they went home and laughed about you, and to find out it wasn't true, shook Sophie. She felt both heavier and lighter, and her brain shorted with the crossed signals.

"Well, I remember what I said to you," Sophie offered. "And it was really not cool. I'm sorry, too."

Ella's lips twitched into a grin. "Clean slate?"

"Definitely."

TWELVE
ELLA

Ella had to hand it to Sophie—when she said clean slate, she really meant clean slate. Whatever Ella said to Sophie when they first met remained buried, and gratitude flooded through her that Sophie had let it go. Post-seizure, during the post-ictal phase, Ella always sludged through brain fog, extreme fatigue, and severe irritability. Everything pissed her off, and she had little control over her emotions. Like a black-hazed nightmare, she rarely remembered what she had said. A few years back, she'd viewed some security footage from their house for an unrelated reason, and cried when she heard the way she'd spoken to Thomas. Her stomach sickened with the thought that she might have treated Sophie in the same manner.

The rest of the week morphed into a solid working relationship. Ella stood hip to hip with Sophie reviewing creative, nibbled on granola in the cafeteria, discussed project tiers, and grabbed a quiet room to pore over dozens of pages of notes.

Earlier in the week, Sophie ordered Pad Kee Mao takeout from *hands down, the best place in the International District.* She had handed over a set of chopsticks, and explained why you couldn't have the same social media message on all platforms.

The TikTok crowd differed from Facebook, which differed from Instagram, she explained. The following day, needing air after four hours of back-to-back meetings, they walked over to Red Lava for coffee (Sophie) and crepes (Ella). While sitting near the corner window, Sophie let Ella in on why the SEO team was notoriously hard to pin down, that the creative director's tell when she didn't like something was to tug on her earlobe, and how last year the stuffy-ass VP got drunk at the Christmas party and did the actual Hammer dance. *Surprisingly well,* Sophie had added.

Last night, Ella stayed late with Sophie. Over a few slices of pizza, an unfortunate episode of ultra-bubbly cream soda spilling on Ella's chest, and an explosion of tired giggles, Sophie showed her how to build a project template based on day duration instead of dates. When Ella clicked a button and cascaded information to the team, she felt like a total badass.

A hefty bump in the road jarred her from her thoughts as Thomas navigated through the Friday morning rush-hour traffic. He peeked at Ella in the rearview mirror. "Work or coffee shop?"

"Coffee, please."

The SUV eased over and Thomas jumped out to open her door. She stepped onto the sidewalk in front of the coffee shop and snugged her laptop case higher. "Want me to grab you something?"

"Not today. One more cookie and my pants won't fit. The wifey is going to trade me in for a younger model."

Ella rolled her eyes. Thomas was the fittest older man she'd ever seen. Sure, he was a driver for her family. But deep down, she had a sneaking suspicion he was some sort of government operative with John Wick-style fighting skills. "I'm going to walk to the office from here."

"You sure? Fourth day in a row. I'm thinking I'm an embarrassment for you."

His voice carried a smile, but she didn't want to tell him that he was right. "Never." She waved goodbye, knowing damn well he'd wait until she made the trek into the office building before he took off.

Thomas's presence *was* embarrassing, but that wasn't the only reason she didn't want him to drop her off. The quick jaunt to the café, waiting solo in line for coffee, and the walk to work was fuel for her dream of a new life. All week, she'd marched the sidewalk like other workers, juggling a mug, pastry, and cell phone, and felt connected to people in a way that had been missing for so long. She was part of an invisible commuter community, a fellow worker amid the daily grind. She tipped her chin at people she passed, or partook in the standard Seattle greeting—a flicker of eye contact to make sure she didn't run into them and then completely ignoring the passerby. Finally, slowly, she felt like she belonged.

Ella stuffed a stopper into the hot drink, bit into a chunk of chocolate hazelnut croissant, and made her way to the office. As she passed, she grinned at a double-parked Thomas, stepped into the building, and rode the elevator to her floor.

After firing up her laptop and starting on emails, the door opened. *Sophie.* Her heartbeat kicked up a notch. How did one always look so effortlessly cool? Ripped black skinny jeans, Doc Martens, a T-shirt with a cat shooting a rainbow laser beam from its eyes, and a cardigan. No one else could rock a mismatched outfit like her.

"You're seriously going to turn me into Pavlov's dog if you keep doing this." Sophie accepted the coffee cup and sipped. She flicked at the foam remnant on her lip and Ella pretended the motion didn't have quite the effect on her that it did. "Yum. Freaking delicious. What is this? I think I taste cardamom, but it's not chai."

Ella couldn't help but grin. She'd been bringing Sophie some type of flavored coffee all week. And she'd continue doing so for the rush she got seeing Sophie's face light up. "Edible rose. Cool, huh?"

"Very cool." She took another sip. "Seriously yummy. Thanks, Ella."

She said my name. Ella had heard her name from Sophie's mouth before, but not like this. Not layered with ginger and honey and sounding all dreamy. *Snap out of it.* After getting along for a week, Ella slowly realized the last several days that she'd developed a bit of a crush. She knew it was ridiculous. So much so that she was going to add this to her manifesto for why parents needed to stop controlling their adult kids—because the first hot queer woman who was nice to them, they'd go gaga after.

"Ella, Sophie!" Malcolm's voice filled the room as he strolled through the office doors. "My favorite PMs assigned to the Devil's ad."

Ella glanced at Sophie. "Does he mean—"

"Yep. Exactly as he said. He'd never play real favorites."

Malcolm plucked out his AirPods and snapped them in the case. "Gather around, friends. New Gracie photo." He dangled the phone in front of Ella and Sophie. "I think she's trying to read in this one." He pinched the screen to scroll tighter to the baby's face. "If you look close, she looks like she's concentrating, right? And right behind her, we have a framed phrase from Alice Walker, so..."

"Do you think maybe..." Sophie stared at the photo of the drooling baby.

Malcolm shoved the phone back in his pocket. "Maybe what?"

"Maybe she just had to poop?"

He overexaggerated a glare at Sophie and turned to Ella. "Hi, Ella, my favorite PM on the DD ad."

Ella grinned. She really liked Malcolm as a manager. She'd never had one before, and wasn't sure what to expect. But she'd pictured some stuffy guy in an obnoxious checkered tie, barking orders from a desk like her dad probably used to do. Even though Sophie was the one training her, Malcolm was their leader, and he perfectly executed a hands-off/hands-on approach. A few times a day he'd swing by her desk, ask her and Sophie if they needed anything, then leave, trusting them to do their job. "Don't need me getting in the way, messing anything up, but I'm here if needed," he'd said her first week.

He snaked a leg around a rolling office chair and pushed it near the women. He plonked down, crossed his legs, and tapped the corner of his crisp white Jordans. "Give me a five-minute status update."

Ella remained quiet until Sophie gave her a gentle nod. "Go ahead." Her voice was encouraging and warm—exactly what Ella needed.

No matter how informal Ella's mind knew this meeting was, her insides didn't agree. Her tongue turned heavy, and she exhaled a low, very unsteady breath. "The leadership team signed off on the strategy. The core target is eighteen to thirty-five, of course, and the sub-targets within that are millennials and Gen Z. The creative lead approved the first-round messaging but hasn't presented it to the director. First-round web landing and banners are developed, and the social cadence accepted."

Ella cleared her throat and glanced at Sophie. Her eyes had softened and her lips were curved up. She looked... proud. The feeling of validation settled somewhere deep, somewhere untouched in so long, and Ella committed that look to memory. "The last we heard, though, the copy team were struggling to come up with consolidated messaging," she continued. "We're hoping to complete that by tomorrow, or Monday at the latest, for preliminary approval."

Malcolm lifted his brow, glanced hard at Ella, then Sophie, and back to Ella. "Well, my job is done here." He chuckled and pushed himself back from the desk. "Great job, you two. Really. Keep at it, and Sophie will get on that cruise ship knitting circle after all."

"Rude." Sophie grinned through the word and watched as Malcolm rounded the corner. When he did, she rested a hand on Ella's arm. Ella froze, the touch making her belly jump. "Malcolm's the best manager in the world. But trust me when I say he doesn't hand out compliments very often. When you get them, hold them close."

I'm straight-up beaming. Out through her chest, up her neck, and square on her cheeks. Ella tried and failed to pull in her smile.

Later that afternoon, Ella stretched and rolled her neck after a two-hour-long project-timeline working session with Sophie. The doors to the east burst open and nearly slammed against the wall. George stomped in with two employees clipping at his heels, carrying an armful of red-and-black pastry boxes.

"Christ. He's the least subtle human in the world," Ella said to Sophie, who didn't really respond but drew her lips into her mouth like she was suppressing a smile. The agency was his place, after all—one would think he'd treat the infrastructure gentler.

"Devil's Doughnuts crew meet in conference room A-14." He cupped his hands to amplify, which was not needed as his baritone voice already shook walls. "Time to double-click into this campaign."

Sophie grinned at the remark, scribbled a quick note on a Post-it, and shoved it in her desk drawer.

"Does this happen a lot?" Ella asked as she snapped shut her laptop.

Sophie unplugged the docking station cord and stood. "What? Free doughnuts?"

"No. My dad being so extra."

Sophie snickered. "Um…"

Ella followed the sweet smell of fried dough down the hall and into the conference room, which was already buzzing with excitement. Red-and-black boxes sprawled over the bare U-shaped table, and the executive assistants hurried stacking paper plates and napkins.

Several staff members gazed at the selections, then puppy-dog-eyed her dad, no doubt waiting for an invitation to eat.

"All right, everyone," her dad bellowed with a clap.

If he were a kindergarten teacher wrangling kids, clapping would be acceptable. Great, even. But being CEO, the loud snap was jarring.

"During yesterday's leadership briefing meeting, it came to my attention that the creative team is stuck on messaging." He crossed his arms across his hefty chest and pointedly glanced at each member, who glanced away. The tone wasn't completely scolding, but even Ella shrunk against the sound.

"Sophie," he barked.

She straightened her spine. "Yes?"

"How many weeks until launch?"

"Five."

His head snapped to Ella. *Oh God, don't call on me. Please don't do it.*

"Ella."

He did it.

"How many weeks until creative presents to leadership?"

Ella swallowed. "Four." Saying it out loud drove home the message. The team had absolutely no time to waste, considering the magnitude of ads on multiple platforms. All the bickering and power matches occurring needed to end, and everyone had to focus.

Co-workers shifted in their seats as the time constraint settled across the room. The air turned heavy before George smiled. "All right. Time to light a spark. Everyone, dig in." He waved Vanna White-style to the pastries. "Sample, share. Get high on sugar. I don't care if you're the creative partner, project manager, web producer, or designer. Cancel the next two hours, brainstorm, and come up with some decent shit so we can hit this deadline. Capisce?"

Ella cringed. She'd told him before that he sounded like a dick using the word, but he couldn't understand why. George rubbed his palms, then hovered his meaty finger over the boxes. Finally, he plucked one from the center and took a hefty bite. "Good. *Creamy.*"

Sophie's face held the same expression as Ella's: *Ewww.* Ella leaned into Sophie's ear. "Thank God he's not part of the creative team."

A giggle squeaked out from Sophie's lips before she put her hand to her mouth and expelled a horribly fake cough.

"You can use that line." He chuckled from deep in his belly.

The team stared in response. Ella glanced at everyone, inspecting if they were passing along whatever judgement they may have for her dad on to her. But most eyes focused on her dad or the doughnuts. Another excruciating minute passed of George droning on about the need to "roll up sleeves" and "pass the baton when needed" and "take care of the low-hanging fruit" (whatever the hell that meant). Finally, he grabbed a second doughnut and waved everyone to the table. Soon, chatter filled the room.

Sophie tugged at Ella's sleeve and stood. "Come on, let's grab one before all the good ones are taken."

Facing Ella was a spread of the most spectacular doughnuts she'd ever seen. And the variety... Who developed this and were they some sort of gluten genius? Chunks of brownies on top, a full candy bar sticking upright with an edible golden spring, fruity colored cereal, bacon and maple glaze...

Ella reached for a red velvet one with black icing and shaved chocolate. She sunk her teeth into it, the sugar practically making her teeth sweat. The shaved chocolate hit Ella's taste buds, sending a sweet spike through her veins. It had been forever since she had a proper doughnut like this, made with craft and precision. Probably not since she was a teenager and she and her dad took an impromptu day trip to the Edmonds Farmers Market and hopped on the Kingston ferry for specialty doughnuts on the pier.

Sophie bit into a chocolate one with whipped berry filling. "Oh God. Delicious." She gestured to the chairs in the corner. "Let's take notes if the team says anything interesting."

"Think the team will come up with some good stuff?" Ella asked as she scooted up to the table.

"Puff the magic powdered doughnut?" a voice called from behind.

Sophie pulled up a chair next to Ella, licked the powder from the corner of her thumb, and hovered a pen over a notebook. "Um, let's hope they have some better than that."

Ella wiped her hand on a napkin and began capturing the conversation like a court reporter. The room soon erupted in a collage of animated conversation and elevated voices.

"A spindle of doughnut holes? A hole in one?"

"Aye, matey, grab yourself a fried golden nugget and..."

"Aye, matey?" Someone in the room laughed. "We're not building a pirate ship."

"Safe space, safe space! Rule number one. Don't be an asshat and no knocking ideas."

"Stick a pitchfork in me, I'm done. Delicious and moist."

"Nope. We can never use 'moist' with an ad."

"What is it with that word?" a guy in the back called out. "Spongy?"

Sophie pulled her shirt over her mouth and giggled. "Just when you think it can't get any worse." She bunched up a napkin and stood. "I need coffee. Be right back."

A full doughnut down and Ella grabbed number two. God,

it was *so good*. Devilishly good, which was too cheesy of a line, otherwise she would've offered it. A designer put on music and the space shifted into a happy hour-like atmosphere. A few team members sketched on the whiteboard, two guys bunched up napkins and tossed them into a wastebasket like basketballs, another group threw their feet up on the chairs and stretched.

Maybe, just maybe, her dad knew what he was doing. He had left without announcement, leaving the group alone with the food, and without the pressure of the CEO watching their progress. It was possible this wasn't only about getting the team together to brainstorm. Everyone was stressed, over-worked, and snapping at each other like bickering siblings. Right now was the first time in two weeks where people laughed.

Sophie returned, a sparkling water tucked under her arm, and juggling two coffee cups. "Here." She handed Ella the water. "Stay hydrated. The last thing we need is for either of us to slip into a sugar coma."

Ella downed the water, then re-poised her fingers to transcribe.

"We bake it, and you will come," a web producer called out. When the room turned silent and stared at her, a solid three seconds passed before her face screamed red and she slapped her hand across her mouth. "You all are seriously perverted. Damn sickos." She laughed and fanned her face. "I was talking like the Field of Dreams, jerks."

Ella laughed along with the woman, deep in her belly, and her body shook. The sugar was probably soaking in, and her stomach gurgled with dough. The afternoon fuchsia sun lowered a smidge and danced across Sophie, who was laughing, too. That full, devastating smile had been buried under pursed lips and worry lines. But now, the dimples were on display, the lip ring shone under the light, and... *oh boy*. She was really, really cute.

"What do you think, Ella?" a designer called as he cut a lemon-crusted doughnut in half.

She flushed with heat. "Oh no... I'm not a creative. I strictly work on project plans."

He whooshed her words away with a wave of the hand. "Forget that. Come on, first thoughts that pop into your mind."

First thoughts, first thoughts. She took another bite. The chocolate was smooth, pillowy even, and she swore she saw stars. *Heavenly.* "Heaven in my mouth."

Sophie's eyes lifted. "Whoa. Where did this tigress come from?" She laughed. "Sorry, sorry. Too easy."

Ella lightly smacked her on the arm. "So unfair. Fine, you try."

"EEK. I don't know." Sophie licked the top of the frosting. "Juicy devil land? Strawberry heaven? One-way ticket to sugared hell? Sugar hole? Oh! A glazed hole in one, no, someone already said that."

"Oh my God, make it stop," someone called from the corner, then ducked from a torpedo-launched napkin aimed at their head.

"I want to lick my glazed fingers," Ella called out, layering with the others the not-so-subtle sexual innuendos.

"Ella wants to lick glazed things. Sophie wants a sugar hole." One of the creatives slumped in the chair with a grin. "I don't know... this conversation has gone to hell in the best possible way."

"Devil's Doughnuts: A one-way ticket to the best possible hell," someone in the back yelled.

A blush swept Sophie's cheeks as she laughed. Maybe it was from the room heating up, or the coffee, but her giggle was high-pitched, and squeaky, and completely adorable. But then she snorted, and Ella lost it, her belly jiggling from hearty laughter.

This was fun. *Fun.* Ella could not remember the last time she had actual fun. Hour one melted into hour two, and the sun bored through the window as it lowered. Rustling papers, and a smattering of really terrible drawings and phrases, filled the whiteboard. Some shifted in their seats while a few hopped on the counter, dangling their feet. Others had their heads on the table, fighting off sugar-induced naps.

Sophie pulled a leg up on the chair and rested her chin against her knee. Her laughter slowed to a soft grin, and her eyes turned glossy. She stared out the window, like in a trance, and her tongue swept her lip. The way the flecks of hazel in Sophie's green eyes sparkled, and the tiniest uptick of her lip, made Ella want to know her thoughts.

A few people left the room, suppressing yawns as they lagged to their last meeting of the day. The conversation winded down, and soon only Sophie and Ella remained. Ella looked across the space, with napkins, crumbs, and plates scattering the conference area. "I'm going to throw up." She held her belly, the sugar gurgling her insides. "I ate so much."

"Ugh, me too." Sophie groaned and rested her forehead on the table. "I need milk to neutralize the monstrosity, but I can't even think of adding any more to my stomach."

A yawn tore through Ella. She stood and tossed plates and napkins into the garbage. "All this sugar has knocked me out. I'm *soooo* tired."

"Same." Sophie joined her in cleaning and combined the doughnuts into one box. "I know you don't drink coffee, but want to grab a Coke or something?"

Ella grabbed a sanitizer spray from the corner and wiped the counter. "No, I can't have caffeine. It's a seizure trigger, so I try to avoid it." Definitely too much sugar. She wouldn't normally have divulged that so casually.

A little nod, a quirk of a smile, and no follow-up questions was Sophie's reaction and Ella appreciated it. Sophie probably didn't care. Not that she *actually* didn't care... but she was probably disinterested in what it was like to have epilepsy. Which was good. So far, Sophie hadn't treated her any different, except maybe being a little nicer, which Ella contributed to their truce.

Sophie stretched on her toes, her arms reaching for the ceiling. Her shirt lifted, and the smooth white lower belly at the corner of her hip stuck out. Ella bit the urge to bury her fingers into the dip in her hip, just to see if it was as soft as it appeared.

Oof. Too much sugar, too little sex, and a lifetime of repression. That was what this was... this burning want to have Sophie lift her arms just a tiny bit higher, just a little longer. She wiped the counter down one last time, forcing herself to focus. She was here for one reason only: finish this job so she could move on.

THIRTEEN
SOPHIE

Temporal lobe, generalized seizures, tonic-clonic, cluster, absence... Sophie's eyes burned. After crashing hard on Friday from a self-induced sugar coma, and using Saturday for chores, errands, and catching up with Maya, she'd spent most of Sunday researching everything she could on epilepsy. And the more she learned, the less she knew.

It wasn't Sophie's place to ask questions or find out what type of epilepsy Ella had. However, her urge to learn more consumed her. What was it like the first time she had a seizure? Did it hurt? How could a kid handle that, go to school, and deal with all the shitty social pressure that comes along with being a kid? How was college? How often did it happen?

Sophie continued reading as the metro bumped down to the office. *Focal onset aware.* People can be awake during a seizure? After hours of reading yesterday, she definitely understood that what she knew as a "grand mal" seizure was now called a tonic-clonic seizure, and not every person with epilepsy had these types of seizures.

The bus pulled up to the corner, and Sophie hopped off. She turned the corner and saw Ella making her way up the sidewalk, and Sophie's heart skipped a beat. *Skipped a beat?* She breathed through the sensation. Since last week, it felt as though a barrier had broken. The lines, the boundary, had somehow blurred, and Sophie loved it. She saw glimpses of a personality that she hadn't known existed, absorbed sparks and tingles she hadn't felt for years. Ella had made her laugh, hard, on Friday, and it felt damn good. And she was *funny*. Who knew? She played off her deliciously devilish innuendos as playful and innocent, but a flash, something twinkly and mischievous, sparked through her gaze, and Sophie went home desperate to know more.

And it didn't help that the vision of Ella saying "licking glazed fingers" had seeped somewhere deep and warm into Sophie's subconscious, producing pretty incredible dreams Friday night. Although, admittedly, it might have just been the sugar eating at her brain cells.

"Ella! Hey!" Sophie called out, and increased her steps.

Ella turned around and smiled, and *dammit*. Now the skipped heartbeat took a lunge and morphed into thumps.

"Hey!" Ella pushed her glasses up with her index finger and moved toward Sophie, with a full, white-toothed smile.

Maybe it was how Ella walked, or because she was at an incline, but Ella had a bounce to her step that Sophie hadn't seen before. In fact, Sophie could swear Ella was damn near jumping.

Damn, she's pretty adorable.

"I was thinking about you this weekend. I almost sent you a text," Ella said as she joined Sophie.

Hmmm. Sophie kept her face neutral, refusing to show how much she thought of Ella over the weekend as well. She sincerely doubted Ella had the same thoughts as Sophie did, or prompted the same internal energy. "Oh yeah? Got visions-slash-nightmares of project plans in your head."

Ella let out a soft chuckle. "No. I was wondering if you

recovered from Friday. My dad and I stopped at Alki Bakery on Saturday, and I couldn't even imagine having any more sweets."

Sophie held the building door open for Ella. "Man, he must have a gut of steel. I had to stop by the grocery store on Friday and grab some Tums. My belly hurt so bad." They stepped into the elevator and ascended. "But I think it was good to go through that exercise. So many ideas got tossed around, something must have sparked the team."

The office was still, even more than usual, and the motion-detected lights flickered alive. Sophie tossed her bag on the chair next to her and pulled out her red marker to cross off the date on her calendar. Twenty-five days left until launch. Her stomach lurched into her throat. So much still had to be done, but at this point, most was out of her control. She could confirm statuses, mediate, set timelines, and funnel information. But she wasn't a creator.

"What's on the agenda for today?" Ella asked as she plugged in her laptop to the docking station.

Sophie turned on the monitor. "I have to clean up all the notes I took on Friday morning. Honestly, I should've sent those Friday night, but after the doughnut fiesta, no one was going to look at them." Talking about delayed notes caused a pinch in her chest. After the massive working hours the last several weeks, and gorging on sweets, the last thing the team was going to do was review anything she sent. But she needed to send them ASAP, because as soon as 9:00 a.m. hit, the team would need the information to continue with their work.

"Perfect." Ella clicked against her keyboard. "I can work on updating the task assignments."

Sophie checked her watch. *Dammit.* The metro had been delayed this morning, which pushed everything back by fifteen minutes. She needed a full hour to edit, review, and send the notes.

She clicked her mouse over the screen and froze. *Wait...*

what? No. No... this couldn't be. Her fingers flew, clicking and clicking. Where the hell were the notes? She *always* used this app. But instead of notes, facing her was a big, fat blank screen. Her heartbeat clouded her vision. Did she take them somewhere else? No... she wouldn't have. She searched, clicked, global searched, and clicked, again. *What in the actual hell?* She was the most diligent, organized person she knew. How had she messed this up? Sickness snaked through her stomach.

Gone. Everything was gone. Not a single thing had been captured from arguably one of the most important meetings of the week and she wanted to puke. "Shit."

Ella glanced up from her screen, her eyes narrowing in concern. "Everything good?"

"No." Her tongue was sharp, as heated panic spread across her chest.

Ella's eyes flickered down, and Sophie's gut turned. Sophie laid a gentle hand on Ella's arm. "Sorry. I'm not mad at you. I'm livid with myself and in total panic mode." Without those notes, they were royally effed. She could try to recreate them, but she couldn't recite the finer details from memory. Maybe she should go to IT to try and recover what was lost, but that would be a minimum of a few hours and she didn't have any hours. She didn't even have seconds.

"What's happened?" Ella asked.

Sophie slumped back into her chair, her eyes refusing to meet Ella's gaze. She loved her role, loved being hyper-organized. The validation she received daily from her work filled her inexplicably. But now, she wanted to curl into a ball in the corner. "I lost the notes I took Friday morning. Everything's gone." The words felt like sandpaper ripping her throat.

"The notes from the round-one call on Friday?" Ella straightened. "I took notes. Maybe I can help?"

Sophie's ears perked. "You did?"

"Yes. You told me to take notes on everything, remember?"

A smile filled Ella's tone. She tapped the keyboard, turned the laptop to face Sophie, and scooted closer. A waft of rose and mint hit Sophie, and she tingled against the scent, before something else hit her. *Shock.* Right before her, on Ella's screen, lay perfectly buttoned-up, time-stamped, highly organized, master class-worthy notes. The air returned to her lungs.

"Ella! What? Holy sh... These are amazing." She threw her arms around Ella and squeezed.

Ella went stiff.

"Oh my God." Sophie yanked herself away. As a staunch supporter of consent before touching of any kind, she felt icky. "I'm so sorry. I didn't mean..." Her palm flew to the back of her head.

"No, it's totally okay." Ella cleared her throat as her cheeks swept with pink. "I'm really glad I could help."

For the last week or so, Sophie had found herself looking forward more and more to work, knowing she'd spend time with Ella. Even though years had passed since something like this happened, Sophie wasn't in total denial about what was bubbling inside—the electric zings, the extra care in picking out outfits, the lightness in her chest when Ella arrived. Besides the one-night stand with the nameless woman from the happy hour last year—which didn't count as having *feelings*—it had been a long time since Sophie festered like this. Everything happening inside was certainly more than what one should feel for a co-worker. But as Sophie re-scanned the pristine notes, something else took over—gratitude. She was thankful she and Ella were on the same team. "Do you want to send this out?"

Ella's mouth opened, then closed. "Are you sure?" Behind the chunky frames, her eyes grew wide. "This is your project. You're the lead. I'm just a bystander."

The humility in her voice struck a chord. Ella did not realize the level of ass-saving she just performed. Beyond that, she'd gotten zero credit for all the time she'd spent in the office working on this project. "You deserve everyone knowing they came from you."

Ella tucked a dark lock behind her ear, and her lips twitched into a grin. She leaned toward the screen and squinted hard for several moments while scrolling through the page. She poised her fingers, hit a few buttons, and leaned back with a satisfied sigh.

The next few hours blurred. Sophie's fingers and brain struggled to keep up with the pace. Pings bounced in from everywhere, carrying messages like "what's the timing?," "where we at with approval?," and "client meeting set for tomorrow." People buzzed by, juggling laptops and coffee as they rushed to their next meeting, while chatter and swearing filled the space.

Mid-message to the legal team, Ella tossed a granola bar on Sophie's desk.

"How did you know?" Sophie ripped open the wrapper and chewed, hoping to quiet the rumbles in her stomach.

Ella blew the top of her bangs from her face and opened her own wrapper. "You're like the Snickers commercial, where the person is hangry."

Sophie huffed through her nose. "See? A proper ad. How long ago did that come out and you still reference it?"

"Good lesson. Got it." Ella nibbled on the granola bar. "Sure is quiet without my dad here today."

Sophie coughed. She may have warmed up to Ella, but not enough to where she would talk smack about her dad. She fully subscribed to the universal language that you can always talk crap about your own parents, but never about someone else's. "Is he back tomorrow?"

"Yes. Sounds like this week is heavy on—"

Crunch. A shrieking, violent sound of shattering glass and a sickening metallic crunch ripped through the room. Sophie's toes gripped into the shaking floor. The faint sound of Ella gasping and clutching her chest sounded next to her. Sophie blinked the room into focus and touched her limbs to see if they were intact, as her pulse thudded in her neck. One, then two, then three full seconds passed before the room boomed back to life. People yelled across the room and bolted to the window.

Ella remained frozen, her cheeks nearly stark white, her eyes unblinking.

The fear traveling Ella's face made Sophie want to hug her, but she refrained this time. Instead, Sophie pressed her fingertips to Ella's shoulder. "Are you okay?"

"Yeah... I, uh..." Ella patted herself and her gaze darted the room. "Was that an earthquake?"

It was definitely something, but an earthquake seemed unlikely. Sophie joined her co-workers, who were pressed up against the window. Her breath fogged the pane, as the scene unfolded. Nine floors below, chaos had erupted—billowed smoke, a gaggle of yelling onlookers, and honking halted traffic. Sophie squinted and leaned in, making out what looked like three or four collided cars, and a delivery truck that had slammed into their building.

"Oh my God..." Ella whispered, with her hands flattened against the glass. "I hope no one got hurt. Did anyone see what happened?"

A man ran down the sidewalk carrying a fire extinguisher, people paced like caged animals with phones glued to their ears. Panicked pedestrians pulled people from the cars, doors flung open, a woman's scream reached them all the way on the ninth floor.

"Everyone all right?" Malcolm asked as he rounded the corner and joined his team at the window.

Sophie nodded as murmurs swirled the surrounding space.

"That guy must've come out of nowhere."

"Should someone call 911?"

"Someone down there probably did."

"Don't want to overload the system."

A piercing alarm cut through the conversation, and Sophie threw her hands over her ears. "Warning. Fire. Warning. Fire." The speakers roared with the mechanical voice and the security lights flashed. Ella's brows knitted so close together they almost became one, as she covered her ears and closed her eyes.

Sophie pulled Ella close to her, the deafening siren slicing at her eardrums. Beneath her palms, Ella trembled. "It's going to be fine, okay? I got you," Sophie whispered. The blinking lights didn't engulf the entire room, but she didn't know if they could still trigger a seizure. "We have earthquake and fire drills every quarter. It's probably not even a real fire, more a precautionary measure."

Ella kept her eyes closed and chewed her lower lip. "Okay." The words sounded pushed out, with no level of confidence attached.

Within a few seconds, the office team emergency response snapped into order, fixing neon hats on their heads, and bellowing orders through a bullhorn. "Everyone needs to evacuate. This way please. Stay calm, move quick."

Ella opened her eyes, fear filling her face. Her chest lifted in heavy breaths, and she slammed her left eye with her palm. It took Sophie a moment to recall an article she read about closing one eye during strobing lights to help stave off the trigger.

"Come on." Sophie tugged Ella towards the desk as the team hurried to grab a few items and follow the line out the door. "We don't know how long this will last. I'll grab our laptops and backpacks and we can work from Starbucks or something until they let us back in."

The calmness in Sophie's tone was a bit of a farce, but it wasn't the car-accident situation making her uneasy. Riding the metro alone since she was ten, she'd seen the most random things in the city, and little frazzled her. Accidents, drug use, fights, film crews, protests, unicycles. But seeing a normally poised Ella with a flushed face and fear-laced eyes tore through Sophie.

After shoving their belongings in a bag, Sophie led Ella to the door, and walked hip to hip with the other building mates down nine floors. Sophie carried both bags as Ella gripped the side of the railing with her free hand, still covering her eye with her other. The shuffling of workers filled the stairwell. Moans that people were being too cautious, some jokes that folks were getting out of a meeting they didn't want to attend, and others wondering if people got hurt filled the cement echo chamber. The faintest sensation of claustrophobia took over as Sophie tried not to imagine what would happen if someone tripped.

Outside, Sophie inhaled a mist-filled breath and peeked at Ella, who blinked open her left eye. First responder sirens wailed in the background, and the emergency response team waved people away from the scene. "This way! Keep walking!"

Ella's color slowly returned. She grabbed her backpack from Sophie and slung it over her shoulder. "Thanks for carrying this."

The tone was too sheepish, and Sophie tried hard to push away the sympathy, but she couldn't help it. Even before her epilepsy research rabbit hole, she knew flashing lights could trigger a seizure. Obviously, Ella was human and had feelings just like other people, and seeing her like this, obviously scared, fragile, and uncertain, made Sophie want to wrap a blanket around her and sit with her until she returned to her normal, feisty self.

After walking for a block, Sophie pointed across the street. "Let's duck into that coffee shop by the lights." She pushed the chirping signal, then scooted through the intersection.

Apparently, the entire building had the same thought as every coffee shop on the block had lines out the door.

"Keep walking?" Ella asked.

"Looks like it."

They crossed the next street and headed closer to Belltown. The surrounding traffic was still gridlocked, but idle motors took over the honking. Ella's braced shoulders returned to a less militant stance, but her smile was gone. "Are you sure you're okay? Things like that freak me out, too."

Ella's chest lifted in an inhale. "I thought for a second I had a seizure."

Huh? Sophie's head cocked. "Really?"

"Only a split second." Ella sidestepped an approaching pedestrian. "It's probably more PTSD than anything. But when something way out of the norm happens, it takes my brain a moment to reconcile the disorientation, you know? It was just shocking, that's all."

That actually made sense. When Sophie was around twelve, she and her dad were in a minor fender bender. She had that same reaction, wondering for a hot second if she was hurt. "I get it. I mean, I'll never fully understand what these situations are like for you, but I can conceptually understand. But the sound of the truck hitting the building..." She shuddered. "So scary. I've never heard anything like that before."

Yes, she researched over the weekend about epilepsy, but she was hungry for more knowledge. How did Ella manage her symptoms? What did it actually feel like? Was she awake or unconscious during a seizure? All the questions seemed so invasive, and the very last thing she wanted Ella to think was that Sophie felt any less about her. In fact, Sophie's feelings were nearly the opposite. Ella was rising to superhero status. But she refrained from telling Ella that, as she didn't want to be seen as glamorizing the disorder.

At this point, no words was probably the best option.

Sophie stepped over a dip in the sidewalk and turned the block. *Great.* Another line out the door. "Good God. It's the coffee-apocalypse."

"You going through withdrawals yet?" Ella raised her

eyebrows, and *oh*, if that teasing tone didn't do something to Sophie's insides.

"Not yet." Sophie jutted her chin to the opposite street with a public park. "We could sit on a park bench and hotspot from our cells, but the mist is going to shift to rain any second and we're gonna get cold and wet."

"I'm no expert, but I think they frown upon laptops getting wet."

"Ha. True." Sophie slowed her steps. Heading back home was the most logical decision. But she'd grown used to spending more time with Ella than anyone else in her life, and the idea of working solo from her apartment didn't sound fun. She liked having a co-worker she could rely on. She refused to allow her brain to think it was anything but that, but the belly tingles had other ideas. "I guess we could work from home. I know we need to be locked at the hip, but we could just do a Zoom call and share our screens?"

Ella slowed to a full stop. She glanced at Sophie, at her watch, then back to Sophie. "I have an idea." A grin spread, wide, full, and beautiful. "Want to come home with me?"

FOURTEEN

ELLA

What a strange reality I'm in. An hour or so post-seizure, Ella usually felt like she was in a lucid dream. She could control her actions. She knew, sort of, where she was, but reality was tilted. She'd often look for something she thought she lost but was unsure of what the object was. Or she'd say yes to random things (*"Do you like black licorice?" "Yes!," when really, black licorice is disgusting*).

Having Sophie in the back of the SUV as Thomas navigated them to her house, was not what it felt like after a seizure. But it definitely messed with her reality.

Sophie was mostly quiet as they exited the highway. After walking almost two miles to a spot where Thomas could pick them up, Sophie dove into panic mode of how much time they'd lost since being evacuated. She instant messaged everyone and tossed the phone to the side when no one responded. Her phone pinged and she snapped it up.

"Malcolm said the fire department hasn't cleared the building yet. Tow trucks have arrived, and we should all take the day off." She pushed her head back into the seat and pinched the bridge of her nose. "It's nice and all, but we don't have a day to waste. Everything will be pushed back."

Sophie's work ethic was one for the record books, and Ella could understand the need to succeed. And she'd been more than vocal about wanting to take the cruise, which wouldn't happen if they didn't complete the launch on time. Ella had a strong inclination to offer to pay for a cruise for her if they missed the deadline. But she hated the idea that Sophie might see that as a condescending offer, not a genuine gift.

As Ella's neighborhood came into focus, Sophie stared out the window with her lips pressed together. It was impossible to gauge what she was thinking. When Ella first had Jasmine over, she droned on about the home sizes, the intricate landscaping, and asked, "Is it true Dave Matthews lives in this neighborhood?"

But Sophie wasn't asking about who may or may not live in the neighborhood, she wasn't lamenting about the gardeners, or the houses, or if everyone had "maids and a bell." She was just... neutral.

The car pulled into the driveway and Sophie reached for the door.

"Wait." Ella pressed her hand against Sophie's. "Thomas opens the door for you."

Sophie tilted her head. "Why?"

"Ah... because that's the rules?" As soon as the words came out of her mouth, she wanted to laugh them back in. She had never questioned why Thomas opened the door.

"Hmmm." Sophie popped open the door with a sly grin. "I've never been one for rules."

Thomas pivoted with a chuckle and stepped quickly to open Ella's door. "Your new friend is going to get me fired."

"Oh, stop. My parents would die without you." She crossed the driveway toward the front door and motioned Sophie to follow. "Please tell me my mom's not home."

Thomas shook his head. "She's not."

If she didn't know any better, she'd think that Thomas had the slightest scolding in his microscopically lifted brow, and maybe she deserved it. She'd been pretty hard on her mom these last few weeks. She was trying to show her grace, after her conversation with Colleen, but her mom had turned clingy as hell after she started her job and it was grating on her more and more.

"She's having a late lunch with friends in Elliott Bay." He checked his watch. "I'm going to head back to the city and wait for her if you two are okay?"

"Yep, we're good." At least, she was good. Sophie looked a little pale-faced and uncomfortable as she scraped at her nail polish. Ella paused at the door, taking a breath. This whole sweaty-palm, dry-mouth thing happening was totally uncalled for. Even though Sophie was drop-dead gorgeous, she was still just a co-worker. And yet, something about the day felt reminiscent of when she brought Jasmine here, when her heart thudded in her chest, when she couldn't wait to run up to the bedroom to feel Jasmine against her and taste her skin.

She didn't miss Jasmine. Not really, anyway. Her heart had mended and healed, but the sense of betrayal lingered, grazing beneath the surface like an old, faint scar.

Sophie followed her into the room and stopped at the foyer, her gaze traveling up the grand staircase and across the room. Her shoulders lifted in an inhale when she firmed her shoulders and dropped her backpack. "Where should we set up?"

Work. Yes, obviously they were here to work. "Um, we can go into the den off the kitchen. Are you hungry at all? We can grab snacks, or our housekeeper, Lydia, could make something for us?"

"Housekeeper?" Sophie's eyes widened. "Oh, uh. No, I'm good. Thanks, though. I'll just follow you."

These heart palpitations needed to slow down, or Ella was going to pass out. Why was she so nervous? Was it because she had very few friends and limited guests? Or was it because of who she was with? She needed to get out of her head, stop acting weird, stop tensing her shoulders. For nearly a month, she'd sat next to Sophie every day. They ate together and ran for coffee breaks. She knew that around 10:00 a.m. Sophie got hungry and reached for a snack, that she adored Malcolm but didn't like the lead designer, and that she cracked her knuckles after typing for too long. But here, now, felt different.

She led Sophie through the entryway and down to the kitchen, motioning to the custom oak corner table. Even though Sophie said she didn't want anything, Ella still grabbed a few bottles of water, and joined her. The rustling of backpacks and notebooks filled the otherwise silent space, and soon, the clicking of keyboards took over.

The nerves burned off and Ella focused on the timeline review, finished the water, and grabbed snacks. Mid-crunch, Sophie slammed the laptop shut and groaned.

"No one is responding to anything." She plucked a grape from the fruit bowl and popped it into her mouth. "This is useless. We are at a complete standstill."

"So now what?"

Sophie stretched and her gaze shifted to Lake Washington. Her eyes traveled across the courtyard, stopping at the garden, when she tugged on her lips. "Can I ask you a question? Like a really personal one?"

This could go one of a million ways. Was this a sex talk? Socioeconomic talk? A getting-to-know-you-on-a-deeper-level talk? "Sure."

"Is it hard to have epilepsy?" Sophie's cheeks turned red, and she pressed her palm into her forehead. "God, sorry. What a dumbass question. I can't believe I just asked that."

Ella tugged on a grape and focused on the fruit in her hand. "Yes, it's hard." A replay roll of her life flashed in her mind. Doctors, meds, invasive exams, the sickening fear and helplessness she felt the moment right before a seizure hit. But recognizing her resiliency over the years, knowing she could power through anything, was a gift. "I missed a full year of school, *twice*. In the sixth grade, I literally couldn't absorb anything. And in college, it happened again. I missed so much class, nearly failed some courses, constantly retook tests, and asked for accommodations... Yeah, it's hard."

Sophie bit the side of her lip. "I've never known anyone with epilepsy. I think there are a lot of things I take for granted."

"Probably." Ella plucked a few more grapes from the vine and slid the bowl closer to Sophie. "Like, I can't take a bath or go in a pool without supervision. We have this amazing hot tub outside, and the only time I can use it is with my mom or dad. I mean, can you imagine how fun it is to sit in the tub with King George?"

Sophie's eyes flashed wide. "King George? Um..."

"You all are not as discreet as you may think." She'd heard the term rumbled through the hall a few times. "I'm not mad, though. I think he'd like it."

"Whew." Sophie overexaggerated wiping faux sweat from her brow. "But yeah, not sure I'd want to go hot tubbing with your dad, either."

"Right? Or, like, I don't know. I can't get drunk, or have too much sugar, or go to a rave because of the blinking lights." Although, admittedly, a rave never sounded fun. Too loud, too many sweaty bodies smooshed together, the fear of a fire hazard and trampling over each other. "Driving a car. That one kills me. I've always wanted to but can't."

Sophie tapped her fingers against the water bottle. "I hate driving. I have a car, but I hate it so much that I take the bus most places."

"But you have the option, you know?" Ella stood and leaned against the window, watching the water below. She'd long ago accepted she had epilepsy. It was part of her, a piece of her identity, woven into the fiber of her being. But the restlessness of her restrictions weighed heavily, seeping into her bones. "Sometimes I feel like I have no options. I'm just... Ugh. I'm so restless. I'm so just over it all. I want to drive so bad. I know it seems super simple, and I have all this." She jutted her arms to the view outside. "But I want to feel what's it like to push a gas pedal and make something move. I want to turn a wheel. I want to hot tub without my dad!"

God damn her lips trembling in front of Sophie of all people. She turned her back to Sophie and stared out the window, hoping the mist hitting the trees would distract her. Besides the fateful night with her parents when she forced them to let her work, and the breakup with Jasmine, and a couple of weeks ago in the office, crying actually was not a norm. She swallowed back the urge to kick Sophie out, while fighting the longing to hug her.

Sophie joined her at the window, standing so close she felt their skin brush. A subtle, cedar-laced scent traveled from her, and Ella wanted to melt. So many moments passed Ella wasn't sure what would break the silence. "Such a beautiful view," Sophie finally said. "Do you ever worry a dead body will wash up on your lawn?"

Ella broke into a giggle. "That's so random." The relief that Sophie had broken the icy moment was enough for Ella to *really* want to wrap her arms around her. Sophie's lips split into a wide grin, her lip ring rising. That mouth... those lips. So pretty, so soft... "Come on. Let's raid the pantry."

After loading up on cheese, crackers, berries, and chocolate-covered almonds, Sophie dug into the food as Ella fetched more drinks. The conversation turned to movies, music, and a discovered shared love of plain potato chips dipped in sour cream. Because, obviously.

"Can I ask another question?" Sophie asked as she palmed a few almonds. "Do people with epilepsy know when they're about to have a seizure?"

Ella spread fig jam on top of a Brie chunk. "I do, but everyone is different. I have an aura." She bit into the cracker. "Have you heard of it?"

Sophie shook her head.

"For some people, like me, I smell something sort of like metallic or sulfur. I used to tell my parents that something smelled funny, and they'd know it was coming." She dusted the crumbs from her fingertips, thinking of how to articulate the sensation right before a seizure. "Have you ever walked down the stairs and you think you've reached the bottom, but really there's one more step? There's a sort of panicking feeling right before you trip, like you're not sure if you're going to fall and break an ankle. That happens immediately before a seizure for me. But it's not enough warning for me to take my spray."

Sophie lifted a bottle to her mouth. "What spray?"

"If I seize, I have emergency nasal spray, it helps stop the seizures within a minute or two."

"Will you show me how to use it?"

Sophie asked so quickly, with no hesitation, and it warmed Ella. This whole conversation, Sophie leaned on her elbows towards Ella, like she was memorizing words, or in class with a world-renowned professor. Nothing appeared to be grossing or freaking her out or giving her some disgusting savior complex.

It wasn't Ella's intention to bring up the spray to teach Sophie how to use it, but it made sense. Her parents had been harping on having Sophie or Malcolm learn to use it since she started her job, and she knew her dad always had one in his pocket. Him popping by several times a day to "check on the team" was probably not the norm, and she had a sneaking suspicion it was in case she needed the medication. She dug out the spray from her purse and gripped it between her pointer and middle finger. "Just like saline spray for a cold. Hold here. Plunge here."

Sophie reached out her hand, and Ella placed it in her palm. Her eyes scanned the back as she read the fine print instructions, and she juggled it between her fingers.

Heavy mist tapped against the window, a steady, rhythmic stream as the silence grew in length but also in comfort. Besides her aunt Colleen, most everyone in Ella's life had treated her as fragile, a case, someone who needed help. Sophie treated her as an equal.

Ella moved closer, consumed with the need to brush Sophie's cheek with her fingers. To see if her skin was really as soft as it looked. The mist and low hum of water hitting the pane was hypnotic. Ella felt like she was floating, only anchored by the thought that if she could just touch Sophie once, she'd be good. She could satisfy her curiosity and stop thinking of her so much.

The German-made, historic grandfather clock in the entryway chimed and Sophie swung her head toward the hallway. She checked her watch and Ella knew this moment, this time together, was ending. She wanted to elongate it but how to do that without seeming needy? But *God*, she didn't want Sophie to leave. Maybe she could ask her to watch a movie, and they could curl up under a blanket with buttered popcorn. Something, anything, to not break this feeling.

"Well, I think work is done." Sophie moved back to the table and unplugged her laptop. "We haven't had a single email since noon. I guess the team just called it a day."

The sinking in Ella's gut was fierce, like a lust roller coaster that just plummeted. "You're probably right."

Stop being so sad. This is what happens when you don't spend time with people.

"Hey..." Sophie's tongue flicked across her lip. "I have a crazy idea."

The tone in Sophie's voice made Ella's heart perk up. "Oh yeah? What's that?"

Sophie glanced behind her, almost to confirm they were alone, then inched toward Ella. "Got an extra suit?"

FIFTEEN

SOPHIE

If someone over the weekend asked Sophie what she'd be doing on Monday afternoon, she would've said she'd be elbow-deep in a web production-review meeting, drafting an email, or checking on an asset status. She would've never imagined she'd be naked in Ella's room, her body aching, buzzing, and *beyond* excited for what they were about to do.

Hot tubbing.

Inside Ella's all-white bathroom the size of Sophie's living room, she slipped Ella's swimsuit over her hips. Was it kind of weird to wear her co-worker's swimsuit, that was once up against Ella's most intimate parts? Sure, a little. But Sophie had been wearing thrift-store clothes almost her whole life, so it wasn't as strange as it might be to others.

Ugh. The mirror confirmed she looked ridiculous. Ella had beautiful, incredible curves. A round butt. And according to that hookup site photo Sophie had peeked at too many times, Ella had boobs, too. Sophie by contrast was boxy, built like a prepubescent boy. No real hips, no real butt, and she could definitely go for an extra scoop of boob.

A knock sounded outside the door. "Did you find the towels?"

Sophie opened the linen closet near the half-standing wall and waterfall showerhead. Everything in the closet was at a Home-Edit level of organization. Various towels, cosmetics, and lotions were aligned by height, and there were so many products she thought she was at Sephora. Even her soaps looked to be in alphabetic order. "Yep. I'll grab you one."

She picked up two of the thickest, plushest towels and gripped the door handle when she paused. *I'm standing half-naked in Ella's room.* Not only that, but seeing Ella's bed was almost more intimate than wearing her suit. She'd have to fully process this bizarre moment later. Right now, there was a hot tub waiting.

Holy hell. Sophie's gaze lingered, way more than it should have, before she forced herself to look away. She no longer had to ogle the dating site photo like a horny teen if she could retain this image of Ella, spilling out of the tankini in the most scrumptious way.

Nope. Stop. Unprofessional, not okay, must stop this train of thought immediately. She tossed the towel to Ella and wrapped hers around her waist as she crossed the room. Her gaze flickered to a canvas propped on an easel, with deep hues of magenta, violet, and orange, creating a warm sunrise over an ocean. "Wow... did you do this?"

She waved Sophie to the door. "Um, yes. It's not finished at all. I just like to dabble. Not sure if I'll keep going or—"

"It's beautiful."

Ella's pale cheeks flushed, and Sophie wanted to burn that image, this moment, into her memory.

Outside, the mist hit Sophie and goose bumps popped up on her arms. The covered area to the east-side courtyard provided little reprieve from the chill, and she wanted to dive headfirst into the tub. On the marble table next to the hot tub, she tossed her phone next to Ella's glasses, water bottle, and nasal spray, and dropped her towel. A bleachy chlorine scent reached her nose, and she held back the urge to wrap her knees in her arms and cannonball off the table.

"Bubbles?" Ella's fingers hovered over the levers.

"Um, is there any other way?" Sophie asked, but she didn't actually know. If her body could salivate, that'd be what it was doing, the anticipation of soaking her limbs reaching a fevered pitch.

"I hate to state the obvious," Ella said as she dipped her hand into the water, "but if I drop or go underwater, please scoop me out."

She released a deflecting giggle, but Sophie knew her well enough that embarrassment laced her tone. "Is there anything else I should do?"

Ella shook her head. "My nasal spray is on the table, but not sure, logistically, how that would work. Don't try to stop it from happening, by holding me down or something. Make sure my head is tilted and that I don't crack my skull. And you know, make sure I don't drown."

The tone may have been jovial, but Sophie saw the vulnerability in Ella's eyes. "Got it."

Ella stepped in first, slowly, and scooted to the side. Sophie followed, tentatively dipping her toe to check the water before she slipped under the bubbles. *Ahhhhh.* The water did not disappoint. Her body melted in the heated oasis. Work stress—gone. Meeting agendas—gone. Deadlines and cranky designers—gone. She pushed herself lower until the water reached her shoulders. "This... is... heavenly."

"Mmmm, sure is. Feels amazing." A sigh escaped Ella as she lazed deeper, and Sophie would be lying if she said the sound didn't do something a little jumpy to her insides. Ella lifted herself up and Sophie's hungry gaze took in the way the water dripped between the deep plunge of her cleavage and the bright glow in her cheeks. Sophie knew she shouldn't look, but tummy flipping and the desire to touch Ella negated any sober thoughts about maintaining a professional boundary.

Ella flicked at a bubble. "God, this is *so* much better than being in here with my dad."

"I bet." Sophie studied Ella's long neck, the slope of her jaw, the wide brown eyes with eyelashes she could see from across the tub. "You look different without your glasses."

Ella raised her eyebrow. "Better?"

She's stunning either way. "Just different." Sophie's fingers skimmed the top of the water. Her whole life she'd wanted to go in a hot tub, but never had the chance. None of her friends had one, she'd never stayed at a hotel growing up, and the one hotel conference she attended last year had a hot tub, but hell if she'd take a dip with co-workers.

The irony of sitting here with Ella was not lost on her.

"I've never been in a hot tub." She wanted to suck back in the words. Opening up was never a strong skill, and she braced herself for the inevitable pity look.

But Ella didn't drop her mouth, tsk, or mumble something like "must be so hard to be disadvantaged..."

"Huh. Interesting." That was Ella's perfect response.

Sophie's insides softened. "I've always wanted to, but our family trips usually involved camping."

Ella grabbed a water bottle from the ledge and sipped. "I've never been camping, but I think it'd be fun. We have an outdoor fireplace, but it's not the same. It doesn't even use real wood. I want to smell actual wood burning, sleep in a tent, watch the stars." She flashed a grin. "I bet you've had a lot more experiences than me."

"I guess it depends on your definition of experiences." Sophie twisted the lid from her bottle. "I've never been to Hawaii or to Europe. Or really anywhere besides the Pacific Northwest."

A bubbling water misted Ella's face and she splashed more against her cheeks. "I've never skydived, visited a houseboat, or drank beer. I've never even been to Pike Place without my parents."

Sophie's mouth dropped. Pike Place Market? The most iconic, most frequented place in the city? Flashes of the million times she went there as a kid with Maya to buy clam chowder, watch tourists gawk at the guys throwing fish, or browsing handmade gifts popped through her mind. "Aren't you my age?"

A sad chuckle left Ella's mouth. "I'm twenty-four, so yeah. But ever since my first seizure, my parents turned super controlling."

"Overprotective?"

"Yes, but like to the highest degree. I'm rarely alone, and even when I'm alone, I'm not *really* alone. Thomas is around, or a staff member who not-so-coincidentally needs to clean a room near mine, or dust the office when I'm in the den. I'm in a Martha-Stewart-prison-like hell."

Since Sophie was little, she had been independent. Partly due to life circumstances—with no siblings and parents who worked doubles, she'd been pitching in with laundry and cooking since she was eight. But another part was an inherent need to fly. Relying on herself was hard. But not being respected enough to think she could run solo would have been harder. "Besides never traveling, there's a ton of things I've never done that you probably have."

Ella propped her elbows against the tub lip. "Like what?"

"I've never been in a convertible. Or flew somewhere exotic for a vacation. I've never been to the ballet or symphony. I've... I don't know... I've never tried caviar."

Ella scrunched her nose. "It's gross."

"Really?"

"Yes. Think of jelly, but instead it's salty and fishy. I seriously hate it." Ella tossed a glance behind her shoulder. "But we probably have some if you want to try, or the chef can get some."

Chef. Housekeeper. This world was so beyond foreign to Sophie that it wasn't even the same galaxy. "Do you recognize how totally bizarre it is to have someone who does these things?"

Ella rolled her eyes. "I'm not nearly as obtuse as you think I am. Of course, I know this isn't typical." She flicked at a bubble, and a grin tugged at her lips. "But I mean, if you're too scared to try it, you can just say so."

"I don't do scared." Sophie smirked and spread her toes under the water, letting the water slip through them. "What is it you want?" She turned warm, thinking of the caption from the singles ad last month.

Ella's legs floated to the surface, and she treaded at the water. Several moments passed before she stopped kicking at the suds and shifted a little closer. "So many things. I want to see the world without shackles. Go to a nightclub. Drive a car. Dance at a country bar. Go home with someone from the country bar." She glanced shyly at Sophie as if to see if the words landed.

They landed.

"Sorry, is that too far?" Ella asked.

Yes. But not because it was too personal. More because being half-naked in the tub with Ella's glistening shoulders and glimpses of her chest through the bubbles gave Sophie some seriously unholy thoughts. And now Ella brought up sex and all Sophie wanted to do was close her eyes and have a little alone time with her right hand to neutralize her heat waves.

Sophie wanted to inch closer, to look closer at Ella's lips. Every day Ella wore a dark ruby red, but with the snacks and now the hot tub, her soft, natural pink lips shone. Sophie wanted to swipe her thumb across the outline. The nerves settled in her throat, and she cleared them away. "No. Not too

far. I haven't dated much for the last, you know, five, six years."
She pushed out a deflecting smile. "You?" She tried to keep her
voice light, but it was anything but as she shamelessly dug for
intel.

Ella's fingertips skipped the top of the water. "I haven't
dated a lot, either. But I was with my ex, Jasmine, for a year."
She tugged her bottom lip between her teeth. "Breaking up was
the right choice, but it still hurt so much, you know? She
cheated, and it kind of destroyed me."

Sophie's belly sunk. "Oh God, I'm so sorry. I can't even
imagine how hard that must've been."

"Like, how do you go from saying you love me in one breath,
then fucking some random woman next?"

Ella's breath sputtered and Sophie paused, waiting to see if
she'd continue.

"She told me it meant nothing. Said it was a heated, one-
night thing. Like that was somehow so much better." Her eyes
focused on her fingers. "It took me forever to get over it. But the
memory of how it gutted me... I don't know if that will ever
disappear."

Screw the distance. Sophie moved closer until she was right
next to Ella. This wasn't a sexual advance, just an intrinsic need
for Ella to know she was amazing. "I'm so sorry she made you
feel anything less than the freaking rock star you are." Sophie
tapped her thigh against Ella's underwater in a playful nudge.

At least, the intention was playful. But the moment she did
it, Ella's eyes locked with hers, her sprinkling of freckles above
her nose prominent and fierce against the rosy cheeks. The jets
clicked off and the bubbles evaporated, slowly exposing everything under the water.

Ella dipped her head, her dark hair framing her face. She
tucked a lock behind her ear and glanced at Sophie. "You think
I'm a rock star?"

"Absolutely."

Ella's lips curved. Several moments passed as the water turned tranquil. The mist danced on the rooftop, the sound mixed with the heated water making Sophie's world buzzed and hazy.

What was happening here? Did Ella feel the same electricity? Her body was so warm in the hot tub, verging on overheating, but she didn't want to leave. She was liquifying in the best way possible.

Ella draped her arm against the lip of the tub and rested her head against her bicep. "What else have you never done?"

Something filled Sophie's chest. A truth serum, and sense of safety, of wanting to open up to someone besides Maya. Was that someone Ella? Everything felt inexplicably natural. "I've never been in love." She swirled her arms in the water. "What was it like for you?"

All lightness in the air vanished, sucked in like a crater, filling the entire space with an electric heat.

"Like your heart is going to be ripped out at any minute, but the adrenaline rush makes you not worry about the inevitable pain," Ella said. "It's warm and gooey and amazing."

Ella's leg touched Sophie's so softly it could have been a mistake. She drew it away and Sophie instantly wanted it back. The pink deepened in Ella's cheeks, a glow highlighted by the steam, and Sophie's insides sparked. Everything about her reaction triggered something deep and Sophie felt her leg floating higher, drawn towards Ella.

Yes, she'd been thinking of Ella more than she should. From the moment Ella stormed into her life like a Gucci-laden tornado, all hips and lips and sass, Sophie couldn't get her out of her mind. Those devastating eyes, that full mouth, death-gripped Sophie and refused to let go.

Ugh, she shouldn't do it. It was a bad idea, but just one touch was all she wanted, that would fulfill her. She let her pinkie fall, a whisper of a touch, and grazed the soft flesh of Ella's lower leg. Ella pushed into the touch.

Sophie dropped her eyes to Ella's full mouth. Her heartbeat pounded in her chest, exacerbated by the heat of the water and the glazed look in Ella's eyes. Sophie's gaze fell, skimmed the top of Ella's chest, and she licked her lower lip. This shouldn't be happening. Right? Maybe? It wasn't technically against the rules, but it was wrong. Or was it? The thoughts clamored, a tug of war between practical and animalistic. And then Ella dusted the back of her hand across Sophie's leg, and the tingles flew to her scalp.

Dammit. She wanted to taste Ella's mouth, to feel the dip between her collarbone, the roundness of her hips, the satin skin. But she shouldn't. She couldn't. Tomorrow, they needed to return to work and normality, which would be impossible if they did what Sophie wanted to do.

But maybe, this was just a little innocent flirtation. Maybe Ella was not having these same thoughts, and later Sophie could dismiss this moment as a blip in the office matrix, intoxicated with chlorine and a scary car crash.

A grin crept over Ella, and her lashes fluttered to her cheekbone. "I think you're beautiful." The voice was barely above a whisper, but it hit Sophie like Ella screamed it across the yard.

Oof. "Thank you." *Thank you? That was it?* Sophie felt the same about Ella, but the words would fall flat. Ella was so much more than her sultry eyes and a full mouth. She was a damn warrior, wicked smart, and carried this devilish, delicious sense of humor.

How does Ella say something like that and allow this unbearable energy to fester? Sophie didn't know what to say. She didn't know what to do. Leave? Stay? Move closer. She froze, staring at the water, her pulse pounding in her ears.

And then... Ella moved. She inched closer and pressed her leg against Sophie, and everything in Sophie's body tensed.

Water droplets dangled from Ella's straps, trailed her arms, her neck, her chest, and Sophie licked the corner of her lip ring.

Chlorine-laced steam, mist, and the smell of cherry blossoms collided. The pull toward Ella was so strong that Sophie didn't know who moved first. But there she was, staring at Ella's shoulders, the crook of her neck, the slope above her lips. Was Ella's heart beating as fast as hers? Was her mind swirling between deep want, fear, and uncertainty? Time clicked by, with the only sounds of mist on pavement, the gentle gush of water lapping the sides of the hot tub, and increased breaths.

And then... holy shit... Ella lifted herself and straddled Sophie.

"Whoa."

Ella paused, caught Sophie's eyes, and held her gaze. When Sophie lifted her hips to press into her, Ella flattened her hands behind Sophie, gripping the end of the tub, caging Sophie. She hovered over Sophie's lap, her eyes darting between Sophie's eyes, like she wanted to read her soul.

Touching Ella was a hard no. They were co-workers. Never once had she mixed business with anything but business. But it had been *so long*, and Ella's voluptuousness and curves were so perfectly *right there*. Her face was fearless. Shyness, awkwardness, evaporated. Ella was in full control.

Ella lowered herself more, her bottom settling on Sophie. Her chest rose and pressed against Sophie, and Sophie wanted to crumble. God, she smelled so good, like sand and beach and fresh flowers, and Sophie wanted to bury her face into her neck and consume her scent.

This felt good. Too good.

Warm lips grazed Sophie's ear. "If you want me to stop, all you have to do is say it."

Jesus Christ. Honey layered Ella's whispery voice, and Sophie's pulse nearly clouded her eyesight. She was useless, powerless, as her hands rose and she pressed her fingertips into Ella's hips.

Did she want Ella? Did Ella want her? Sophie had seen the ad Ella posted, firmly stating she wanted a one-night stand only. Sophie wanted a lifetime. And this, no matter how amazing, would not help her meet that goal.

"Do you want me to stop?" Ella whispered again.

Sophie's breath hitched. "No." The words were breathless, fleeting, escaping her mouth like her willpower. The water was charged, dancing, and Ella's legs tightened around hers. Sophie trailed her palms, reaching higher, holding Ella close.

Ella's lips swept Sophie's neck. One kiss, two kisses... higher. She pushed her body against Sophie's, and Sophie's legs trembled. Yes, she was scared. But it was more than fear. She dangled her fingertips in Ella's hair, the sensation of Ella's mouth on her skin nearly unbearable. This was complicated, yes. But right now, she didn't want to worry about complications or conflicts, or anything but warm, wet skin pushing into hers and the feel of Ella's lips as they moved from her neck, to her collarbone, to her shoulder.

She was collapsing, a useless, squishy entity that dissolved beneath skillful touches. Ella hooked her finger below Sophie's strap and lowered, kissing her shoulder, behind her ear, the line of her jaw.

The feelings were too much, the need to taste Ella's lips burned her mouth. Sophie gripped Ella behind the neck now, staring hard into those dark amber eyes, her pulse pounding so hard she was sure Ella could feel it through her veins. Ella sighed, staring at Sophie's lips, looking at her like she was heaven, and leaned.

Sophie closed the gap, pushed her lips on Ella's, and *ahhh...* her soft, pretty mouth was everything. Strong, full, smooth. Ella relaxed into the kiss, her tongue gently pushing against Sophie, and pressed her chest against Sophie's.

Fuuuu... God, this all felt so good. The missing piece in Sophie's life. She explored Ella's luxurious, velvet tongue and soon Sophie didn't know whose breath was whose and she didn't care.

Ella pulled back again, and stared at Sophie, her cheeks flushed. Was she thinking the same? Almost as if she could hear her thoughts, Ella pressed her mouth back against Sophie, her hands dragging against her shoulder, her fingertips gliding. She filled her mouth with Sophie's lips, her tongue circling Sophie's lip ring, her air coming out in spurts. Her fingertips swiped Sophie's dip in her lower neck, and trailed lower. Sophie's insides heated, her legs tensed.

So much time had passed since Sophie had been touched like this, with purpose, with strong, heated desire. She wanted Ella. Now. She tugged on Ella's bikini top, loosening the strings as Ella's fingers dipped even lower, her thumb grazing the sensitive skin on her side. A little lower, they slid more, so close...

"Ella! My God, are you in the hot tub alone?"

A screeching voice and the hard crack of heels against a wood deck slashed the moment. Sophie dropped her hand as quickly as Ella hopped from her lap. A flurried moment passed in embarrassed blushes and clearing throats.

"Mom, no," Ella called out. "I'm here with a friend."

Ella's mom bolted down the stairs, all crisp blouse and crisp hair and crisp heels, and Sophie wanted to dive under the water and not come up. The heat in her body turned cooler, but still tingled, which Sophie decided was a terrible way to feel. She couldn't look at Ella as she tried hard to act normal.

"Thank God!" Her mom clasped a hand over her heart. "I thought you were in there alone. I should know you're more responsible than that."

Sophie cringed at the probably well-intentioned, but terribly delivered words, as her libido officially shriveled.

"I'm good." Ella's voice had morphed from sex kitten to full-on irritated daughter. "Mom, Sophie. Sophie... meet my mother."

This was not how she'd picture a meet-the-mom moment, nor meeting the CEO's wife—with a lingering horny-charge.

Ella's mom did a quick double take. "Sophie from the office?"

What did that mean? The delivery was not unkind, per se, just... unreadable. "Yes, that's me."

"Well, I've certainly heard about you." Heels and all, Ella's mom trampled through the grass to shake Sophie's hand. "I'm Claire."

Sophie shook her hand with a firm pump. "Nice to meet you." Her voice displayed a nonexistent confidence. She'd never been comfortable around wealthy people, especially ones like Claire who looked like they stepped out of a high-end yacht magazine perched on the end of a Whole Foods aisle, with her blond bob coiffed to perfection, and her simple strand of pearls not actually that simple.

"Well, are you girls almost done? Want to come in for some food?" Claire asked. "Lydia is prepping some fresh fruit and snacks." She made no movement to leave.

Claire might look bougie, but she had a kindness to her voice and worried eye crinkles.

Ella tossed a look at Sophie. "Yep. We were just about to get out."

Why did those words hit like that, like lemon seeped into a paper cut? Obviously, the moment between them had shattered. But Sophie nearly flinched as Ella lifted herself from the tub, wrapped her towel, and gathered her items without another word.

The drive back to her apartment was the first reprieve Sophie had from the most quiet, awkward hour of her life. Ella had hardly spoken since leaving the tub, except to say Sophie could use the shower to wash off the chlorine, and to remind her to grab her charger still plugged into the wall. After getting dressed and gathering all her work items, Sophie wanted to bolt. She thanked Claire for the hospitality and Ella summoned Thomas to take her home.

Ella did not offer to come with.

When Thomas dropped her off, she dragged herself up the three flights to her room. After kicking shoes to the side, she dropped her bag near the door, and flopped onto the couch.

"What in the hell?" she said to her fake ficus tree. A lifetime had passed since the accident in the office this morning. How could everything have changed so quickly, so intensely? She glided a fingertip across her lip, savoring the leftover tingles from Ella's mouth. The kiss had been more than any kiss she'd had before. Purposeful and full, soft but intense, passionate and sweet, filled with trembles and promises.

Her body squirmed, replaying every moment. She lowered her hands, resting them on top of her belly, picturing Ella's neck, her arms that glistened with water, feeling her body on top of her. Ella was fearless, much more than Sophie thought.

Sophie sprung from the couch. She shoved boots into a closet, tugged off sweatshirts hanging on the chair, and put away dishes. Was Ella okay? She had definitely been the instigator, right? Okay, it was a mutual instigation, but maybe Ella just wanted to scratch an itch. Get one night in, quench the thirst, and move on. And here Sophie was entertaining visions of date nights, their times in the cafeteria, and how Ella's tortoiseshell glasses highlighted the amber in her eyes.

Ella's reaction after their kiss was... unexpected. Sophie couldn't stop thinking about the way Ella's body felt pressed against hers, the taste of her lips. But Ella was so dismissive, so casual, so utterly nonchalant.

Putting away dishes, scrubbing the countertop until her

forearms ached, and asking Alexa to blare Amy Winehouse did nothing to dull the internal monologue. What if Ella was how she portrayed herself in the ad? Maybe she really did just want a hookup and Sophie was convenient.

Sophie needed more than convenience.

So now what? Go to work tomorrow and pretend it didn't happen? The thought made her heart squeeze. After scraping off all her nail polish, folding laundry, and getting ready for bed, she blinked at the ceiling, willing it to provide her with clarification.

Fuck it.

She grabbed her phone and searched her contacts. She and Ella had exchanged numbers weeks ago for work-related purposes, and this was definitely not work related. But it would most likely not violate any HR rules. Technically speaking, she wasn't Ella's manager. She had seniority, sure, but Ella's dad was the boss. This might be considered a bigger infraction for Ella than Sophie.

Now she was overthinking as her thumbs shook over the hovered screen. She should just not do anything, let it go, and chalk it up to an emotional day.

Perfect—decision made.

In a stunning betrayal of the mind/body connection, Sophie's thumbs flew off a message before she could stop.

SOPHIE:

For the record, I REALLY didn't want you to stop.

SIXTEEN

ELLA

So that happened.

Ella stared at her phone, willing another message to appear. When Sophie had texted her a few hours ago, a thrill shot through her chest. She responded immediately with a blushing emoji and a follow-up:

ELLA:

I didn't want to stop, either.

And then... nothing. Just nothing. Not that she expected a ton more, but she hoped this would kick off some sort of banter. Maybe flirty messages, maybe some sexting. Who knew? Being in her luxury prison, she was a master at curating sexy messages.

But Sophie didn't respond, so Ella didn't send any more, either. No way was she going to give off stalker vibes to the co-worker that she'd been hard crushing over for the past few weeks.

Ella swiped the canvas, adding a bold crimson to the golden sunrise. The brush slid across the fabric, and the bristles embedding into the canvas allowed her mind to rest. She worked another hour, detailing the crests in the waves, touching up the shadowed images in the sand, and perfecting a cloud.

Normally painting put her in a spell, but her eyes kept flickering to the phone to see if she somehow missed a message. Finally, she gave up and tossed her brush into the water. She shoved her feet into slippers and bounced down the stairs in search of a snack.

Like a guard dog sniffing out a potential treat, her mom appeared from wherever the hell she was stationed. "Hey, honey." A mild frown appeared. "You really should wear those bangs away from your face at night otherwise we're going to break out like in high school."

Whatever. Ella wanted to tell her mom that adding the word "we" to these types of statements did nothing to soften the blow from reminding her of her acne-ridden teenage years. She pulled open the fridge and grabbed a container of leftovers. "You heard from Dad?"

"Yes, his flight got delayed. Won't be home until late." Her mom popped open a yogurt lid and was uncharacteristically quiet. She inhaled and cocked her head at Ella.

Oh, no. Here it comes...

"So, Sophie." She wiggled an eyebrow. "She seems nice."

Nope. Ella was not having this conversation. Her mom would try to squeeze every single detail, then push for more. Five minutes in, she'd beg Ella to have a spa day and "dish" about the "cutie." And her mother had a freakish level of intuitiveness, she would decode every syllable spewed from Ella's mouth. No doubt she'd take one look and know something had shifted within Ella. Her mom would ask when Sophie had transitioned from a massive pain in her ass, to her coworker, to someone she thought about *a lot*. Ella would have to cover up the fact that Sophie had evolved from a mentor to someone she'd... straddled. God, Ella couldn't believe she had been that bold. The freedom of being in the hot tub alone, her parents gone, the rain... something had taken over. And she'd loved it.

"Yes, she's nice." Ella bit into the tangy chopped salad and moved to the window. The landscaping lights illuminated the courtyard and paved a path to the water. She rarely took the time to enjoy the view, but today, the yard's beauty clicked.

Her mom's throat rolled with a swallow. "This is the first time you've brought someone over since Jasmine."

"She's not *someone*." Such a lie, and Ella quickly shoved another bite in her mouth to deflect her words. Sophie was absolutely someone. "She's just a co-worker. It's not like I brought her over to..." *To taste her mouth, sink in her lap, press my lips against her dewy skin.*

"I think whatever you two are working on has certainly been the needed spring in your step." Her mom scraped the spoon against the side of the yogurt cup. "You had us worried there. We haven't really talked about what happened that night."

Ella breathed out. Three months had passed since *the incident*, when she scared herself and her parents enough that her dad had no choice but to hire her. And yes, she regretted her behavior, but it had been the only way left to yield the desired result. Being at the office was everything she craved. It had started as a way to earn money for her own place, to free her from the shackles. But it morphed, becoming a place where she belonged, where she felt needed and included and worthy.

"I know I scared you guys." She finished the last bite and rinsed her bowl.

The vision of that night flew through her mind. Snot-filled crying, ripping at her shirt collar, because everything suffocated her. She couldn't take it anymore, she'd screamed. She couldn't breathe. Even her hair drowned her. In a fit of desperation, she grabbed the kitchen scissors and cut off her waist-length braid, as her horrified parents shrieked. She'd only seen her dad scared a few times in her life, and that moment was one of them. He froze, helpless, as his daughter transformed. He faltered between coaxing, yelling, to nearly tackling her in order to rip the scissors from her hand.

Her actions that night were uncalled for, and shame burned into her chest reliving the moment. She knew she'd scared her parents, and that hadn't been the intention. She simply had endured too much, and she needed them to listen. "I never apologized for what I did. I... I should have handled it better."

"Yes, you should have."

Her mom's words were firm, but not harsh. She tossed the yogurt cup in the trash and joined Ella at the sink. The rose-scented night lotion she used reached Ella's nose, and for the first time in forever, Ella wanted to hug her and have her tell her that everything was going to be okay.

"I've reflected on that night, too." Her mom pressed her hand on top of Ella's. "A lot, actually. You've been trying to tell us for years how you felt, how you feel smothered. I know it's not easy, and it's not always fair. But you are *different*, Ella. And I know you hate to hear that, but it's the truth. You will always have greater needs than others, and that's just fact. Does that feel horrible? Yes? Do I wish you were any other way? Absolutely not. Because this is part of you, and I love you."

Ella reached over and consumed the hug she wanted earlier. Her mom squeezed her and kissed the top of her head.

Yes, her mom could be difficult and judgy and frustrating. But deep down, she wouldn't have her any other way, either. "I love you, too." Ella tucked a bottle of water under her arm. "Good night."

Back in her room, she clicked on the lamp and snuggled into bed. She clasped her fingers behind her head and stared at the ceiling, evaluating the emotional day. God, feelings sucked. Since Jasmine, she'd convinced herself the only thing she wanted was a one-night stand. No strings attached meant no broken hearts. It meant no puffy eyes, no burning stomach, no obsessively evaluating the things she hated the most about herself and what caused Jasmine to stray.

And now here she was, thinking... no, *feeling*... things for Sophie, and even though it was scary, she didn't want to stop. She checked her phone one last time, but Sophie still hadn't messaged back.

Should I...? She tapped the phone case, running through a list of worst-case scenario outcomes. *Yes I should.*

ELLA:

hey, now that Thomas knows where you live and all, want us to pick you up tomorrow for work?

Bubbles appeared on the screen, and she held her breath. The message was easy enough, a cross between professional and friendly which could be waved away depending on the response. If she said no, then whatever happened in the hot tub was a fluke, and she could chalk it up to the emotional day.

SOPHIE:

You mean swap a 45-minute commute for a 10-minute ride and give up all the metro's morning special smells? Sounds great, thank you.

Ella poised her fingers to respond, but before she could, another message popped up.

SOPHIE:

♥

A heart emoji. There was no mistaking the message's intention. Ella closed her eyes for the evening, a full smile spreading at the same rate as her heart filling.

The next morning, Ella showered, took her meds, and bolted to the driveway in record time.

Was the sun a little brighter today? Only a sliver of sunlight cracked through the dusky clouds, yet it seemed the brightest morning in forever. She pulled in a breath of springtime air, the mineral, earthy scent of Lake Washington hitting her nose.

Thomas held a tire air pressure gauge in his hand and glanced up from his squatting position. "You're ready early. Big day today?"

Sure is. "Just the usual." Such a damn lie, and she fumbled with her bag to avoid any eye contact. Right now, this little whatever it was with Sophie was a magical secret secured in a twinkly box, and she was not ready to share it with anyone. Much less Thomas, who was a master at uncomfortable silences and would just wait it out until she cracked.

She hopped in the back seat and shoved her laptop bag on the seat. *Be cool, be calm.* "Can you swing by Sophie's place and pick her up for work today?" *Dammit.* Her voice had a squeak to it, and she cleared her throat.

"Ah," Thomas said, with a tone like "I knew it!" But he didn't know it. Or maybe he did. Maybe how she radiated inside was seeping to her outside, and soon everyone in the world would know she had a big, fat crush.

The ride to Sophie's house took forever. She tried to distract herself by scanning emails and scrolling social media, but she eventually gave up and tossed her phone back in the bag.

A car zoomed by and she grabbed her phone to snap a picture. "Is that a '69 Mustang Fastback?"

Thomas's eyes widened in the rearview mirror. "How in the world did you know that?"

"Over lunch last week, Sophie told me how she used to work with her dad on cars. He was obsessed with this old, broken down '69 Mustang. Apparently, he spent like ten years fixing it up, but all he ever does now is polish it with a cloth diaper." She grinned, remembering the conversation from the café. "I didn't know what it was, so she showed me a picture."

"Ah. Sometimes it's more fun to collect the car than drive it. Especially one that's such a beauty." He rolled to a stop at the light and tapped his fingers against the steering wheel. "Sophie sure is a nice young woman. We ended up chatting the whole way home last night."

Ella's ears perked up. "Yep, she is." Why hadn't she just gone with her last night? But her confidence was still bruised from Jasmine, she wasn't sure where they stood, and the idea of a thirty-minute awkward AF conversation had knotted her stomach.

He bumped over a pothole and turned down a block, where Sophie stood with her leather wrist bands, multiple rings, ripped fishnets, and plaid skirt. God, she was so damn pretty.

"Morning!" Sophie hopped in the back, her cheeks pinking when she smiled. "Thanks for picking me up."

"Anytime," Thomas said as he pulled into traffic.

"Hey, you." Sophie's eyelashes fluttered with the whisper.

Damn if Ella didn't feel that tone to her toes. "Good morning." Could Sophie feel this charge in the air? This heaviness, this urge, to reach out and touch her again? She desperately wanted to recreate the hot tub moment in the back of the SUV... if Thomas weren't sitting right there. She wanted to ask Sophie so many things but knew good and well that Thomas might appear as if he wasn't listening, but he heard everything.

"I can't believe they got the building cleared already for us to return." Sophie's office-professional voice returned, much to Ella's dismay.

"I know. It'll be so weird to see it all boarded up, though." The traffic slowed to a roll, and Ella checked her watch. "We're going to be putting out fires left and right with the loss of time yesterday."

"For sure." Sophie glanced out the window. "We'll set a quick scrum call when we get in."

Small talk was dumb. Ella didn't care about status meetings, calls, level setting, or if the copy editors agreed on a proper comma placement. She wanted to pull Sophie to her, taste her mouth, trail the pad of her fingertip up her silky smooth arm.

Once Thomas dropped them off at the office, with the purr of electric cars and traffic humming down the street, Ella tugged her cross-body bag over her shoulder. She moved toward the building when Sophie laid a hand on her forearm. The hand was warm, the gentle touch telling Ella everything was okay.

Sophie glanced behind her shoulder. "Hey, um, so about what happened at your house..."

She wanted to do it again? Maybe go into the alley and make out against the wall? Could Ella pull her into a single stall restroom, throw her on the counter, and show her what her hands could do? Ella was open to just about anything.

Sophie bit the side of her lip and her gaze dropped to Ella's mouth before it snapped up. "My job is really important to me. Like, sometimes, I feel it's the only thing I have, you know?"

A bus screeching to a halt at the corner perfectly mirrored Ella's insides. *Her job is important? Obviously. But what does that mean for what happened?* Ella hated that her hands fidgeted. She tugged her purse tighter to her chest to hide the motion. "Yes, I get that. It's important to me, too."

Sophie looped her thumbs in her backpack straps. A thin red stripe ran through her neck, and she glanced at the sidewalk. "I just think it wouldn't be appropriate if we said anything or... did anything... at the office."

Rejection hit hard and Ella's stomach curled into itself. Was this about work only, or ever again, or what? Ella squared her shoulders. "What about when we're not in the office?"

Sophie's lip turned up and her tongue swiped at her lip ring. She wrapped her pinkie around Ella's and moved her mouth to Ella's ear. "Outside of the office..."

The breath was warm against Ella's ear, and she nearly collapsed from the rasp in Sophie's voice.

"... all bets are off."

SEVENTEEN

SOPHIE

Sophie turned off the engine and rested her head against the seat. After taking the metro most days, she almost forgot how to drive. She dragged herself from the car and slugged up the cracked micro-driveway to her childhood home.

She loved her parents—good, hardworking people, who did the best they could. But she hated when she visited. It felt like a chore. Because normally it *was* a chore. Growing up, her life was filled with laughter, friends, school, and adolescent shenanigans. She'd skip school to drink beer at Alki Beach, or hop on the bus to the International District to eat dim sum, or she'd hang out with Maya and Harper.

But this house represented a darker side of her upbringing—the lonely nights at ten years old eating her mom's Lean Cuisine microwavable dinners by herself in front of the TV. Walking home from the bus stop when she was in kindergarten because her parents were still working, and they couldn't afford daycare. Gluing the straps on her sandals because her dad's payday was every other Friday, and sometimes the checks were spent before they arrived.

A bucket, broken shingles, and old flowerpots scattered the

unstable, chipped wood porch. She stepped over a toolbox, most likely holding space while her father attempted to fix yet another cracked, broken, or dangling item. Fixing the house was like playing home renovation whack-a-mole. Every time he fixed one thing, two others would break.

The door handle jangled in her grip, and the hinges creaked as she cracked it open. "Hello?" she called into open space. *Jesus.* Every month or two, when she stopped by, she swore her mom added another knickknack to the limited space. A shelf in the corner, normally overflowing with framed family photos, books, and random jars from garage sales, now held a family of porcelain dolls. *Yikes.*

She toed off her shoes on the wicker mat and stepped into the house, inhaling the familiar scent of sweet pea laundry detergent.

"Soph?" Her mom stepped into the living room from the hall, wrapping her long dark hair up in a bun. "Hey, honey. Didn't expect to see you today. Everything okay?"

Everything was okay and not okay. The hot tub moment from Monday was still fresh, and the last couple days at work, everything felt different. Amazing, yes. Heart zings and pings galore. But also scary as hell. She and Ella had seamlessly snapped back into work mode, which was exactly what Sophie wanted—at least she thought it was. She'd even told Ella they could not even hint at flirting in the office. But she had no idea Ella was some sort of disassociation master and could apparently click off her emotions in a second.

Forty-eight hours into whatever was happening with Ella, and Sophie was already exhausted. For years, she thought work kept her from meeting someone special. She blamed late hours and the drive for success for keeping her from finding a partner.

Now she wasn't so sure. Did she know deep down she was her own worst enemy? Maybe she knew she'd be struggle-bussing like she was now, buried under an avalanche of insecurity, wondering if every single breath Ella took, every word she muttered, was filled with regret.

"Yep, I'm good." She finally responded to her mom. "Just wanted to stop by and see you guys."

Her mom studied Sophie's face for several long moments. She tugged on the strings of her hooded sweatshirt and moved toward the kitchen. "Want something to drink? Pop? Tea? Hungry?"

"Nah, I'm good."

Her mom stepped away and returned with a box of Goldfish crackers and two cans of root beer—Sophie's favorite. She followed her mom to the couch and sunk into the cushion. The couch had to be pushing twenty-five years old, covered in decades-old Kool-Aid and grease stains. But it perfectly cradled Sophie's butt and she secretly hoped her parents never upgraded.

A part of Sophie was uncomfortable that her apartment was nicer than her parents' entire home. She had a stainless-steel dishwasher, new furniture, ultra-modern gray wood flooring, and a floor-to-ceiling stone fireplace. Her parents had old, original hardwood floors, a drying rack for their hand-washed dishes, and a refrigerator that squealed when it kicked on.

Her mom scooted next to her and winced as she unwrapped the brace nestled around her wrist. She massaged the joints with some medicinal lotion that reminded Sophie of how her grandmother smelled.

"Is it getting worse?" Sophie popped a cracker in her mouth and held the box to her mom.

"It's not gettin' better, I'll tell ya that much. I might need surgery, but the doctor's hoping with buckets of ibuprofen and some arthritic gel, I'll be okay." She dipped into the crackers. "Occupational hazard, am I right?"

Sophie hated seeing her mom in pain, but she wasn't wrong that after serving for over thirty years, something like this was bound to happen. With the amount of trays carried, coffee poured, and tables cleared, it was a miracle she hadn't injured herself worse at this point. "Dad at the library?"

"How did you know?"

Sophie grinned. "What did he finish last night?"

"Who knows? Could've been an Ashley Herring Blake romance, Stephen King, or a non-fiction on the industrial revolution. Never know with that man." Her mom chewed slowly, letting silence fill the air. "All right, spill it, woman. You never just pop by to say hi. What's going on?"

So many things. She was tired. She wanted this cruise so bad. And she was currently battling a severe love-hate relationship with her insides. The waterfall of tingles that happened when Ella's glasses slipped on her nose when she was concentrating, or when she put a pen in between her plump red lips, or when she glanced at Sophie with her doe eyes after speaking at a meeting, was overkill.

Sophie cracked open the soda, the fizzy bubbles burning as they traveled her throat. She wasn't sure she was ready to dive into this with her mom, as the feelings for Ella were fresh and raw. But also, what would her mom's reaction be when learning Ella was the CEO's daughter, who lived in a mansion on Lake Washington?

"You know what?" Her mom squeezed Sophie's knee. "I was just about to polish my fingernails. Let me grab the box."

No, she wasn't. Her mom never wore polish, worried it would flake into the food she was serving. But Sophie loved nail polish.

She excused herself to use the bathroom and go look in her childhood bedroom. Even though she moved out so many years ago, and her parents only had two bedrooms, they'd kept her room almost exactly the same. There was a sense that any time she wanted to move back, she could.

Mixed emotions filled her as she scanned her room, noting

the posters of the Ramones and Violent Femmes still hanging on with masking tape above the plastic bins used for a dresser. She closed the door and returned to the living room. The house made her both happy and sad. Familiarity brought comfort, but this was the end—her parents had reached the top of what they would do with their lives. And was this really a way to live? In a shitty, run-down home, with creaky floors and loud neighbors, while working at a diner and mechanic shop.

Towels and extra soap from the overstuffed linen closet fell to the floor as her mom dug around. A few grunts later, she grabbed a shoe box full of different shades and brought them to Sophie. "Pick one."

Sophie scrummaged through half-crusted bottles and clearance price tags, and plucked out a deep, shimmery violet. She flipped her legs crisscross-style and held out her hand as the room filled with the stinging scent of nail polish. Gently, her mom guided the color across Sophie's fingertip, and soon Sophie's shoulders relaxed. "Remember the trainee I told you about? Ella?"

Her mom focused on swiping color across Sophie's thumb. "Yeah?"

Why was Sophie nervous? She wanted to confess. Feelings, insecurities, thoughts gurgled inside like a shaken-up carbonated drink, and if she cracked it the tiniest bit, she'd overflow. The fact that she hadn't even told Maya about what happened in the hot tub scared her. "I, uh." She cleared her throat. "We've been getting along a lot better and working really hard on the new campaign."

"That's great." Her mom pulled Sophie's left hand onto her lap. "It's always easier to get along with co-workers than not. Remember when we had that cook, Bob? Such a prick. And boy, did it make the days drag."

Sophie remembered this guy, who had toddler-level emotional regulation and screamed across the kitchen on a whim. She blew on her right hand to dry the polish, stalling. "So, she's George's daughter, and I, we, uh, we are getting close. Like really close."

Her mom stopped and stared, her brows scrunching together. "George the CEO?" After Sophie nodded, her mom took a breath. "I see."

I see? That was all her mom's response, and a fine thread wrapped around her chest and pulled tight. She knew exactly what her mom was thinking, because Sophie had thought the same. Her deeply held beliefs about money and privilege were not just something she picked up on her own. It was generational intolerance, passed down from her parents.

Sophie's eyes flickered to the corner, passing from the torn fake palm tree that had been there since Sophie could remember, to the ratty blanket tossed over the chair her mom surely got at Goodwill, to the scratched-up wood paneling on the wall. "Why didn't you and Dad ever do better for yourselves?"

"*Excuse* me?"

Her mom's shocked voice hit Sophie hard, and she so badly wanted to retract the question. But, she had to ask. Her dad was the smartest man she knew. Her mom worked so hard, busting her ass on the regular to serve food. They could have done so much more with their life. Yet, they were trapped a step above poverty, and they'd always be there. She needed to know why. "I'm sorry... I'm not trying to offend." Jesus Christ, she sounded terrible. "But why didn't you get a different job? Or Dad? Or move from this place?"

Her mom now squinted and folded her arms across her chest. "Why would we?"

"Because..." How did she say this, without really sounding like the people she despised? Was she now the elitist, pigeon-holing her parents, putting them in a box *she* thought they belonged in? "You guys could have done so much more. Had more things. Gone on trips. Bought a bigger house."

The heat of her mom's gaze bored into her, and Sophie's insides burned.

"Why do you think your dad and I wanted a bigger house, or trips, or more things?"

Because wasn't that what everyone wanted? Aren't you supposed to strive for that while disliking the people who had it? Sophie glanced back at her fingers.

"Do you think you had a terrible childhood?" her mom asked.

Sophie shook her head. "No, of course not."

"Tell me your worst childhood memory."

The worst? How did she answer something like that? She scoured her memory bank, remembering when she sobbed on her eighth birthday into her Minnie Mouse cake. That whole year she had begged Santa Claus, the Easter Bunny, the tooth fairy, and even the God at the church her grandma attended that she would give up everything if she could go to Disney for her birthday. "I always wanted to go to Disneyland, and we never could."

"*That's* your worst memory?" Her mom scowled.

"I mean, I was left alone a lot, and I just didn't have the things other kids did. I didn't go to college, I couldn't shop at the mall, sometimes all we had was mac 'n' cheese for dinner."

"You love mac 'n' cheese."

"That's not the point!" Sophie exhaled a shaky breath, and her mom braced her shoulders.

After so many moments where the air felt tight and Sophie thought of the million ways to apologize, her mom pulled Sophie's hand back into her lap and continued polishing. "Growing up, all I ever wanted was to go camping." She finished swiping and twisted the cap back on the bottle. "It was my dream, but the idea of my parents affording a tent and the gas to drive to the coast was unheard of. That's probably why we camped so much in the summers and made so many forts in the living room during the winter."

Forts in the living room. How had Sophie forgotten that? She and her mom would destroy their space, piling blankets across the back of chairs, tying sheets to hooks her dad put in the ceiling, and pulling her mattress onto the floor. They'd prop themselves up on their elbows, eat through a bag of marshmallows, and read books with flashlights.

Her mom wrapped the brace back around her wrist and snugged the Velcro tight. "When I got a little older, I dreamed about one day leaving the trailer park and getting my own house. I mean, I couldn't even imagine. An actual house—*in Seattle.* It was unheard of in the park."

Sophie's neck grew tight.

"Your dad loves working on cars so much. How he can go from working in the shop during the day to coming home and doing the same thing at night is beyond me." She grabbed the root beer in her hand and took a small sip. "How many people are lucky enough to work at a place that is also their hobby? *That,* Sophie Squirrel, is a dream come true. Your dad and I live our dreams every day. It may not be your dream, and that's okay. You own your dreams. We own ours."

Oof. The words clobbered her over the head, and she bit back a tremble in her lip.

Why did she focus on the negative parts of her life? The money, the time spent alone, the lack of *things.* And yet she'd had two loving parents, who also loved each other. She couldn't even remember them yelling, except for the night she got caught sneaking out as a teen.

"Now, about this Ella girl."

Sophie smiled through her moistened eyes and reached for her mom. "I don't think I want to talk about her right now."

Her mom dug into the cracker box and popped one in her mouth. "Okay, but let me just say one thing. You've always accomplished what you've set your mind to. You're a fighter, always have been." Her mom kissed the top of her head. "Just make sure she deserves you."

Make sure Ella deserves me. A few weeks ago, the concept of someone like Ella deserving her was unfathomable. She would have thought about everything she lacked and compared it against everything Ella had. She would have convinced herself she wasn't good enough while pushing herself to prove otherwise.

But knowing Ella the way she did now, it wasn't about who deserved each other more. It was about opening herself up to the possibility of happiness.

Sophie lifted herself from the couch and stretched, fatigue setting in. "Is it okay if I sleep in my old room tonight?"

Her mom smiled and folded the cracker box closed. "Of course. Anytime."

EIGHTEEN

ELLA

Six shampoos later, and the glue still would not come out of Ella's hair. She tangled her fingers through the brittle pile of burned ends, her scalp raw from scrubbing. Shaking out her aching arms, she exhaled, and scrubbed one last time.

Not that she was surprised this had happened, of course. Ever since her first seizure, she'd had twice-yearly EEGs to monitor her brain activity. But the glue sucked. Tacky, flaky, and nearly impossible to remove.

The timing of her doctor appointment the previous evening wasn't ideal. She'd skipped the final meeting to make it to the doctor's office on time, and Sophie was mostly MIA for the evening. Ella had sent her a few text messages after the appointment and received delayed, brief responses, which frazzled her nerves. Later in the evening, Sophie finally shot a quick message that she was spending the evening with her parents, and Ella calmed.

After confirming she looked respectable, she hopped down the stairs to the kitchen and pulled out a yogurt parfait. One bite in, her father's heavy footsteps sounded around the corner.

"What's up, kid?" he asked, straightening his tie and reaching for a cup of freshly brewed coffee.

Kid. She tried hard not to roll her eyes. "Nothing." She may not have rolled her eyes, but the annoyance was thick in her tone. He didn't mean the things he said, like calling her kid. But that was the crux of their relationship—well-intentioned, but horribly executed, dialogue.

He lowered his phone and stared at her, his eyes folding with concern. "You okay? Did you have an episode I don't know about?"

"I'm sure with the secret service level of monitoring you have from my smartwatch you would've been informed already." She grinned and rolled the spoon over her tongue. "No, I'm good. I just had all that gunk in my hair from my EEG last night and it took me longer to get ready than I hoped. And right now, we don't have a second to waste."

How did her dad do this, day in and day out, with a smile? Not only a smile, he thrived on the intensity. A level of excitement was attached to the chase, for sure, but the stress was so much. She didn't want to admit to Sophie or her dad, but she'd been sleeping pretty terribly lately, plagued with nightmares of being in the wrong building, or that they pushed an ad out without the proper legal sign-off and she'd single-handedly bankrupted the company.

"And the results were fine, I assume?" her dad asked as he twisted the lid on his to-go mug. When she nodded, he patted her on the shoulder. "Good. Why don't we head in together today, then?"

Ella grabbed an apple for the road and followed him to the car.

The office buzzed more today than was typical. Ella wasn't sure if it was because she was fifteen minutes later than usual because of the glue debacle, or because they were getting close to sending the creative to the clients. As Ella rounded the corner, Sophie's face lit up, and Ella's breath halted sharply in her chest.

"Morning, sunshine," Ella whispered as she slid into her seat. "I can't believe it's Thursday already. I feel like the week flew by, but also like we must be in July by now."

"Same. I'm so done." Sophie reached into her bag and handed Ella a teal cupcake with edible pearl sprinkles. "For you."

Ella opened the compostable container and inhaled. "Smells amazing. What's this for?"

"I had so much nervous energy this morning, so I stopped at a bakery by my parents' house. Figured I'd load us up for the day we're about to have."

"I know. I'm a little nervous to be honest." Ella dipped her pinkie in the frosting and licked. "I keep refreshing my email to see if something came in overnight, but nope."

Yesterday, they had multiple meetings with the creative leads to do internal final approval. And not surprisingly, but also not welcome, they asked for a few tweaks before they sent it to the client for initial approval. The team had worked themselves to the bone and created some pretty cool images and copy. But. And Ella would never tell anyone, especially since this was the first ad she'd ever worked on, something wasn't landing with the images. But she was a PM, not a creative, and Sophie mentioned so many times to trust the team.

"Do you think we should pre-set a meeting with the client?" Ella asked.

Sophie's head tilted side to side. "It's always so hard to know. When Malcolm gets in, let's see if he thinks we should do a placeholder. It looks terrible if we move the placeholder because we couldn't get our shit together, but would be equally as terrible if we couldn't get all the right people in a room because we were delayed."

"Got it." Ella bit into the cupcake and murmured an approval. "Love your outfit today. You look amazing."

Sophie's face screamed "swoon" as she patted the frayed-edged, scissored neckline of her David Bowie sweatshirt. "Ah. This old thing?"

Within an hour, voices boomed around Ella, as the team forwent a formal meeting space and resorted to shouting across the open workspace.

"Insta and Facebook updated and sent."

"Banner ad, initial approval. Sending to our contact in legal for a quick peek before the meeting."

"Conference room changed for an increase of team members."

"I'll send the agenda if you want to recap for the web team the digital-display update."

"Web producers approved dimensions. Sending ticket over now."

Ella's head spun, but the energy was intoxicating. This modern-day Mad Men-type feel, where caffeine flowed and heels stomped, and the pinging of instant messages became a symphony in the background. She stole glances at Sophie, marveling at the way her lips pouted when she was in deep concentration, how her fingers typed at rapid-fire speed, and how she peeked up and did a quick scan of the room, then winked at Ella, who melted under the split-second motion.

Clap, clap, clap. Her dad's signature palm smacking broke up the chatter and folks quieted. "All right, guys, we're getting close to the finish line here. The leads are knee-deep in presenting to the VP right now." He stomped over to Sophie and checked his watch. "Sophie. Burning the midnight oil—er, the mid*day* oil, I see."

Sophie sat upright. "Yep."

"I told the program manager to circle back with you right

after the meeting concludes." He pivoted on his heels and pointed at the lead producer. "Joel! Can I get…"

As he thumped to the nearest table, his words became lost in the oblivion. Ella leaned toward Sophie. "I gave him that one."

Sophie's nose scrunched. "You gave him one what?"

"For the bingo card." Ella took so much pleasure in Sophie's jaw dropping she was inclined to take a picture. "I told him to work in the words 'circle back,' 'finish line,' and 'synergies.' Two out of three isn't bad."

A red stripe raced up Sophie's neck. "I, um, not sure what bingo card you're—"

"Like he doesn't know." Ella cut her off with a smile. "He's known about this game forever and made it a personal mission to drop as much business jargon as possible. We used to google things he could say, or when we watched a workplace movie and a good one came up, he'd jot it down in his little notebook. I think it's like his contribution to the office shenanigans."

Sophie's mouth remained open before her lips lifted into a smile. "Your dad just became one of the coolest leaders, ever."

Ella had appreciated this trait in her dad, thinking it took a lot of humility to essentially be the butt of a five-year-long joke. Her dad may have the emotional intelligence of a ferret, but he took his work seriously. He wanted to keep up morale in the way that he knew how. Even though he fell flat sometimes, he at least tried.

Two hours flew by, coffee was drunk, refilled, drunk, and refilled again. Knuckles popped with the fatigue of typing. Ella nearly broke out in a sweat with the fevered pitch. She wasn't even sure when they ate, until she realized a half-eaten slice of pepperoni pizza was on her desk, and she vaguely recalled a manager tossing them some food on the way to a meeting.

When the leads rejected a headline for not being "punchy enough"—whatever the hell that meant—the whole room groaned, and some seriously creative spins on the f-word funneled through the air. She booked an emergency working-session conference room while Sophie literally jogged down the hall to knock on the door of the legal team.

The time clicked away, three o'clock ganging up on them. Her heart thudded in her chest. Landing this today was critical. If not, they were in serious danger of not executing on time, and the real possibility occurred of Sophie and the other team members not going on the cruise. She glanced at Sophie, her cheeks red, her lip ring tucked firmly between her teeth, all lightness and warmth gone as she dashed to and from group to group, with her laptop tucked under her arm.

Malcolm burst into the room and cupped his hands. "Approved!"

Approved? Like approved *approved?*

Sophie slumped in her corner, her face like she finished a marathon. She gripped Ella, her fingers fanning across her arm. "It's done. Oh, thank the sweet baby advertising angels for looking down upon us during our time of need."

The energy in the room shifted from scowls and groans to cheers and sighs. "Approved?" Ella glanced at two creatives hugging each other, and Malcolm patting a guy on the back. "But what does that mean?"

Life filled back in Sophie's face. "That means we wait for the client approval and then we're good to go."

Nice. After all the work, time, and preparation, they were inches away from the finish line. From the first week of training, she remembered after client approval, which usually took a few days, they'd typically request minor tweaks, send back to legal for approval, and then prep the producers to code on the website. The running, the chase, the marathon was complete, and a lightness that Ella hadn't felt in so long filled her. "So now what?"

Sophie leaned toward Ella. "Now we celebrate."

Celebrate. With Sophie? Every part of this sounded intriguing. "Any ideas?"

Sophie's eyes dashed across the space and her lips curved into a grin. "Yes, I do."

NINETEEN

SOPHIE

"Are you sure this is sanitary?"

Ella's cocked eyebrows and the hesitation in her voice made Sophie crack up. How could Ella, a Seattle native, have never planted a fat one on the wall? "It's literally the least thing from being sanitary." Sophie chuckled. "You're looking at a decade's worth of saliva. I mean, spit dries, right, but think of the sheer amount of germs attached to this wall."

"Not sure I want to think of that." Ella's jaw worked overtime on the three pieces of bubblegum Sophie gave her as she studied the wall. "It's kind of pretty if you take out the whole bodily-fluid part of the equation."

"Agreed." The gum wall, tucked away in an alley outside of Pike Place Market, was pretty in its own way. Colorful blobs of pinks, blues, and greens laced the brick, chunks and layers of gum dripped from the surface. A few years ago, when the sugar from the gum started corroding the brick, the city had scraped it off, apparently gathering over two thousand pounds of gum. Sophie remembered being so bummed to hear about the city cleaning the area. The wall was iconic, part of the heartbeat of the city, and shouldn't be bare. Thankfully for locals and tourists, but probably not for the maintenance crew, it filled back up pretty quickly.

After leaving work early, Sophie wasn't sure why the gum wall was the first thing that popped in her mind. But after learning about Ella over this last month, and her severely limited life experiences, Sophie wanted to show her everything. Sophie loved her city. And Ella appreciated Seattle, but only knew it from afar. She didn't know what made Seattle, well, Seattle. She didn't know what it was like to stand outside of the El Corazón music venue amongst the smell of hot dog vendors and marijuana. She had never been to the International District, besides the fancy places, and eaten the best pho in the city at a hole-in-the-wall restaurant. She'd never sat under the Alaskan Way Viaduct on top of a truck, listening to the sounds of the city and sharing a 40 with friends.

"Who ever thought of this in the first place?" Ella asked, moving aside for a few tourists.

"Rumor has it gum wasn't allowed in the theater, so people would stick it on the wall. Not sure how that continued to grow, though." Sophie popped a fourth piece in her mouth, chewing until the gum broke apart.

Ella winced. "Isn't your jaw sore yet?"

"My jaw has more stamina than you could imagine." She meant it as a joke. But the heat in between them sparked.

Ella stopped chewing, her gaze dropping to Sophie's jawline.

"You ready?" Sophie dug out her cell phone from her pocket. "We have to take a selfie, obviously. Especially as a gum-wall virgin." Sophie spit the gum into her palm.

Ella pinched the gum between her fingers. "Okay, ready."

"One, two, three!" Sophie pushed the gum into the wall and snapped photos as Ella squealed and ground the gum into the wall with her thumb.

"Ewww." Ella giggled and wiped her finger on her pants.

"Okay, now that we crossed that off the proverbial bucket list, what's next?"

So many things... Sophie's grin dropped as she studied Ella, the freckles above her nose, the tiny curve below her earlobe, the dark eyes that captured Sophie, the voice that shook her core. The pale cheeks that looked so ridiculously soft that she wanted to feel the cotton skin under her fingertips. She needed to know more about this woman who'd morphed from a solid pain in the ass to someone she wanted to show the world to.

Sophie tucked a swatch of hair behind Ella's ear and really, really looked at her. Smart, strong, bold, feminine. Ella captured Sophie with her strength, with her humor, and with her heart.

Ella inched forward, her eyes flickering between Sophie's, her tongue swiping her bottom lips. She laid her hands on Sophie's hips and tugged her closer.

Tourists clamoring for their own photo op, the sound of the market, and a guitarist strumming a slow-ballad version of "Heart-Shaped Box" faded into the background. Sophie cupped Ella's face in her hands, her heart thumping against her chest. She swiped her thumbs on her cheek and touched her lips to Ella's, and... *this*. This was what Sophie was missing in her world. As Ella sighed into Sophie's lips, Sophie's skin prickled. She moved her tongue, opened her mouth, and deepened the kiss.

"Oops, sorry!" A tourist with the worst possible aim bumped into Sophie.

Ella groaned at the break in the moment. "Way to ruin the moment." She slipped her hand into Sophie's with a grin, intertwined with her fingers, and tugged her down the alley. The case was settled—Sophie never wanted to walk any other way.

For the rest of the day, Sophie reveled in the way Ella moved through the world outside of the office. Among the shuffling of the crowd, vendors calling out prices for flowers and fruit, and the smell of seafood, they strolled Pike Place, their hands seamlessly attached. Ella shifted between quiet observance and squealing excitement, depending on what she saw.

Her fingers glided across handwoven beanies, stroked the side of glass bongs, and she stared at a hand-painted picture of Jimi Hendrix across a canvas. She unabashedly sampled the entire spectrum of dusted hazelnuts, from cinnamon to ranch, even when Sophie tried to tug her away. "I think they only want you to taste one or two," Sophie whispered.

"But how can I make the best choice?" Ella purchased one of every kind. They stepped out of the way of screaming toddlers in strollers, people carrying woven canvas bags filled with vegetables and flower bouquets, and teenagers being, well, teenagers. Sophie bought them honey sticks and caramel popcorn, and they nibbled on cheesecake samples while listening to a man play Tchaikovsky on a sidewalk piano.

"I know we've eaten nothing but shit today, but I'm hungry for some real food." Ella stretched her neck, still clinging on to Sophie's hands.

What was happening here? Why did everything feel so natural, so comfortable, as if they'd walked no other way except with their hands molded together? She didn't want to break the magic of the market, but her belly was nudging her for some protein. "How do you feel about eggs and hash browns? Like diner-style?"

Up the steep hill past Post Alley, with the scent of the cheese makers and piroshkis following them, they made their way to one of the gazillion souvenir shops, to grab an Uber to Green Lake.

An hour later, Ella scooped up another serving of the saltiest, greasiest hash browns this side of the Olympics. "Oh my God," Ella murmured through her food. "Why is this so good?"

"'Cause of the sheer amount of butter used to fry it up and the decade-long remnants of bacon grease imbedded into the flat-top stove." Sophie grabbed the pepper from the condiment holder and doused her eggs. "Not to mention the guy at the fryer has been cooking here since I was little."

The heavily tattooed server with flaming orange hair juggling an armful of white ceramic plates walked by and Ella tapped the side of the plate. "More, please? If you don't mind?" She grinned at Sophie. "How can they have all-you-can-eat hash browns and still make a profit? I might move into this place."

"I can't believe you've never been here." Sophie spread homemade raspberry jam across a dense chunk of sourdough bread, then scooped eggs on top.

She wasn't sure what Ella's reaction would be to coming to the local-favorite, true dive diner in Green Lake. They'd swapped the sounds and smells of Pike Place for fryer grease, dough, hearty butter, and sticky floors. This place was iconic. A known cure for hangovers, the last pit stop after raging all night, the Saturday morning breakfast spot for families and college kids alike. And she'd be lying if she said she wasn't a tad worried Ella would grimace, as she was probably used to truffle-oil-laced egg soufflé with organic crème fraîche.

But as Ella dug into her third plate of hash browns, all worries ceased. This unlocked yet another new side of Ella, and Sophie was hungry for more. She wanted to know about Ella's dreams. What did she really want to do for a career? Where was her first kiss? Did she ever have a dog? She stared at her mouth, wanting to taste the sweetness again. "Can I ask you something?"

Ella wiped the side of her mouth and reached for her glass. "Sure."

"Can you tell me about Jasmine?" Nothing halts a first date-ish like bringing up an ex.

Ella's smile faded. She stabbed her fork against the food and exhaled. "She was exactly what I thought I wanted when we met. Spunky, spicy, and fiery. Kind of like a human jalapeño popper. I almost idolized her in a way. She was outgoing and fun and just so confident."

"You're confident."

"It's an act." She lifted the fork to her mouth. "But, for quite a while, I really loved her. But then I saw certain things about her, and I started to question who she was as a person. She was obsessed with money. After a few months, she started ordering the staff around, almost like she was joking. But you know how people joke around and say things with a smile, but deep down they mean it?"

Sophie nodded. She absolutely knew people like this, the same people who started conversations with, "No offense, but..."

"And, well, she broke my heart." A gloom passed over Ella's eyes. She set the fork down without taking a bite and bit the side of her lip. "I know it sounds intense or whatever, but I had real dreams for us. I wanted to see the world with her. We looked at apartments together. I saw a future, like a real future, with her. And when our relationship ended, the *way* it ended, it ruined me. I lost her, my world was shattered, my future was gone in a snap."

"I'm so sorry." Why did she have to bring this up now? All lightness was siphoned from the room, swapped with darkness. No one had ever cheated on Sophie before. But she could imagine the sense of betrayal, the inability to trust again, the gut-wrenching sense of rejection, would cut deep.

"But... think of this." Ella chewed on another bite, and the side of her lip twitched into a grin. "Had that never happened, I would have had no idea how delicious fried, shredded, overly buttered potatoes were."

Sophie laughed. "That is an excellent point."

. . .

Sophie didn't want the evening to end. But after polishing off an obscene amount of breakfast food, having a hot make-out session in a terribly un-sexy spot in the alley near the dumpster, and strolling around Green Lake, when Ella yawned, Sophie knew she had to end the evening. But the logic of knowing she needed to end the evening didn't make it any easier to say good night. When Thomas dropped her off, the bounce in her toes morphed into trudging up her stairs, and she flopped hard on her bed.

She liked Ella. *So much.* But was the timing right? She was George's daughter, for God's sake. Oddly, though, that didn't scare her. So, what *was* scaring her? Sophie stuffed the fabric of her knitted blanket in between her fingers and rubbed, her belly corkscrewing with the images of Ella, her mouth, her laugh, and the way she fought through her nerves to command a room. She relished the joy in Ella's eyes at the dive diner, and the flicker of her eyelashes when Sophie leaned in to kiss her. These last few weeks had been the best she could remember.

But did Ella feel the same squeeze in her heart? Did she feel like her breath ripped from her lungs when she saw Sophie? Did she go to bed the way Sophie did, thinking of Ella's eyes, the freckles ridging her nose, or the slope of her long neck? She yanked her phone onto her chest and dialed. "I'm completely freaking out and don't know what to do."

"Whoa, slow down there, slugger." Maya's chipper voice came through. "Break this down for me step-by-step. Do I need to shank someone? What happened?"

Everything had happened. In a few weeks, Ella had flipped Sophie's world upside down. And now she was scrambling amidst the carnage. She wanted to take a leap, but she had so much work to do. She still had her five-year plan to rise the corporate ladder, and become manager someday. "No shanking required." She exhaled into the phone. "I'm just spinning out about everything."

"Ella, huh?"

Sophie stopped vigorously kneading the blanket in her hand. "How did you know?"

"*Really?*" Maya chuckled. "Ella sucks. Ella is ruining my life. Ella is spoiled and rude and poopy and *oh so dreamy.*"

Okay, fair. Regardless of the actual words Sophie may have spoken, Maya had an innate ability to read into everything. Sophie didn't even try to argue with her best friend that she never once uttered that Ella was dreamy.

"I don't know what to do." Sophie flopped her wrist over her eyes. "I really like her. She's so different than what I thought. And it feels so damn good and natural, but how can it feel this good so quick? But is it really quick if you break down the amount of hours actually spent together? But the timing is terrible, I have so much work to do, and this launch and the cruise—"

"*Jesus*, you're absolutely spinning." Maya's voice cut through the verbal tsunami. "Let's just take this one thing at a time. You've established that you've got it super bad for this woman. Great. But you're freaking out because you think you don't have time. You're the hardest worker I know. You fight for your team, your company, and whatever project you're managing. You fight like hell for me, Harper, and your family. But you refuse to fight for yourself, Soph. I love you, you know this. But have you ever once considered that you use work as an excuse to avoid getting into a relationship?"

"But I'm busy!" Sophie protested. It's not like she didn't want to date before, she just didn't have time.

"Do you think you are any less busy than any of your co-workers?"

"I don't know... no, probably not."

"And are they all single?" Maya continued.

Sophie paused. She could clearly see the point that Maya was making, but Sophie's life differed from her co-workers'. She didn't have a degree to fall back on, or a family with money and connections. She pushed herself because she had no other choice.

"I love you so much. But you crack through certain barriers, and shield yourself behind others. You deserve to be happy." Several long moments followed. "Do something spontaneous. Something absurd. Just *do something*, for you and only you."

The words sunk in, uncomfortable and squirmy in her chest, before her spirits lifted. She did deserve happiness, dammit, and being with Ella made her happy. All she needed was to take the plunge.

Maya sat with her in silence. The only sound coming through the phone was the faint sounds of breathing. Sophie mulled the words in her head, broke down her dating life, and soon, a smile spread. She had an idea. "Hey, is Remi there?"

"Ah, yeah. Why?"

Sophie hopped off the bed and paced the bedroom. "Can I talk to her?"

"Hmmm. Suspicious. I love it. Yes, let me get her."

Ten minutes later, Sophie hung up with a satisfied grin. She could not wait for tomorrow.

TWENTY

ELLA

Ella grinned into the mirror as she flat ironed her bangs the fifth and final time for the morning. She tugged on the bottom of her shirt and frowned. The lace-panel sleeveless top was not giving the right vibe. Four shirts later, she settled on a cotton short-sleeve top that carried the message she intended—*I'm ready for our not-quite-sure-if-this-is-a-date day together.*

This was a date, right? She reread her text exchange with Sophie from the previous evening.

SOPHIE:

> I had so much fun today! So… how about we do something totally wild. Let's ditch work and go out.

She used the words *go out*. That was what one used to articulate a date. Most likely.

ELLA:

> Ditch work? Ugh. Sounds amazing, but makes me a little nervous. I don't want to let anyone down. Nor do I want to get fired.

SOPHIE:

Um, isn't your dad the boss?

ELLA:

Stop! Yes, obviously, but…

SOPHIE:

I'm kind of teasing. I talked to Malcolm. Client said it would be Tuesday at the earliest before we hear from them. So as long as we have our phones on us for urgent questions, we don't need to come in.

ELLA:

So, what I am hearing is…

SOPHIE:

Pick you up at 10?

ELLA:

YES!

A knock at the bedroom door made her jump, and she leapt to grab it. "Colleen?

"Hey, sweet girl." Colleen opened her arms, and Ella lost herself in a warm, patchouli-filled hug. "Don't you look adorable."

She did look kind of adorable, if she said so herself. "What are you doing here?"

Colleen crossed the room to look at Ella's painting and nodded with approval. "Your mom and I had some paperwork to look at, and then we're grabbing breakfast. But more importantly, what are *you* doing here on a Friday?"

Oh, nothing big. Just meeting the woman of my dreams for a date. She spritzed perfume in the air and walked underneath, fanning the mist. "Our manager said we only needed to be on call. So, Sophie and I are going to explore the city." *And maybe, if I'm lucky, each other.*

Colleen's eyebrow lifted. "Sophie, eh? The beautiful co-worker? Glad things worked out between you two."

A lifetime had passed since she was at Colleen's, brushing Mocha-Tina and holding back tears from her first few weeks at work. So much had shifted, and the air smelled like hope and opportunity. She shoved her emergency nasal spray in her purse and strapped it across her body. God, she was nervous. Excited, yes, but also, this was a huge step. "Can I ask you something?"

"Yup. Shoot."

"Why didn't you date again after Dottie died?" She swallowed, knowing the level of invasiveness in the question.

Colleen tugged at the sleeves of her sunset-colored muumuu. "Who says I didn't?"

"Wait, what?"

"I don't tell you everything, my love." Colleen sat on the end of Ella's bed and twirled her multi-colored ring. "It took years, but I do date off and on. But right now, I'm fulfilled with myself, the farm, family, friends. I'm not missing anything."

Ella considered all of this. "Okay, so when you did date, what made you take that leap? Weren't you scared of getting hurt?"

"Of course I was. I think everyone's instinct is to protect themselves from getting hurt. I know when things with you and Jasmine ended, you thought the world ended. It was really shitty what happened. But does that mean you're destined for relationship purgatory?" She set her fingers in her lap. "The biggest lesson I learned from Dottie's death is that life is too short to not do what makes you happy. So, if going out with a co-worker today makes you happy, then live your life to the fullest. We don't get second chances. Well, of course until we're reincarnated, but that's a totally different subject."

The doorbell rang and Ella perked up. "I love you." She hugged her aunt. "I gotta go. I need to save Sophie from my mother."

She bolted down hallway one, then hallway two, then nearly floated down the stairs when she saw Sophie at the entrance, engaged in what was surely terrible small talk. Ella stopped at the bottom step to breathe in the moment. A real date. With Sophie. Who looked amazing by the way, in a cropped sweater, tennis skirt, and purple fishnets. She kind of wanted to devour her on the spot.

Sophie looked up with a grin. "Hey!"

The blush rose fast and furious to Ella's cheeks. "Hey, you." She glanced at her mom and not so subtly jutted her chin in the upstairs direction. "I think Colleen wanted to talk to you. In the other room."

A nod and a smile followed. "Yes, I'm sure she does." Her mom winked, and for the first time in forever, Ella was not annoyed. "Nice chatting with you, Sophie. Have fun today, you two."

"Nice to see you again, Mrs. Northwood." Sophie's eyes followed Claire out of the room.

Ella wasn't sure how Sophie would react to her today. Yesterday, they spent the day holding hands, and stealing kisses. But today was a new day, with the high of closing the last phase of the campaign and a spontaneous day off disappearing. Things might just go back to nor—

Whoa. Sophie took two steps and pulled Ella in for a kiss. "Hey." Her words were soft and low, and her fingertips grazed Ella's waist.

"I demand to start my day every day just like that," Ella joked. She grabbed Sophie's hand and dragged her outside. "Come on. I cannot wait for today."

Ella slunk into the front seat of Sophie's car. "So, you going to tell me where we're going?"

Sophie pulled out of the driveway and drove from the neighborhood. "I figured I needed to finish the proper tour of the city, since all you've seen is what your parents have shown you. First stop, International District."

The ride tested every ounce of willpower Ella had. She wanted to skim her palm up Sophie's thigh. Trail the skin on her wrist. Hold her hand, or snuggle into her arm, or *something*. But she settled for the sweet kisses that Sophie planted at the red lights.

Sophie parallel parked like a champ, then gripped Ella's hand as they strolled the sidewalk. The sun was warm today, topping at nearly seventy degrees, and the air filled with the smell of spring and fried chicken. Sophie pointed to a place at the end of the street and held the door open.

So many options filled the menu and Ella wanted to eat everything. Was she always this hungry or was this the result of sitting in a cloud of sesame, garlic, and dough? Fried pork wontons, soup dumplings, cucumber salad, xiao long bao... Her mouth watered so much she needed to swallow.

After ordering and digging into their first few bites, Sophie lowered her chopsticks. "Did your dad take the day off, too?"

Ella snorted. "My dad never takes a day off." She added more soy sauce into the ginger, and dipped a cucumber. "Sometimes I wonder when he'll retire. Not to sound crass, but the family money comes from my mom's side. I think growing up the way he did, he always feels the need for a backup plan or something. He wouldn't have to work if he didn't want to, so he must really, really want to."

"I swear, the more I learn about your dad, the more I resonate with him. Words I never thought I'd ever say." Sophie grinned as pork-scented steam rose from the soup dumplings. She popped the whole thing in her mouth, and cleaned a drip of soup from the corner of her lip. "Why do you work? I mean, I'm so glad you do, but do you get a personal fulfillment from project managing or something?"

"Nope, sure don't." Ella laughed. She loved being in the

office, part of a team, and she actually didn't mind the work. But her dreams, what fulfilled her, were not found in the office. "I can see how much joy you get from work. All your organizing, and keeping the ship running, and commanding a room, is really impressive." *And hot AF, but I digress.* "The only thing that fulfills me is art."

"Why didn't you major in art?"

"My parents thought a business major would be more practical. Which is kind of funny, because they also never wanted me to work." She shrugged. "I essentially had to force my dad to hire me."

The reason for wanting to work, to escape her parents and have her own place, had faded in the past month, though. An urgency to leave no longer seemed as all-consuming as it had several months ago. A few weeks had even passed since she'd looked at apartments online. She thought it was because she was so busy at work that when she got home, she had zero interest in looking at a screen. But maybe there was more to it.

Sophie's mouth had dropped open, and she closed it. "You forced your dad to hire you? I just assumed... I guess I thought he just handed the job to you."

"Hell no. He respects his company too much to just toss this job to me." She bit into her steamed bun and chewed. "But he was scared of me, for me, and I... well, I didn't really give him a choice."

Ella spent the next hour polishing off wontons, potstickers, and finishing the final bite of sweet taro bun, while she told Sophie everything. How claustrophobic she'd felt, about the meltdown that led to her chopping off her braid, how her parents were terrified. Sophie listened, peppered in minimal questions, and let her talk. She didn't try to say she couldn't believe it happened, or that Ella had overreacted, or that her feelings weren't valid. She didn't try to point out her amazing house, or Thomas, or her bank account. When she was done, Ella felt raw and exposed.

"Thank you so much for sharing that with me." Sophie rested her hand on top of Ella's. "Honestly, I feel really honored you trusted me enough to tell me all of this."

Ella swallowed, her skin flushed and hot. Never had she opened up like this and she tried to read Sophie's eyes to see if she went too far. Sophie leaned over as if she knew what Ella was thinking and gave her a soft, reassuring kiss. And when she did, Ella exhaled.

This was better than any date she'd had before.

TWENTY-ONE
SOPHIE

This day was for the record books. Dim sum, a water taxi ride to Alki Beach, a visit to Golden Gardens, and a late dinner. Sophie drove up I-5 with the sunset fading in the west, and a comfortable silence filled the space. No more spinning thoughts, no more wondering how Ella felt, no more second-guessing everything. She felt closer to Ella right now than everyone in her life except her parents and Maya.

She threaded her fingers with Ella's and kissed the top of her hand. When she released it, and Ella leaned her head against Sophie's shoulder, the most real of all realities hit. This was what happiness looked like. This was what happiness *felt* like—all warm and gushy, with belly tingles and jumping heartbeats. But there was a calmness, a stillness, to the happiness. For once, she was beautifully content.

Ella's eyes furrowed as Sophie pulled into a parking lot. "We're going golfing?" She turned her head toward the window. "There aren't any cars here."

"Yeah, they're closed for the night." Sophie turned off the ignition. "Do you trust me?"

"Of course," Ella responded, but cocked an eyebrow. "Why?"

Sophie's eyes dashed across the parking lot and to the building. "Come with me, but we have to be super quiet."

A slow grin spread across Ella's face and she hopped out of the car. Sophie interlocked their fingers and guided Ella down the stairs. The sprawling, lush, green golf course was so peaceful, she barely registered they were still in a city. She tugged Ella against the side of the building and put her finger to her mouth in a "shhhhh" motion.

The office door was on their left, and Sophie saluted her palms to peer through the window. She squinted, making out a faint light in the distance. She jiggled the door. Unlocked. *Whew.* Her hand froze on the handle. "Still trust me?" When Ella nodded with a grin, Sophie squeezed her hand. "Once we're inside, we have to be totally silent. But if you hear or see someone coming, get my attention and we'll bolt."

Sophie squeaked open the door and tiptoed inside, then waved in Ella. She motioned her to stay put as she Pink Panther-ed her way to the office. Her heart pounded against her chest wall as she stepped inside the office door and stared at the wall of keys hanging from tiny hooks.

Ella was in the corner, her face flushed, her chest lifted, and Sophie flooded with the thrill of seeing Ella with what seemed to be a similar adrenaline rush. Already, this was going better than she expected. No alarms, no unexpected facility person, no lingering golfers who could question what she was doing here after-hours.

After plucking key #16, she crept backwards, and her gaze flickered across the hall. "Got it," she whispered, and crossed the room back toward the door.

Ella tossed her a confused glance, but followed her outside, down the opposite side of the building and back up the hill.

Sophie spoke no words until they were a good fifty feet from the clubhouse. She escorted Ella past a few sheds and moved to the cart barn, where rows of parked golf carts waited. "Here."

"Huh?" Ella palmed the keys in her hand. "What are we doing?"

"You've always wanted to drive, right?" Sophie licked the edge of her lip ring. "Let's drive."

A solid four to five seconds passed before Ella squealed. "Whaaaat? Here? Now? Which one? What?"

Sophie pointed to #16 at the edge of the lot and hopped in the passenger seat.

Ella sat in the driver's seat and ran her hand across the steering wheel. She thumbed her glasses back up her nose. "I don't even know what to do."

Her voice contained all the excitement Sophie hoped it would. "Okay, accelerate on the right, brake on the left."

"I mean, I know that..."

"Just turn the ignition to 'on' and push the gear here to drive." She tapped the gear button. "Then press the pedal to change how fast it goes. Smooth and slow at first until you get comfortable."

Ella nodded at the instructions, reminiscent of her first week at work. But this time, her nods contained a smile that Sophie wanted to remember forever. Ella's tongue swept her lip, and her eyes furrowed in fierce concentration. Her left hand's knuckles turned white as she gripped the key and pressed the pedal.

Sophie flew back. "Whoa!" She flew forward when Ella slammed on the brake.

"Ah! Sorry. Shit!" Her hand fumbled and she twisted in the seat. "Okay, okay, I got this." She eased them out of the parking lot and followed Sophie's instructions to the end of the pavement.

A few minutes into it, Ella's knuckles returned to a normal color and soon she squealed. "I'm driving!" She screamed into the night air as she reached a max speed of maybe five miles an hour. She turned in a large circle, returned to the lot, and accelerated.

Yes, Ella was not supposed to drive. But Sophie figured the risk was pretty low in a golf cart, when the max speed was twenty miles an hour and there was no one else around. If Ella had a seizure, Sophie was pretty confident she could get them to safety.

"I'm fucking driving! Whooo!" She screamed again and increased the speed to about ten miles an hour. She looped the lot and after a bit loosened up. She turned, looped, reversed, looped again, while bouncing in her seat and yelling.

The rush was obvious. Ella's body lifted, and she yelled with such animation that Sophie felt Ella's joy in her soul. Meadow smells filled the breeze and the bumps in the pavement were no match for Ella. She gained more confidence and completed the slowest doughnut known to humans. "I've always wanted to do that! Do you think I left skid marks?"

Going the speed of a sloth, Ella absolutely had not created any marks. Sophie nodded anyway.

Ella bumped them down to the edge of the parking lot when shouting started behind them.

"Hey! Stop! Hey!" A man with a polo shirt boasting the name of the golf course ran toward them, waving.

Ella slammed on the brakes. "Oh my God, what do we do?"

Sophie turned around. The man inched closer, his yells stronger. "You speed it up and outrun him."

Ella's eyes turned as wide as Sophie had ever seen, before she pressed on the pedal and floored it. They bumped over the parking lot, swerved in between cars, and Sophie clasped on to the rack with both hands.

"Go! Go! Onto the greens." Sophie glanced over her

shoulder as the man dug out keys and hopped in a cart, chasing after them.

The cart jolted over the lip and they went down the green. "Ahhh!" Sophie yelled, the elation filling her belly. "You got this! Just circle around, bring us back to my car, and we'll make a run for it."

"Got it." Ella's chest rapidly lifted in quick, sharp inhales. She firmed her grip and swerved down the meadow.

The man screamed. "Stop! You two! Stop. I'm gonna call the cops!"

Over the hills, to the left, on top of a few lone branches crunching beneath them, Ella navigated the cart. "Over there!" Sophie pointed to the right exit. "He's gaining on us. Can you go a little faster?"

Ella pushed down, and the golf cart trudged up the steep hill. "Is he getting close?"

"Yep, but we got this."

The sound of sirens rang in the background and Sophie's heart thudded. "Come on, almost there. Once we stop, hop out and run like hell."

"Okay." Ella navigated to the right, down the slope, and to the exit.

"The sirens are getting closer. Get ready to run." Sophie shifted her legs towards the opening, ready to bolt the second the cart slowed. "Hundred more feet... fifty... twenty... okay, stop! Get out, go!"

Ella pushed on the brakes, Sophie threw the gear into park, and they both leapt out.

"Don't look behind you. Just keep running!" Sophie's lungs emptied, and she scrambled to get the keys out of her pocket. The key fob took more than one click to open, and her heart nearly stopped. She dropped into the car, Ella did the same, and Sophie squealed out of the parking lot.

"I can't believe we just did that!" Ella pushed the back of

her head into the seat and brought her palms to her cheeks. "I've never done anything like that before... and shit... God, this feels good. This feels so wrong. Does this feel wrong to you? But also incredible? I can't believe we outran the cops!" She dropped her hands from her face and her legs stomped against the floor, glee transferring from her voice to her legs. "This is AMAZING!"

"It feels good to be bad, huh?" Sophie pulled back onto I-5 South. "What would your dad say?"

"I think he'd be proud." Soon her breath evened out. "Holy shit. Do you think the police will find us?"

Traffic surrounded them, but no police cars. "No, I think we're good." Sophie actually knew they were good. The sirens were a happy coincidence, and nothing to do with her and Ella's little escapade on the greens.

When Sophie talked to Remi yesterday, everything had fallen into place. She'd remembered Remi telling a story a few months ago about one of her regulars who managed a golf course, who said he owed Remi his life after Remi had introduced him to his fiancée the year prior.

All Sophie asked was if Remi could find out if she could drive a golf cart without being a member. That inquiry morphed into a three-way text string where the manager jumped on the first-date bandwagon. Soon, the three devised a plan where Sophie would pretend to break in and he'd pretend to chase after them after giving her enough lead time. He mapped out the office location, which key to take, and said he'd put the golf cart in slot 16. Everything else simply fell into place.

Maybe Sophie would tell Ella sometime about how tonight came together. But for now, she fed off of Ella's excitement.

Ella stroked her thumb on Sophie's upper thigh. "I think we've packed everything we could into today," Ella started, and looked down at her hand grazing Sophie's leg. "Is there anything else on the agenda?"

The agenda, work, this, us, *has all led to the now.* She was ready, she was sure, as sure as she was ever going to be. A hard lump grew in her throat, and she tried to discreetly swallow. As the car lights drove by and she neared the exit, she inhaled a quick breath and exhaled through her nose. "If you want, we can go back to my place."

TWENTY-TWO

SOPHIE

Well, she said yes. And not just any yes, but an enthusiastic, breathy, sugar-dripping, resounding yes. Sophie held Ella's hand from the garage to the elevator to outside her apartment door. When she had to drop it to open the door, she missed the warmth of her touch immediately.

"Wow... this place is so warm and homey. The colors, everything. I love it." Ella tugged her shoes off at the door and continued scanning the apartment. "It's great."

Sophie's place *was* great. After she'd saved for a year to make sure she had a proper nest egg, she'd moved into this apartment at twenty-one and couldn't imagine moving out. The place was everything she wanted—modern, warm, quiet. Yet, she couldn't help but think of Ella's gazillion-square-foot bedroom, her kitchen island the size of a king bed, and wondering if Ella was secretly comparing it to her own place.

But as Ella stood in the corner, a genuine perma-grin forming, all signs indicated that she really did like Sophie's apartment.

"Can I get you something to drink? Eat?" Sophie fidgeted with her key before placing it on the hook. Everything sludged in slow motion. She was pretty sure if Ella felt the way she did, they could skip all this formality and just move toward the bedroom. But suggesting that felt like a player move, and Sophie was seriously out of practice.

Jesus, her hands needed to stop sweating. She was a career woman with a great apartment, great job, great friends... not some teen about to lose their virginity. She'd had sex before, dammit. Sure, infrequent at best, but she wasn't clueless how this happened. "Not sure what I all have. Life of a bachelorette, am I right? Probably like raspberry soda, coffee, which I know you won't have, um..." Sophie rested her forearm on top of the open fridge door and strummed her fingertips across the top. "Let's see... let's see... leftover Chinese, but we might want to skip that. Probably way past its expiration. Oh, cheese? Scrambled—"

A gentle hand on her hip broke her last words. Ella's fingertips fanned her side, and she rested her chin on Sophie's shoulder. "Raspberry soda sounds perfect." Her voice was a whisper, calm and collected, and everything Sophie needed to drop her rigid shoulders.

She grabbed two sodas and moved to the couch. Ella's footsteps followed her, and once they sagged onto the sofa, Ella skimmed her finger across Sophie's stockings.

"Are you okay?" Ella asked.

Sophie took a sip, the bubbles fizzing her throat. "Honestly? I'm freaking out a little. Like, I love this." She motioned between the two. "I've had the most incredible time with you. And, ahem, I think we're maybe thinking the same, but I'm not sure, and sometimes I get super in my head about things, and it's been a long time..."

Ella rested her elbow on the couch backing and leaned her head into her hands. "Do you want to have sex, with me, tonight?"

Wow. Well, she just said it. Bluntly, firmly, with zero trepidation in her words. "Well... um... if we're both feeling that..." She scraped her thumbnail against her other thumbnail. "It's kind of been a long time."

Ella raised an eyebrow. "Oh yeah? How long?"

Why was she embarrassed? She felt the pink rise to her cheeks, and she gulped down more drink to counteract the heat filling her face. "Like a year ago, just a quick, one-night thing. And before that, honestly, a handful of times in my adulthood."

The information seemed to settle on Ella as she slowly grinned. "Oooh... was it hot?"

Huh?

"The one-night thing. Was it hot?" Ella's expectant wide eyes flickered with deviancy.

"You don't really want to hear this, do you?" The last thing Sophie would want to hear was about a partner's former escapades.

"No, for real. I do." Ella turned her body more toward Sophie and licked her lips. "I'm a little freaky like that. It's like being a voyeur without the whole invasion of privacy thing."

God, this woman is incredible. No jealousy, no nerves, just curiosity. At work, Sophie was on top of everything. She owned that space, confident in the way she spoke to her team, in the way she moved her body, in the information she disseminated. But relationships, sex, being joyful with someone besides her friends, was foreign. "It was really fucking hot."

"Gah! Tell me everything." Ella strummed her fingers together and bounced in her seat.

Sophie laughed and leaned back. She told Ella about a happy hour event last year—which she was not feeling at all—so she distracted herself by making flirty eyes with a woman across the bar who looked equally as miserable. When she excused herself to go to the bar, the woman followed her. She was funny, sexy, and they chatted. Ended up making out in the bathroom, then getting an Uber to her place, and doing things she only read about in spicy lesbian romances.

Ella peppered in questions, leaned back, and fanned her face. Sophie had never opened up so much about a past sexual relation, and frankly wouldn't want to be on the receiving end of this information. But Ella clearly loved every second of it, and the room heated several degrees as she kept talking.

The room quieted, and Sophie set her empty can on the coffee table. This felt so good, too good. Was it too good? Or was this just how relationships worked? Right now, she felt she could tell Ella anything, and she'd nod, ask questions, and be genuinely interested in what she had to say. She didn't want to lose this moment, this feeling, ever. She wanted to be happy. She *deserved* to be happy.

Ella clicked on the top of the soda can. "What are you scared of?"

Not *are you scared*. But *what*. It was like she could read Sophie's insides. "So many things." Sophie let out a chuckle, but it was true. "Getting hurt. Getting too happy. Feeling what I'm feeling right now forever. *Not* feeling what I'm feeling right now for the rest of my life, and what it will do to me if that feeling fades." She took a deep breath, the words constricting in her chest. "I, er, I saw your profile on an app looking for a one-night-only type relationship. And you do you, for real. But I'm looking for more. I need more."

Ella's head tilted to the side. Her eyes narrowed, widened, and she grinned. "Oh my God, I totally forgot about that profile. I deleted that app like a week after I set it up." She set the soda on the coffee table and crisscrossed her legs. "I did that more out of spite than anything. It was right after Jasmine and I broke up and I tried to convince myself I didn't need anything more than a hookup."

Ah. "And now what do you think you need?"

Ella's eyelashes dipped to her cheek, and for the first time tonight, she looked sheepish. "I need you." The words ghosted the room with their delicacy but hit with the weight of a thousand pounds.

Sophie dangled a finger in Ella's silky hair, before she tucked the strand behind Ella's ear. She pulled her close, gripped her head lightly, her thumbs swiping her cheeks. The air quieted, still, and Sophie could hear her heartbeat thud in her chest. She pressed her mouth against Ella's, savoring the raspberry on her lips. Ella pressed back into her, sliding against her mouth, her fingers scraping gently up Sophie's arm.

A waterfall of shivers fell from her arms to her belly to her toes, and Sophie pressed for more. Ella's smooth, velvety tongue met Sophie's, and she moaned into Sophie's mouth. Sophie's hands grazed Ella's thigh, her neck, her shoulder as Sophie searched for more open skin.

Ella's collarbone, the crook of her neck, tasted so sweet, the softest mix of salty skin, and Sophie could have nuzzled there forever. "Is this okay?" she asked as she danced her mouth to below Ella's ear, her forehead, and across her jawline.

"Yes..." Ella murmured, her fingers pressing into Sophie's back.

Ella draped a leg over Sophie, then shifted on the couch. Everything was slow, intense, and also... super uncomfortable. Why did she wear the fishnet stockings that were now digging into her skin? Sophie needed more space, she wanted to explore, to know Ella on every level, and this couch was not doing it.

"Do you want to move to the bedroom?" Sophie pulled back to read Ella's eyes, but barely had a chance.

Ella leapt up, tossed her glasses to the side table, and tugged Sophie to her. "Yes, please, for the love of everything holy." She kissed Sophie, grinning into her mouth.

In the hallway, they got distracted. Ella pushed Sophie into the wall, kissing her with the promise of tomorrow, with the promise of safety, with honesty and encouragement. Sophie's knees buckled under the intensity, and her fingers found the dip in Ella's hip, the curve of her backside. She lowered her hands, cupping Ella's ass, pushing into her hips. Shit, she needed friction. She needed Ella's hands and mouth, her sweet kisses, and her laughter. She needed the confidence, the salty personality, and her smart mouth.

Ella's hands found Sophie's thigh, tugged it up high, and hooked it behind her hip. She pushed her thigh in between Sophie's legs, and the motion was incendiary, lighting her, sparking her alive. "This good?" Ella asked, gripping Sophie's face, sucking on her bottom lip, circling her tongue on Sophie's ring.

"So good." Sophie breathed into Ella's mouth. Her pulse raced, thudded so loud in her chest, in her neck, even her scalp prickled. Dizzy, she leaned into the wall for support. She smiled into the kiss, consumed the kiss. She dropped her leg and yanked Ella toward the bedroom.

Clothes on the floor were kicked to the side, the door wide open, hallway and living room lights on. Sophie needed this now. Her body ached, glorious and fevered, her skin puckered with the anticipation of having Ella in her mouth.

They tripped their way into the bed, frantic and rushed. If Sophie waited another minute, another second, she'd burst. Sophie ripped her fishnets stockings off and kicked them to the side. Ella tugged Sophie's sweater over her head and tossed it to the floor, then ripped off her own sweater. God, she was incredible. So full, so round, and Sophie wanted to put her mouth on everything.

Sophie straddled Ella, her heart thumping against her chest wall, and slowed her movements. She wanted to savor every part of Ella. She pulled back, linking in her fingers with Ella, and kissed the top of Ella's fingertips. When she dropped her hands, Ella sat up, holding Sophie firmly, strong behind her, and put her mouth on Sophie's neck. Breath heated Sophie's skin, and she turned to putty.

Ella traced her finger, a ghost of a touch, across Sophie's chest. She planted a kiss on Sophie's cleavage, her shoulder, her neck. She dragged a finger, tracing the outline of Sophie's breast with the softest of touches. How could something that was a whisper, a graze, make her feel like this? All curled toes and hair on fire and it was like Ella was touching her, *really* touching her, on the inside.

The pads of Sophie's fingers pressed into Ella's back and she let Ella lower her racerback bra straps. She kissed and nipped at the freshly bare skin, then removed the bra. "Oh, Sophie... you're so beautiful..." She cupped Sophie in her hands, her thumbs gliding across Sophie's nipples, and Sophie crumbled under the touch. All the fear of opening herself up melted with each trace, with each kiss. This was all a dream, but she didn't care. She never needed to wake up.

Ella brushed her lips against the sensitive skin around her breasts, leaving the skin wet and hungry. She hovered, then blew a soft flutter of air across the wet skin, and if Ella didn't pull Sophie into her mouth right now, she wouldn't be able to stand it. Sophie's skin scorched, blushed, and... oh shit... yes. Ella's mouth latched around Sophie's nipple, and Sophie's body arched into her in response. "Ella... oh... so good. Don't stop, please don't stop." A delicious symphony of pinching, sucking, licking, and moans swirled, and Sophie could die this moment and be happy.

Breaths and squeaky bedsprings and luxurious sighs bounced from the walls. Ella hopped off the bed and removed the rest of her clothing, with no fear, no hesitation. Sophie saw her future—in her pale skin, in the way her eyes danced, in the curve of her hips, and her mouth, oh... her soft sweet mouth.

Ella straddled her now, and Sophie clutched at her hips. Sophie pulled Ella into her, wanting to touch every part of her skin, wanting, needing to feel closer. She cupped Ella's breasts into her hand, so full, so beautiful. "Are you okay? Still good?"

"Everything is fucking... delicious. We can do everything." Ella moaned into her ear.

Sophie wrapped her lips around Ella's breasts, and oh... Christ... this, her, having her, feeling Ella grip her neck to push into her more... it was too much and not enough and she needed more.

Not enough air existed, but Sophie didn't care. Exploring, learning everything about Ella, what she liked, what she craved, what she needed, was the only thing Sophie needed. Ella pulled Sophie to her mouth, her kisses strong, full, and Sophie breathed her air, gasped against her mouth. Her skin tingled pink. Her chest stretched and filled and... oh God. This. All she needed was this, Ella, them.

Thighs and knees and fingers and tongues danced across flesh. Ella ground into Sophie, lowering herself, and put Sophie's thigh between her legs. Feeling Ella's want on the top of her leg fevered Sophie. She wanted every part of Ella in her mouth, on her fingers, in her hand.

Ella kissed Sophie's belly, trailing her tongue down her side, as Sophie quivered and goose bumps skittered across her body. Hot breaths filled her skin, heated her, and she needed Ella. All of Ella.

Ella hovered at Sophie's center, blushing her fevered skin.

"Can I..." Ella asked through pants.

"Yes, yes, everything, so good, yes..." Incoherent words bumbled from Sophie.

And then Ella's mouth was on Sophie's center, and Sophie lost the ability to speak. Moans and sweat filled the room, filled her skin. She wasn't sure who was louder, Ella or her. Hooking Sophie's leg above her shoulder, Ella was in full, complete control, experienced and driven. When she dipped in one, then two, fingers to join her mouth, her breath, her tongue, Sophie turned to liquid and she gripped at the sheets. With every rhythmic glide, Sophie felt how beautiful she was, how worthy, how wanted. Ella tasted her with promise, with decision, showing Sophie she wanted this as much as her. "You're so beautiful... so incredible..." She hummed against Sophie's core, and Sophie felt whole, complete, powerless, and powerful. Connecting with Ella, feeling this... She was inside out, upside down, no longer feeling human, yet the most human she'd ever been.

What Sophie wanted, true connection, welding together, interlocking dreams, and hopes and desires, unfolded with every motion. Ella's tongue moved more, wider, softer, then firmer. Sophie's body arched and pressed into Ella as she read Sophie's body, a maestro conducting the perfect symphony, knowing when to increase, when to decrease, less pressure, oh God, more... pressure, definitely more pressure. The moment was building, the crescendo tapping against her insides, at first a faint vibration. It grew, heavier now, the trembles increasing, heightening, her moans loud and intense, and she *was so close.* The quivering started harder now, lower in her belly, and then... yes, right there, one more... tension seized her body and she broke, the waves crashing, pulsating, releasing.

On top of Sophie's shivering body, Ella pulled back and rested her head on Sophie's belly, her chest rising and lowering against Sophie's skin. Ella's heart pounded against Sophie, her skin dewy and glistening and perfect. No words were spoken, none needed to be.

She was boneless. A pile of useless mush that had no words, no thoughts, no energy. When Ella rolled herself off from Sophie and lay next to her, Sophie lifted her arm to tug her back, but was useless. Moments passed, breaths returned to stable breathing, and Sophie leaned her head onto Ella's chest.

As Ella's fingertips lazed across Sophie's buzzed head,

thoughts slowly took shape. Sophie knew what this was, and she was ready. She was open. And it was time.

Recovery was much quicker than expected. The need to know Ella in the same way, to make Ella feel as good as she made Sophie, overtook Sophie. She trailed a fingertip down Ella's stomach. "Please, please, let me do that to you."

TWENTY-THREE

ELLA

The sun peeked through the blinds, illuminating a naked Sophie lying on her stomach. Her back rose and lowered with soft breaths. Ella desperately wanted to wake her up and repeat every moment of last night, but also wanted to sit here forever and watch her sleep.

Her phone alarm rang in the other room and she eased out of the bed, holding her breath to not wake up Sophie. A towel lying on the floor from their late-night joint shower provided the perfect cover. She wrapped it around herself and tiptoed down the hall.

Thankfully, she always had extra medication in her purse, in case she ended up stranded somewhere. She'd never actually had to use the extra meds before, but last night was the perfect stranding. She tapped off the alarm, moved to the kitchen, and chugged back her pill with a full glass of water. God, she was thirsty. And tired. And so deliciously sore. Every aching muscle was a sweet reminder of the best day of her life.

Yep, yesterday was the best day she'd ever had. Emotionally, physically, soulfully, she had never experienced a connection like that before. Not even with Jasmine. The feelings she had, the feelings Sophie had, were confirmed, solidified, explored. That missing piece of her now felt filled to the brim. For the first time in her life, she was totally satisfied. Grateful. Hopeful, even.

Her phone showed about a dozen unread messages from her mom, two from her dad, ranging from *Hope you're having fun!* to *Don't forget to rest.* She'd told her parents she wasn't coming home and she was safe, but it didn't surprise her how much they'd blown up her phone.

She plucked an apple from a bowl on the counter and crunched into the fruit, typing a quick message to let them know she was alive. Allowing their child to have freedom had to have been hard for them, and she understood that now. Separation anxiety, the fear of keeping your loved one safe, the need to hear that they were healthy... it all clicked.

Quiet steps entered behind her and lips brushed her shoulder.

"Morning."

Sophie's voice was a hoarse whisper, and Ella melted. She pressed her body into Sophie, feeling the warmth spreading as Sophie spread her fingers across Ella's belly and pulled her close.

"Morning," Ella whispered, savoring this moment. She wanted to savor these moments, to tattoo them into her brain, to capture the tingles in a lockbox and release them anytime she needed endorphins. She took one more bite of apple and turned.

Perfection. Standing in an off-the-shoulder Bon Jovi T-shirt grazing her upper thigh, Sophie was stunning.

Sophie brought Ella's hand to her mouth and bit into the apple. "I'm starving." She chewed and kissed Ella, then bit into the apple again. "Want to grab breakfast?"

Breakfast, dinner, a trip to Paris, a house with a backyard and a rescue Saint Bernard, Sophie could have asked anything, and Ella would have agreed. "Yes, please. But if we go anywhere, I need to go home first and change. I didn't bring any backups."

"You can wear something of mine." Sophie downed a glass of water and wiped her mouth off with the back of her hand.

"You're like five sizes smaller than me. I'd spill out of everything."

"I know." A sly grin spread. When Ella lifted a brow, Sophie threw her hands up in defense. "Okay, okay. Change, then more food."

An hour later, after one more session where Ella filled her mouth with Sophie in the shower, Thomas pulled up to the corner and opened the door. "Good morning, ladies. I trust you slept well last night." His voice was professional and kind, but he had a twinkle in his eye.

"Sure did." Ella slid over for Sophie. The urge to be touching Sophie every moment was powerful, and she moved into the middle seat to wrap her ankle around Sophie's. She swiped her thumb against the inside of her wrist, and wanted to kiss her now, here, on her arm, on her mouth, everywhere, but refrained. Thomas would most likely not appreciate being a spectator.

When they pulled up to Ella's home, Sophie hopped out and took a breath. "Everything feels different. Like the same, but different, right?"

Ella gripped her fingers. "Yes, it does." She glanced at the door and paused. "If you want to keep quiet about this, I totally understand. I know it's a crazy thing my dad being…"

"My boss? Yep, sure is." Sophie smiled, but her eyes turned serious, and her gaze flickered against Ella's. "I don't want to keep this quiet. I thought I did, but now I want to scream it everywhere. I want everyone to know how I feel and hope that someday they feel this way, too." Her face bloomed red. "Oh, shit. See, I told you I was seriously rusty on all of this. That was a lot. Too much? Too quick?"

Ella pulled her in for a kiss. "Not for me." Her chest felt like it was going to burst. "And it's not too quick. I've been feeling this for a while. I only just acted on it now."

"Same." She inhaled a breath. "Okay, let's do this."

The door opened and her parents appeared like overbearing genies just released from the bottle. "My most favorite girls in the world!" Her dad's voice boomed across the open space.

"Women, Dad. Women."

He clapped once. "Oh yes. Of course. Did you all have fun yesterday? What did you do? Break any laws?"

Ella's eyes grew wide. She glanced at Sophie with a smirk.

"Honey, do you need to eat?" Her mom reached her hand out like she wanted to touch Ella's hair, but retreated. "Or maybe take a nap? Sleep is so important, you know that's a trigger—"

"Mom." Normally, she would have snapped the words. But today, she didn't want to snap. And her mom was right. She really did need to get some sleep at some point. Working late, spending time with Sophie, enjoying life, took precedence right now. "I'm good. Going to change and then we're grabbing some food."

Her mother's lips turned into a flat line, but she nodded and surprisingly dropped the subject.

"Sophie." George cleared his throat. "A quick word with me while Ella changes?"

"Of course." Sophie responded before Ella could protest, her voice flipping to professional mode.

Ella glanced between everyone and decided the best thing to do was to change and leave as quickly as possible, before her parents gave Sophie some archaic speech about the importance of treating their daughter right, or her mother listed out all the meds and potential effects of epilepsy. Upstairs, she brushed her teeth, threw on some clothes, and ran a flat iron through her bangs. When she returned, her dad and Sophie were just coming out of the den, where her dad gave Sophie a quick bro-style tap on the upper back.

Ella cringed. "Ready?" She nearly pushed Sophie out the entrance. "Bye," she called behind her head to her parents, but closed the door before her parents could respond.

Thomas opened the back door and escorted the women in, and Sophie leaned in toward Ella. "So... potential idea for today. Only if you're cool with it, and no pressure." She scraped the side of her thumbnail. "A couple of my friends are heading out for brunch and wondering if we'd like to join."

Sophie wanted to introduce her to friends? Already? Something filled Ella, warm and squishy, starting in the chest and sinking to her belly. "I'd love that."

After Sophie gave Thomas the address, she leaned back and pulled Ella's hand into her lap. "You know, your parents are way cooler than I think you give them credit for."

Ella huffed. "Cool is not a word I would ever use to describe my parents. Was it super awkward with my dad?"

"Not at all." Sophie traced the outline of Ella's palm with her fingertips. "I thought he'd tell me to keep business and personal life separate, but he didn't at all. He just told me that he hadn't seen you so happy in such a long time and was grateful I was in your life."

Score one for Pops. "He said that?"

Sophie giggled. "Yes, in a very George Northwood sort of way. But that was the message. I think he even tried to hug me, but then sort of shook his arms out. But I felt the hug right here." She pointed at her heart with a laugh. "He's a good dude. Really."

Her dad had always been in her corner. Sometimes at a distance, sometimes annoying, sometimes very, very loud, but still in her corner. As the traffic and trees flew by outside the window, a peacefulness settled. Ella wanted to call him and thank him.

The SUV pulled over in front of a Thai and Filipino fusion restaurant, with the most delicious sweet and savory scents mingling in the air. Sophie intertwined Ella's fingers in hers, and Ella adjusted her glasses back up the bridge of her nose.

"You're going to do great. Everyone is super nice. Except Remi." She laughed. "I'm totally kidding. It's a long story, and I'll tell you all about it tonight."

Tonight. As if she knew they'd be together today and tonight, and this was the new norm. Ella refrained from skipping into the restaurant.

"Hey!" A chorus of welcomes and nice-to-meet-yous, and hugs came from the table, as Ella shook people's hands.

"I'm Ben, Maya and Remi's roommate, and clearly the best looking of the group." This man, Ben, was beautiful. Warm, brown skin, dark eyes, and dimples that Ella could spot a mile away. The smile in his voice carried to his eyes, and Ella had never liked anyone so quickly.

"Pay no attention to Ben, ever. He likes to tell lies," a gorgeous, full-bodied, strong woman with a head of dark curly hair and a mischievous grin said, while nudging Ben out of the way. "I'm Remi. Really good to meet you." She shook Ella's hand with a strong firm grip.

A woman who was at least a half foot taller than Ella, with long, glass-straight blond hair and a huge white smile, nudged Remi on the hip. "And I'm Maya. I'd like to think I'm Sophie's other half, but I think that title is about to be stripped away."

Ah. So this was the famous Maya, Sophie's best friend and Remi's girlfriend. Everything clicked. Ella took her in, the firmest of firm postures and a radiating warmth.

Ella moved to shake Maya's hand, but she opened her arms and pulled her in for a hug instead. *I can get used to this.*

The next hour flew by, the awkwardness of meeting new

people fading within the first ten minutes. In the past, Ella would have been sweating, hiding a smile because she'd swear food was in her teeth, and freak out that she couldn't believe she forgot to put on her lipstick today.

But now, she was laughing in between bites of ube croissants and pork belly egg scramble as Ben—who was taking the prize for the most animated human she'd ever encountered—talked about a "hell on wheels" nurse who he almost came to blows with after the man blocked him from visiting his favorite patient.

"Wait, aren't you supposed to *not* have favorites?" Remi asked Ben as she cut into her green onion sticky waffle.

"It's not like I'm a teacher. I absolutely have favorites." He dashed pepper over his eggs. "I mean, the dude was such a dick about it, too. And sure, the patient was an eighty-five-year-old woman who was *apparently* tired, but he was so obviously jealous I was the one she liked the most. All flexing his muscles like a bouncer in some Tacoma dive bar, acting like I couldn't take him, but I could. I could for sure take him."

Maya tucked a blond lock behind her ear and cut into her pancake. "So... when are you going to ask him out?"

Ben arched an eyebrow. "I'm thinking tomorrow."

Ella joined in the laughter. This group, this conversation, was what people talked about when they mentioned community, found family, and platonic love. The genuine love and mutual admiration among everyone here were obvious, and Ella felt honored to be a guest.

"Okay, tell us... how did everything go yesterday?" Remi winked at Sophie with a sly grin.

Sophie gave her *the look*, the one that clearly conveyed Sophie was going to tackle her later in the parking lot. "You're busting me."

Huh? Ella's gaze flickered between the women.

"Don't be mad, okay?" Sophie spread her fingers across

Ella's forearm. "But Remi helped me out yesterday with the whole golfing thing." Sophie dove into the story of how Remi, the golf manager, and Sophie devised the stolen golf cart heist.

"Wait! That's what you two were talking about?" Maya's eyes lit up. "Why didn't you tell me?"

Remi rested her fork on the side of her plate. "'Cause you can't keep secrets and I could just see you sending Sophie a text that Ella would see and ruining the surprise."

"Rude. And also, that's totally fair." Maya grinned and continued eating.

Sophie leaned into Ella's ear. "Are you mad? I was worried about liability and everything. I didn't want us to get arrested for breaking and entering. But... I wanted you to have a memorable experience."

So, Ella didn't actually steal a golf cart or run from the cops? This information shifted the evening into a different perspective. She'd flown high off that rebellious act for hours. But that high settled, and was now replaced with something that felt like the warmest group hug she'd ever known. "You all did that... for me?" She glanced at Remi. "You don't even know me, and you used the big favor on me?"

Remi shrugged, her black curls bouncing with the motion. "We didn't know you, but we know Sophie. You'll soon find out we are this funky little family that does random shit for each other. We like to see each other happy."

Maya leaned toward Ella. "And you make Sophie happy. Really, really happy."

Ella gripped Sophie's hand under the table and absorbed this information. Her heart filled, a smile spread uncontrollably, and the blush sweeping her cheeks differed from any other blush she'd felt before. Yes, this was the first time meeting this group, but she already felt like she belonged. True friendship, altruistic friendship, was something that had been missing in her life. And now, she got to peek at what it may look like.

"Ahem." Ben cleared his throat. "I would like it noted, once again, that I may not have fancy connections with a golf course manager, but I'm still the best-looking one out of the group."

A collective groan rose from the table, and Remi bunched a napkin and threw it at Ben. Today was already perfect, and it wasn't even noon.

TWENTY-FOUR

SOPHIE

Seven days had passed since Ella spent her first night at Sophie's, six days since Ella met Sophie's closest friends, two days since they spent all night in bed eating snacks in between marathon sex sessions, and one day since Sophie knew Ella was the one she wanted to be with.

Returning to work was both hard and not hard. Sophie adjusted back to working life and withheld from making out with her girlfriend in the breakroom. She did, however, sneak quick kisses in the elevator, soft swipes of hands when getting water, a nudge of the knee under their desks. At Sophie's insistence, she and Ella had an awkward, grown-up, career-setting birds-and-bees conversation with George on Sunday, about how to handle their relationship. "No hanky-panky in the office, otherwise we should be good. You're not a manager, so no need to bring in HR."

Ella may have groaned at the words "hanky-panky," but Sophie found them somewhat endearing. *George—endearing. Who knew?*

"Hey, were you CC'd on the email from legal?" Sophie asked Ella a few hours into their Friday morning.

Ella scrolled through her email with a twisted mouth and pushed up her frames. "No, I don't think so."

"Here, I'll forward it to you. They need to make the slightest tweak to the copy, but the latest version was already sent to Devil's." Sophie clicked on the mouse. "It's not enough for us to interrupt DD's and let them know, but we'll want to double-check before we return the final assets that we include the message."

"Got it." Ella scribbled a note, then frowned. "Are we worried Devil's hasn't gotten back to us yet?"

Yes. But as the leader of this project, girlfriend or not, Sophie needed to remain calm for everyone, including Ella. "Nah. It'll be fine."

But it wasn't fine. Devil's Doughnuts was supposed to get back to them yesterday morning. Ideally even the day before. They were now over twenty-four hours late, and with this tight of a turnaround time, every single minute counted. Not always, but most often when clients didn't come back within the time frame with a resounding "love it!", it usually meant they didn't love it. And depending on the level of changes requested...

She shook her head. Yes, she wanted to go on the cruise so badly, but this was more than getting a paid vacation. This was proving she could lead this level of campaign. This was making sure her four other colleagues also got the cruise. This was showing Malcolm he was justified in promoting her, and showing the team that all their hard work had paid off.

As the afternoon rolled around, Sophie's anxiety increased. She lunatic-level refreshed her emails, sent DMs to the senior PM, walked by and whispered to the creative lead, and finally knocked on Malcolm's door. "So, when do I push the panic button?"

Malcolm rolled his wrist. "It's a little after two. Why don't we give it, say, one more hour and then let's schedule a sync." He tapped his thumbs on the side of his chair. "I think you and

Ella could use a break. I saw her yawning earlier, and you're a wound-up ball of stress."

"No, I'm not." His deadpan stare cracked her defiance. "Okay, fine, I am. Just a little, though."

His corner lip lifted in a sly smirk. "Besides, I bet you and Ella would like some alone time."

Her face beamed red. "What? No. I mean, huh? Grrr. How did you know?"

"Please." He huffed and pushed up the sleeves to his button-down. "I've been working with you for six years. You'd be surprised at how observant I am."

"*Really?*"

"No." He laughed. "Unlike most of you in this place, I don't get involved with the gossip. *However*, George told me and asked me to double-check his thinking whether HR had to be notified. Spoiler alert—you're good."

Whew. Not that she was really worried, but it freed up a little mental space to not have a potential pink slip hovering over her. She rounded the corner where Ella yawned again, and a tinge of guilt flew through her. They already worked hard during the day. And now, as delicious as it was, they worked hard at night. Since the sex seal broke over the weekend, they had not come up for air. Maybe tonight she'd see if movie and cuddle time would be sufficient.

"Hey." Sophie pulled up behind Ella. "Want to take a walk? Grab a coffee and a raspberry drink?"

Ella locked her screen in a millisecond and stood. "More than anything. I need some non-fluorescent light before my eyes bleed."

Outside the building, the partial cloudy day was perfect. Sophie loved the sun, of course, and she missed it in the winter. But when spring hit along with full sun several days in a row, her body overheated. She locked hands with Ella and strolled, rolling her neck.

"You doing okay?" Ella squeezed her hand.

"Yeah." Sophie tugged open the door to the nearest coffee joint. "I'm just feeling a little itchy, you know. Just want to hear from the partners."

"We will," Ella said with a confidence that Sophie was lacking. After they put in the order and moved to the pickup spot, Ella kissed Sophie on the cheek. "We got this. At least from everything you've taught me, we've done as much as possible. It'll be good."

"How can you be so calm?" Sophie grinned, but it was true. Ella seemed unaffected, which sounded heavenly. The timeline was already aggressive, and now, Sophie felt like she was verging on suffocation.

"You have a lot more riding on this than me. That cruise is within touching distance for you, and you deserve it." Ella thanked the barista for the raspberry lemonade. "Besides, my dad's the boss and no one has the balls to yell at me."

"You are terrible." Sophie laughed and picked up her coffee.

Ella pulled the straw to her lips and sipped. "When I started this job, I was so anxious, so desperate to show I had earned my place. And I still want to do a good job, of course. But that fear is gone. The team is much nicer than I ever thought. And I probably don't tell you this enough, but you're an amazing teacher."

Sophie's insides warmed. How did she get so lucky? For years, her goal was to train. Her other goal was to have an amazing, stable relationship. She now had both, and if she wasn't so damn tired, she might click her heels together Gene Kelly-style as they crossed the sidewalk toward the office. "And you are the perfect girlfriend."

"I kind of am, aren't I?" Ella grinned and kissed the top of Sophie's shoulder.

They'd wandered nearly a full city block when Sophie checked the time. Forty-five minutes was good enough for a break. She was going to head back in and send a client-friendly, but stern, email to Devil's, warning them they were in danger of not executing this campaign in time.

Words, traffic, and pedestrians passed by as she composed the email in her head. Firm warning, grave warning, critical warning, wait... no, this was a friendly reminder. So caught up on the words, Sophie barely noticed the faces blurring in front of her. A full moment passed for the face in front of her to blink into focus.

Holy shit. The one-night-stand woman was walking toward Sophie and Ella. She'd changed slightly in the last year—she now had short cropped pink hair, instead of a dark red, but everything else looked the same. Oh Christ, should she say something? Sophie was the one who'd slipped out that night before the woman woke up, a total dick move on reflection. Maybe she wouldn't remember her. Besides, what would she say? "Ella, meet hot one-night-stand woman, sorry we never actually exchanged names. Woman, meet my girlfriend." Nope, she was going to pull the oblivious Seattle card trick and pretend she was so distracted in her thoughts that she didn't see her.

Sophie peeked up from the sidewalk and accidentally made eye contact. The woman's gaze locked with Sophie's and she approached Sophie and Ella. *Double shit.* Ugh. They absolutely did not need to engage. Sophie wanted to bolt.

"Well, if this isn't awkward as fuck," the woman said in a clipped tone, with a smirk rising.

A million words swirled in Sophie's mind about how to explain who this woman was. She turned to Ella, ready to be as vague as possible until they could talk later, and time shifted into slow motion. Traffic sounds and weaving bike riders whizzing by muddled in the background as Ella's face morphed from joyful to a frozen scowl. Red, angry stripes flashed up Ella's neck and Sophie's stomach rolled in response.

"Good to see you again, Ella." The woman crossed her arms with an amused grin and turned to Sophie. "I guess good to see you, too."

No... Wait, what? Sophie's heartbeat thudded so loud in her ear that she felt dizzy.

Ella's gaze flickered between the woman and Sophie. "Jasmine," she whispered. Finally, she straightened her shoulders and firmed her jaw. "Can't say the same for you."

TWENTY-FIVE

ELLA

Sophie's voice echoed behind Ella, faint and distant, like she was in a tunnel. A horrible, *what the fuck* tunnel that was in serious jeopardy of collapsing and sucking her into the darkest abyss known to humankind.

"Ella!" Sophie grabbed Ella's arm, her breath expelling in spurts. "We have to talk about this."

How could Ella talk about this when she barely processed what just happened? The last five minutes kept playing over and over in her mind. The moment when Jasmine got that look, that stupid effing satisfied grin like she just one-upped Ella, and said to Sophie, "I had a good time with you last year. I don't think I ever got your name." Sophie's eyebrows had cinched. Then her face dropped, her cheeks flushed, and she turned nearly green... and Ella knew. It took all of five seconds to piece everything together. The realization of what had happened slapped her in the face. Neither of them had to say anything else.

Her insides raged, and her belly burned with a foreign sickness, the type that she'd seen in movies, but never felt herself.

"Jasmine, though? *Jasmine?* Of all the women in Seattle, *she's* the one you fucked?"

"I didn't know she had a girlfriend! I would have never done that had I known." Sophie's eyes searched Ella's, caged like an animal, frantic and rushed. "Ella, please. I'm so sorry. I had no idea. You know that, right? How could I have possibly known? I didn't even know her name."

Oh, Ella knew Sophie barely knew Jasmine. She knew *everything* about that night because of course she asked, like an absolute idiot, about the hot, sordid details to feed her voyeur kink. She'd consumed every word Sophie was willing to share and dove in for second and third scoops. How many times Jasmine made Sophie orgasm, the dirty shit they whispered in each other's ears, how Sophie tugged off Jasmine's underwear with her teeth—everything. She was told the excruciating details on how Jasmine bit then blew on Sophie's most sensitive places, that the kitchen counter provided perfect leverage for round one, and that the upstairs apartment banged on the floor to get them to shut up.

She knew it all.

Images of the two of them rolling in the bed flashed in front of her. She squeezed her eyes shut hard, but that only made the picture more vibrant. That night, Ella knew something was off with Jasmine. Jasmine was supposed to come over as she did almost every night. But soon short, sporadic texts replaced their usual long-winded, funny banter. When Jasmine stopped texting and finally went totally silent, it triggered Ella's Spidey-sense.

Ella remembered pacing in her room, bouncing between being livid at being ignored with being sure Jasmine was in an accident and lying somewhere in a ditch. The feeling, the panic, the hopelessness, the worry, was because of Sophie.

When she went to Jasmine's place that next morning, she smelled it in the air—an unfamiliar perfume and the sweat of someone else on the sheets. Then she found the bunched-up fishnet stockings in the corner. Fishnets! How did she only think of this now? Sophie's signature outfit was right in front of her eyes this entire time, and she never made the connection.

She confronted Jasmine that morning, who transitioned from "You're acting crazy" to "Oh, honey, I would never... I love you" to "So obviously you must think I'm the worst person in the world." After every gaslighting trick in the effed-up relationship book, Ella picked up the stockings and threw them at Jasmine's face. Finally, Jasmine had crossed her arms, deviant and unapologetic, and blamed her tryst on Ella being too controlling, too obsessed, too *boring*.

This can't be happening. Ella couldn't breathe. She needed more air. Her collar was tight and gross and constricting her airways. She clawed at it, pulling it away from her sticky neck. Everything happening right now was too much, and she needed to get the hell out of here, far away, and process. She bulldozed her way up the sidewalk, refusing to listen to Sophie's pleas.

Her belly knotted into a ferocious twist and she wanted to cry and hit something and throw up. The crushing devastation was not about ownership over Sophie, not about jealousy. Sophie, the woman she'd fallen for, the woman who she saw a real future with, the woman she'd felt the most intense connection of her life with, now represented the pain Ella had felt for so long. The self-doubt had been so heavy and thick for a year, where she constantly wondered why she wasn't good enough, why someone she loved chose someone else, someone more fun, someone *better*.

She bolted around the corner, her low heels clacking into the pavement. Pedestrians stepped out of her way as she marched straight ahead, searching for oxygen. She needed to not look at Sophie right now. She needed to get as far away from her as possible. If she looked at Sophie, she wouldn't be able to think, and right now she needed to think.

"Ella. Stop."

The sound of Sophie getting closer approached from behind her, and soon she felt fingertips grip her forearm.

"We need to talk about this. We need to figure this out." Sophie's fingers dug into Ella so tight her skin started turning white. When Sophie looked down, she dropped Ella from her grip in a snap.

Ella rammed her thumbs into her temples, the prickles of sweat beginning to brew beneath the surface. She looked at Sophie's watery, regret-filled, wide green eyes. Reflected was Ella's past and future colliding in the most gross, gruesome way, and she pivoted on her heels. She couldn't look at her face. Sophie had captured her heart. She *owned* her heart. But now she also owned her heartbreak.

"I can't... I can't even look at you." Ella's mouth quivered and she drilled her teeth into her lip to stop. She was not going to cry here like a rookie, fifty feet from her office.

"That's unfair." Sophie withdrew her hand and took a step back. Her voice no longer carried the pleading it did a moment ago. "I didn't do it to hurt anyone."

Of course Sophie didn't. She was a good person who didn't know the collateral damage from her actions that night. But that didn't mean the logic in Ella's brain could outrun the crushing betrayal in her heart. Jasmine's cheating had shredded Ella— she'd balled up in a corner, stopped painting, refused to shower, she'd been destroyed. And Sophie, unknowingly or not, was a participant.

Ella needed to leave. But she couldn't. Dammit. She had to go back into the office, pretend that nothing had happened, pretend that she couldn't feel her insides breaking. The sweat bubbled up now, mimicking her tears filling her eyes, and she cried into her hands. "Fuck!" She stomped her foot, angry at herself for being emotional, angry at Sophie, angry at herself for being angry at Sophie, and her shoulders collapsed.

A hand touched her arm and she whipped it off. "Please, just... please don't touch me right now."

What was she going to do? She needed to run. She needed to get away from here, and think, and paint, and exhale, and come to grips that the person she'd been falling for, really, whole-heartedly falling for, was half of someone who destroyed her. How did she reconcile that? Could she? Goddammit, *she knew* these last few weeks were too good to be true. Life was cruel and punishing and unfair. And she was stupid enough to think that maybe this one time, things would work out.

Screw work. She had to get away, flee, go hide in a bunker, something. Anything to avoid facing Sophie, reality, this weight burrowing into her chest.

Sophie's phone rang. Her lips pulled into a flat line. She exhaled through her nose, and brought the phone to her ear. "What's up?"

Her face morphed from narrowed eyes to wide eyes, to an "oh shit" face. She nodded, hummed an affirmative, and then clicked off her phone. "We have to go back." She reached out to touch Ella again, but then dropped her arm to her side. She released a heavy, shaky sigh. "Devil's Doughnuts got back to us. They rejected the entire campaign."

TWENTY-SIX

SOPHIE

Sophie thought Ella would follow her back to the office. Or at least hoped she'd follow her, but no. As Sophie rode the elevator solo to the top floor, she bit her shaky lips. Should she have followed Ella down the street? This was bad, so effing bad. But she thought after Malcolm called, Ella would push aside this terrible, awful, horrible moment and come back to the office to work on the campaign.

But Ella didn't. She ran. Deserted Sophie, without letting Sophie speak, without a mention that they would talk later, without a hint that she was still her partner at work.

She was sick about this. She had no idea the woman from happy hour had been Jasmine. How could she? And what in God's name were the chances? She would *never* sleep with someone who was in a relationship. Except that she had. But seriously, how the hell was she supposed to know?

No, no, no. This wasn't really happening. All of this was some terrible nightmare, and she'd wake up in a second. Sophie chewed on her lip ring and watched the elevator floor numbers rise. Maybe Ella just needed to cool down. Surely, she would think logically about this situation, realize that Sophie had never meant to hurt her, and she would come to her senses. Because this, them... was not done. They had only just started and no way would Sophie let it slip away.

The elevator doors opened and even if Sophie wanted to wallow in the shithole of the last twenty minutes of her life, she didn't have the luxury. The office energy mirrored the one on the sidewalk, but even more frantic. If that was possible.

As much as she didn't want to, right now she had to push Ella out of her mind. "What the hell happened?" she called to Malcolm as she marched to her desk and flipped open the laptop.

"Can you gather everyone in the conference room in ten minutes?" He dug his phone from his pocket. "I'll text George."

"Got it." Her fingers sped across the keyboard, adding names to a large group message.

"All hands on deck, Soph. Let the team know. We're working through the weekend and might need to pull a few all-nighters if we have any hope of launching on time." He was looking at his phone, his fingers tapping the screen at the same rate as his voice. "I'm grabbing the creative director from his three p.m. meeting, and I'll see if George can get ahold of the VP." He stuffed his phone and looked around. "Where's Ella?"

Sophie swallowed. "She, um..." Christ. *We had a fight and she took off, and I know it's not cool, but it was a really big blow and...* "She wasn't feeling well. I got this."

He nodded and stroked the dark hair on his beard as he left for the creatives' desk.

Sophie blasted the message to everyone on the team: *Urgent meeting in conference room G-1.* She grabbed her water bottle and ripped the laptop cord from the socket. After bolting to the conference room to set up, she pulled out her phone.

SOPHIE:

It's super busy, but it doesn't mean this isn't important. We need to talk. Call you after work?

She stuffed the phone in her back pocket and poised her fingers as the team funneled into the room. Squeaky chairs, animated conversation, and opening laptops sounded until she got everyone's attention. "What do we know? Did anyone speak to the client on why it was rejected? Is this something small and fixable? Talk to me. Ideas on how to make it right?"

"This is bullshit," a designer yelled from the corner. "We followed their creative brief to the tee. They cannot come back, this late in the game, and say they want it re-done."

Sophie agreed, but they didn't have a second to indulge in the time-honored group bitching bonding moment. "Is anything salvageable?"

"Malcolm talked to the marketing director. He should know the full scoop," an editor commented from the back.

Sophie glanced at her watch. "Okay, he'll be here in a few minutes. He was going to text George and brief him."

Murmurs surrounded her, some more frantic than others, with tones of how hard they worked.

"The timeline's already too aggressive."

"We just dumped weeks of work down the toilet. May as well throw the entire campaign out the window."

"If we don't hit this, then the team can't go on the cruise."

"Forget your cruise."

Sophie's head snapped to the angry voice. "Seriously?"

The designer stiffened. "Not everyone gets to go. In fact, I could go on about how unfair it was you all were chosen."

"Don't be a dick," another designer chimed in. "Just 'cause they didn't choose you doesn't mean that the ones they did don't deserve it."

"So, you're saying I don't deserve it?"

"Are you saying I don't, either?" The man's tone snapped. "I wasn't chosen, but I have personal integrity and want to see this executed cleanly and on time."

"So now I don't have personal integrity?"

"Jesus Christ, I didn't say—"

"Enough!"

Sophie didn't need to look to the doorway to know the booming voice belonged to George. The room settled like a dad just walked in and caught the kids fighting.

George stomped into the room. "Talking shit to one another stops right now. Capisce?"

Yikes.

George snugged his tie, then crossed his arms. "Now, someone tell me exactly what happened."

Malcolm moved to the front of the room, bringing the kind, calm presence needed. He put his hands in the air like he was blocking the team from yelling. "All right, all. We need to take a breath. We've been under tight deadlines before, and I believe in all of you. But I'm gonna be real, here. We will need heads down, all hands on deck, laser focused if we have a chance to execute on time." He grabbed the marker for the whiteboard and jotted down a number: 10. "We have ten days to redo and launch. Ten. It's not a lot of time—"

"It's no time!" the designer yelled from the back.

When Malcolm turned to face him, tossing him a look like "how dare you question me in my own home," the designer shrunk. "It's not a lot of time," he repeated, "but I've seen you pull miracles before, and this is no different."

Sophie took a deep breath. She believed in the team, but ten days? They spent a gazillion hours to reach where they were now. Malcolm was right, the team had performed some marketing miracles in the past. But ten days was impossible.

"Let's go through the positives here." Malcolm poised his marker over the whiteboard. "Legal has already been reviewed. As long as we stay within the realm of what we said before, a follow-up review will take less than an hour. Headline copy needs to be adjusted, but they approved the messaging on the lower hierarchy. The design, however, was totally rejected."

"Cool." A designer slumped back in her chair. "They rejected the most time-consuming thing."

"Why does everyone think copy takes no time? I'm sick of everyone saying, 'It's just some copy,' with a sense of ease, as if I pull words straight out my a— out of the *air*. Maybe design takes less time, huh? With AI now, it's not like you're creating anything original."

"Are you kidding me right now?"

"Guys!" Now it was Sophie's turn to snap. "Come on! You all are the greatest team I could ever work with. Brilliant, all of you. And we're a family, and families fight. But right now, we need to seriously cut the shit and put heads down."

George gave her the slightest nod of approval. She looked at her watch and nearly choked. This meeting alone was cutting into valuable seconds that should be spent on recreating images.

"The backup files from the creative we rejected internally are attached to the project plan. Step one, retrieve." Sophie continued and Malcolm scribbled on the whiteboard. "We're going to follow standard rush-job protocol. Refresh current assets, pick the three top choices, war room mentality. I'm going to chat with the EA to bring in food and snacks. Design in room B-14, copy in B-25, legal will be on standby. Two team members will be responsible for coming up with something entirely new as an extra fail-safe. Directors, please choose your person and let me know." She took a breath and glanced up at Malcolm, who motioned for her to continue. "One single source of truth. *One*. We can't waste time bouncing back and forth, wondering which spreadsheet or person has the latest information. Everything runs through me, and I will update the project plan in the platform. Any questions?"

The room steadied, all shifting and groans hushed. She'd take that as a no.

George inched closer to the middle of the room. "Everyone, take ten minutes. Call your family to let them know you're going to be late, and gather what you need. Sophie, let's get some food delivered by six." He turned to leave but paused in the doorway. "You guys can do this. I believe in this team."

The room scattered. Some took out phones and talked in their chairs, some bolted from the room. Sophie gathered her items and glanced at her phone. God, she wanted to talk to Ella so bad. But right now was absolutely not the time to try and call.

She stepped out of the room and found George and Malcolm in a hushed conversation.

"Sophie." George motioned her forward, and Malcolm stepped away. "Where's Ella?"

This was why people don't like workplace romances—because when something happens with the couple, the work suffers. Sophie refused to let this happen. "She wasn't feeling well."

George's face dropped, and he reached for his phone. *Shit.* He was a dad with a medically compromised daughter, and no doubt his mind just went to a dark place.

She cleared her throat. "I mean... ah. Look, we had a fight. She was upset and left. But I would love to, um, not get into the details with you."

His face lifted with relief. "Okay. Well, we need her here. You cannot run all of this on your own." He pulled out his phone. "I'm calling her."

Good luck. "I've got this. Really. Just in case she doesn't answer or..." *Just in case she never wants to see me again*, just in case she quit, just in case Sophie unintentionally ruined the best relationship of her life.

George frowned into the phone and moved to text messaging as Sophie scooted back to her desk. Once there, she tried once more to call Ella. The call went straight to voicemail. She left a quick, hushed "please call me back" message, and used her last remaining seconds of the break to run to the bathroom, fill her water bottle, and scramble a text to Ella.

SOPHIE:

We need to talk. We cannot leave things like this, please. We're adults and I know we can figure this out.

Her fingers hovered. Now was not the time to say what she wanted to say, to confess her deepest feelings, to share how much she'd fallen and that she saw a future with Ella. And maybe it was fast, and she wouldn't be the first lesbian this side of the Pacific who U-Hauled. She poised her fingers, fumbling the rest of her message.

SOPHIE:

I don't want to lose you.

TWENTY-SEVEN
SOPHIE

Maybe Ella's lack of response since the blowup on the sidewalk was a blessing in disguise. Because for the last seventy-two hours, she hadn't gotten home earlier than eleven. Last night she didn't even have the energy to floss.

Seven days. They had exactly seven days left to execute a campaign. The team threw everything they could on the wall—changing graphics, updating copy, crying, swearing. Coffee overflowed along with a few frustrated tears, and everyone was exhausted.

Her heart hurt over Ella. But the ache started morphing from pain to anger, splashed with resentment. For someone who was *sooo* supportive of one-night hookups, creating an ad for herself to find a no-strings-attached relationship, and so open with her sexuality, Ella held that night against Sophie this much? It wasn't like Sophie had *tried* to hurt Ella.

But her heart hurt for something else. Maybe it seemed ridiculous, but now that it was so close, she wanted this cruise so bad. She needed sleep and rest and to see the ocean. Her entire life, she'd dreamed about having a vacation like this, and dammit, she deserved it. She'd have to save up for a year to do this on her own and burn through a week of vacation time. Her dream was being flushed away because the team couldn't generate some goddamn proper images of doughnuts. She dug her knuckle into her eye as her spirit cracked.

Unfair. Everything was unfair.

7:00 a.m. of the final forty-eight hours arrived early, but she was not the first one in the office. The design team were unloading their backpacks, all ponytails and sweatshirts and makeup free, looking like they'd barely showered.

Sophie grabbed her phone. One last-ditch effort before she'd be considered a full-on stalker.

SOPHIE:

Can we please talk?

Her breath hitched and stuck in her throat when she saw the bubbles arise. *Thank God.* Hopefully Ella could wait for a week, though. Right now, she didn't have a free second.

ELLA:

No

No? *No?* Was she actually serious right now? Sophie exhaled through her nose and pulled in two more cleansing breaths. Okay, enough. Later, they'd clear this mess. Right now, she couldn't. The internal stress-level barometer reached a fever pitch. She missed Ella, and wanted to know her girlfriend was okay.

But another layer added to the stress. So much work surrounded her. She was getting lost in approvals and documents and asset refreshes and headlines, and she needed Ella to help manage the project.

Her lips trembled. This was all too much. Everything was too much. She slumped, and rested her head in her arms on her desk. She wasn't sure how long she lay like that, but the room increased in volume.

"You feeling all right?" Malcolm's voice sounded behind her.

She snapped her head up so quickly she got a head rush, then pressed her thumb into her temple to stave off the impending headache. "Yep, I'm good."

Malcolm's mouth twisted, then he pointed to his office. "Come with me, please."

Oh boy. That was definitely Malcolm's stern dad/manager voice. She prayed he wasn't about to give her a lecture on how workplace relationships jeopardize the ability to run a project effectively. She couldn't handle that conversation right now. At this point, she could barely handle staying awake. She scraped at the remaining polish on her thumbnail and followed him to his office.

He shut the door behind them, definitely another terrible sign as he always liked his door open. She sat down with her shoulders hunched like she was called into the principal's office.

"Ella is gone for an indefinite period."

His voice was devoid of all playfulness, and she desperately wanted him to break this moment up and show pictures of his baby. "Wh... what does that mean? Indefinite?"

"Exactly how it sounds. George called me late last night and let me know." He sat down and propped his elbows on the desk. "She will not be back to help finish this campaign."

Christ. Taking a few days to reel from the whole Jasmine situation was understandable. But taking more than a week off because of what happened with them was over the top. The devil and angel sat on her shoulder, playing a hearty game of tug of war. Sophie was heartbroken and dealing with what this information meant. However, being a professional, she should know taking a week off was not feasible.

Her anger shifted, quickly and furiously, to anxiety. All her nail polish fell to the ground, and hot tears sprung to her eyes. "I can't do this, Malcolm. I can't."

He put his palms in front of her on the desk. "You can, though. You absolutely can. And... you don't have a choice. It's too late to train anyone else."

"It's too much! I didn't even get half of what I needed to do last night and I was here until midnight. I am totally fried. I've got nothing left to give... I just..." She started crying now, and buried her face into her hands. She was mortified she was crying in front of Malcolm. But she missed Ella, and God, she was so fucking tired. The only thing that made this situation less humiliating was the look of panic crossing Malcolm's face.

He handed her a Starbucks-coffee-stained napkin from under his coffee cup. "I've ruined everything." She wiped her nose with the napkin and her eyes with her sleeve. "We won't get it done on time, and everyone is going to lose out on the cruise, and now Ella is not coming back, and it's all my fault."

Malcolm's chin jutted to the side, and his eyes narrowed. "Ella not being here has nothing to do with you."

How could Malcolm sometimes be the smartest man in the room and also so totally clueless? She wiped her eyes with her sleeve. "Yes, it is. I mean, I didn't mean to upset her and everything, and I don't know how to make it up, but it's one hundred percent my fault, and I wish I could fix it so she could be here with me"—she coughed—"to finish this campaign." The tears bubbled again, and she hiccupped. "I ruined everything."

Malcolm ran his fingers over his tight curls and interlocked his fingers above his head. He exhaled a slow, steady breath. "Look. Ella's gone because of an HR-related issue, and we don't know when she'll return. But I can assure you that you had nothing to do with it."

What in the hell is an HR issue? "What do you even mean?"

"I've already said enough, and this is a sensitive topic. But you don't have to do this one hundred percent alone, okay? Give me an hour to readjust some schedules. I can pitch in, we can see if George's EA can book the rooms, I can have a junior designer upload the assets instead of you. I've got you."

Sophie nodded and stood, her chest allowing a bit more air in than when she arrived this morning. But still, what was an HR issue? George and Malcolm both assured them that dating in the office was okay since they were peers. Sophie checked her watch. A few minutes remained before her next status meeting and she decided to do something bold, ballsy, and something she'd never done. She went to George's office.

"I know we are not supposed to pop by like this," she started as she stared at a heavily annoyed executive assistant who was juggling ringing phones and instant message pings firing on her computer. "Can I please talk to George for like just a minute."

"He's not here."

Of course not. Even in the midst of the deepest shit show, he was MIA. Although, after learning more about him lately, Sophie wondered if maybe he thought his presence was too much additional pressure. For once, though, she wished he were hovering. "When is he going to return?"

"I don't know," she said, without looking up from her computer.

"Well, where is he?"

The executive assistant looked up now and ceased her typing. "I don't think that's any of your business."

That's fair. "Can I please schedule something?"

Her lips pulled into a tight line. "Listen. He's gone, probably for a few days—"

"A few days? We have this campaign and we're going to—"

"I will send him an email letting him know you stopped by." She flicked her hands in a dismissive wave. "If that is all, I need to finish this."

Sophie turned without response. The EA was George's gatekeeper and doing her job well, but she needed to talk to him. *Fine.* But she had to figure out how to talk to him later.

The buzzing of her phone in her pocket was like a yellow jacket. Instant messages and texts hit her at the same rate as her heartbeat. She scrammed back to her desk with more voices clamoring.

"Assets need to pop more. Increase the shadowing on image two."

"Rework bullet one from the copy."

"Where we at with round three and four?"

"Team A and B are working on copy level one and two. Team C and D are joining forces. Going to swap A and C with B and D for a second iteration."

"Send this to legal, see what needs to change. I'll set a teleconference with Devil's team for noon."

Like soccer players in the championship, they scrammed, hurried back, adjusted, and iterated. Sophie went old-school, nearly sprinting between war rooms, grabbing papers and sketches, and hand delivering to the other room.

The moment she'd make an update in the spreadsheet, a new update was sent her way.

Malcolm poked his head in the war room. "Devil's approved the background. Main image and copy still needs work."

Thank God. A small win. She ran back between war rooms, breathless with a grin to relay the message.

The afternoon melted into the evening. Notes, and whiteboard scribbles, people kicking off shoes and eating pizza. She ran, room to room, barking messages, failing to hold a smile. Her throat burned, and her limbs were on fire.

Come on, we can do this. They had exactly one more day. Absolutely no more. Today and tomorrow, to make this work if they had any hope of coding and going live.

6:00 p.m.... 7:00 p.m.... 8:00 p.m.... The sweat at Sophie's hairline temples now felt like a permanent part of her. She ran her hand against her scalp, prickling her palm, and tried to catch a breath. The team around her, with dark-circled eyes, yawning and grumpy, slogged against the keyboards.

"Lead message is approved!" Malcolm's voice cut through the tapping, and a small cheer erupted. "Sinfully Angelic was the winner."

Of all the copy, they chose that one? Clean, simple messaging, which made sense, but was also different than the original direction. It wasn't her place to judge, though, and she said a quick gratitude prayer that she could check this item off the list.

Everyone enjoyed the one-minute celebration, then dove back into the work. With the new copy, the designers need to flip the graphics and create more imagery because of the new blank space. They used what they had, and tried different fonts, colors, and shadows. Edits and scrolling, and swapping images continued through the night. 10:00 p.m. crept up on them. The Devil's team was no longer responding, and Sophie needed to call it an evening.

Twenty-four hours left. Not a second more. No more contingencies, no more breaks.

But Sophie was scrappy. A fighter. And she refused to give up—on anything. She would not let her team down. And she wasn't giving up on Ella.

TWENTY-EIGHT

SOPHIE

5:00 a.m. was stupid early. Sophie squinted into the dark, slapping at her phone to hush the alarm. The shower wasn't refreshing. Her bones ached, her head hurt, her eyes were sawdust. She hadn't worn makeup for a week, she hadn't eaten a proper breakfast in five days, and her outfits this last week were jeans and whatever T-shirt passed the sniff test.

But 5:00 a.m. was essential to get to Ella's house and then to work on time. On the road by 6:00, Sophie joined the smattering of commuters on the 405, pushed aside all work thoughts, and freed her brain to think about Ella. From that first day in her sharp business suit, glaring with that pretty mouth and pouted face, to the level of grace Ella showed her after Sophie allowed the prejudiced demons to cloud her judgement.

Then her mind drifted to the hot tub, to the golf course, to Ella's laugh, to the way Ella's body felt in her mouth. She wanted to bring Ella a cupcake and watch her smile, and taste her lips. God, she missed her so much.

But as she stood outside Ella's house, her hand balled in a fist to knock, she realized how completely invasive standing uninvited and unannounced at 6:45 in the morning might be.

What if they were sleeping? *Nah*. George was usually in the office by seven. But he hadn't been there for several days.

Grrr. Nope. She was not thinking clearly. All she needed to do was be patient and wait for Ella to call. She stepped down to the driveway when the door clicked open.

"Sophie." George's voice was less booming than normal, and not very welcoming.

Flames rose to Sophie's face. Did Ella tell her dad that Sophie had banged her ex? Yes, George was Ella's family, but he was her boss, for God's sake. But King George knowing about her sex life made her cringe. "Um, hey." She raised her hand in the most awkward half wave of all time, then dropped it. "You look different."

Ugh. What a ridiculous thing to say, but it was true. Besides the time she and Ella stopped by and he was wearing slacks and a polo, she'd only ever seen him with a five-piece suit. So, it jarred her to see him in joggers and a zip-up sweatshirt. "Um, I didn't knock. How did you know I was here?"

"We have alarms everywhere. When you pulled up, I got a notification. I saw you standing there and decided to put you out of your misery."

Finally, the faintest smile came through his voice, and the awkwardness cracked. "Ah, is Ella here?"

He crossed his arms, and his mouth turned flat. "She is."

Jesus. She had her wisdom teeth pulled with nothing but local anesthesia when she was sixteen. This felt like a similar experience. "Can I talk to her?"

George shook his head. "She doesn't want to see you."

This moment just won the award for her most humiliating time. Her boss was blocking her like a bouncer sneaking into a members-only club and she wanted to dive into the lake and never emerge. Even though she wanted to see Ella, she wasn't going to confess her undying love at his feet. So, she just nodded, but her chest burned hot and the blush on her cheeks grew to a fever pitch.

"If it makes you feel any better, she doesn't want to see me, either." George smiled now, and these words did, in fact, make her feel a little better. "Walk with me."

George turned and Sophie followed, strolling down the courtyard, toward the water. He kept his hands in his sweatshirt pockets and remained silent, minus the heavy breathing. The slight chill in the late spring air popped goose bumps on Sophie's arm, and she snugged her short cardigan across her chest. George opened the gate and motioned for Sophie to sit on the chair, as a whiff of fresh mineral smell from the lake floated to her nose.

She slunk on the chair and stared at a seagull flying overhead, the squawking breaking up the silence. Silence—with George. If she wasn't so tired and distraught, she'd probably crack some joke about how the apocalypse must be near. But today, she had no life and no energy. She was empty.

A bucket of rocks sat between the chairs. He dug in and handed her one.

"What are those?" Sophie flipped the smooth marble-sized stone in her hand.

"I call them my thinking rocks." He tossed one in the water and his eyes followed the ripples. "Sometimes when things seem... unsalvageable... I toss them in there until I get some clarity."

Who was this dude? This loud, boisterous, voice-could-crack-cement man was sitting like a wise retiree on his dock. He nodded his head, indicating for her to try it. She tossed one in with a satisfying plop and exhaled as the smoothness of the water got interrupted by the perfect circles of the ripples. When the calm returned to the surface, she tossed another.

"Do you think Ella will ever talk to me again?" Sophie focused on the water and not George's eyes.

"I hope so."

Yikes. Not an "of course" or a "turn your frown upside down" or "put your nose to the grindstone" type of pep talk she'd grown accustomed to. Her belly sunk.

"I don't know what happened with you all, but I think she just needs a little time."

She's had time. Sophie refrained from protesting this out loud, and instead nodded. She tossed in another rock when she felt her lips tremble. "I can't lose her. I think I'm falling... I'm, ahem. I really like her so much. She just makes my heart happy. And I can't lose this. I finally have this, for the first time in my life, and I can't lose it."

George didn't seem surprised by her words. He made no sound, except for the clanking of two rocks he rolled in his palm. "Ella had a seizure that afternoon when she left the office. She was hospitalized for a few days."

"What?" She gripped the side of the chair. "Is she okay? Why didn't anyone tell me?" *When? How? Was she home? Did someone help her?* A crushing weight pushed on her, and Sophie buried her face in her hands. She bit back the brimming tears. "This is all my fault."

"You may be pretty powerful, Sophie. Scrappy as all get-out. But even you could not create epilepsy in my daughter." He tossed both rocks in the water and dusted off his hands. Leaning back on the chair, he shoved his hands back in his sweatshirt and took a deep breath. "Claire and I... we didn't listen to her. We *don't* listen. We think we're doing the best for her, but now I'm not so sure. She told me she took this job so she could save money for an apartment, just to get away from us. I forced her into this, threw her into a high-stress position. I should've just given her the goddamn money."

The self-loathing surprised Sophie. She wasn't sure if she should reach out and touch his arm, or say something soothing, or agree with him. So, she remained silent.

"So, if it's anyone's fault, it's mine." He took a deep breath. "And even I know it is not totally my fault. But she was so goddamn determined to prove she could make it in the business world. She pushed herself too hard, not getting enough sleep, so much stress, eating bad, everything. But even saying all that, it may have happened anyway. We will never know."

Sophie straightened and tried to read his face. "But she's okay, though, right? I mean, she's had a lot of these before?"

He nodded. "Yes. She will be. On the way down, she hit the kitchen island, and got pretty banged up—a shiner and a solid goose egg. We had an MRI done and thankfully everything was okay. But it's pretty devasting to everyone. She hadn't had a seizure for so long, we thought the meds were all under control..."

Sophie needed to do something. Run into the house, confirm Ella was okay, check her wounds, call the doctor to confirm her status, *something*. "Please, please, can I just see her?"

George tossed Sophie a sympathetic frown. "I really can't let you. Also, I don't think you want to. Ella's not herself after a seizure. I'm gonna give it to you straight—she's not pleasant. She's angry, irritable, hates everyone. And it's hard to not take it personally. I'm her father. I've seen this a hundred times. I'm made of steel right here." He tapped his heart with a chuckle. "And her words still cut me. I'd hate for her to say something to you that you can't recover from."

As much as Sophie wanted to run into the house, a part of her filled with warmth. King George was protecting her, and protecting his daughter. She kind of wanted to hug him. She leaned back, watching as a bird swooped to the water and caught a fish. Things were not all right. Not at work, not in her personal life, not with anything at this moment. At the same time, it was the most relaxed she'd been in a very long time.

"Every time something happens with Ella, I re-evaluate

everything. Ella's going to move out someday. I know this, Claire knows this. And I'm spending all my time running this company, which is so self-sufficient it doesn't need me. Time for me to seriously consider retirement."

A flicker of panic rose. Not hearing his cheesy jokes, or terrible business jargon, would uproot everything she'd grown accustomed to. Who would clap so loud she'd knock over her coffee? George couldn't leave.

At the same time, she hoped for his sake that he did. "We're not going to make the Devil's timeline."

"I know." George shifted in his chair. "But you all did your best. I'm really proud of you and the team."

Wow. Those words filled her in a way that she didn't know she needed. After tossing in a few more rocks, Sophie lifted herself from the chair, and walked back to the car with George. "Can you let Ella know I stopped by?"

He nodded. "I'm really rooting for you two."

Her heart pinched. She wrapped her arms around his waist and gave him a hug.

"Well then." He patted her once on the back with a chuckle and took a step back. "I'll double-check with HR that I don't need to file a report for this."

Once she was down the driveway and out of eyesight, tears fell. Maybe she and Ella would be okay. She at least had hope.

She glanced at her watch. It was after 8:00 a.m. and she was late. Did it really matter, though? They couldn't finish the campaign. Not unless the mother of all agency Hail Mary passes landed in their inbox.

TWENTY-NINE
SOPHIE

At exactly 1:23 p.m., a potential Hail Mary was exactly what landed in Sophie's inbox. Sophie's stomach lurched into her throat when she saw the email from Ella. Subject: *For you.*

Her fingers raced to open the email and then paused. *For you.* Not *I'm sorry*, or *Hi*, or *Let's talk.* Nope, just *For you.*

What if this was a resignation note? What if it was a breakup note? What if it was both?

She couldn't read it. Not yet. Her palm whipped to the back of her head, and she rubbed her scalp like she was trying to release a genie. Looking around, she saw slanted frowns, creased foreheads, and people barking at each other. Her work family was being torn apart, her relationship was wobbly, everything was a jagged-edged rock. She was one hundred percent over it. Whatever this email contained, she had to deal with it.

A quick, shaky breath left her mouth, and she clicked open the email.

Sophie,

Show the team if you see fit.

Ella

The words lacked even a hint of emotion. Sophie read the email five different times, speaking it five different ways, and nothing. It was factual, brisk, to the point. No smiley face, no heart emoji, nothing.

She exhaled. Was this post-seizure talking? Was this a post-traumatic sidewalk event result? There was no way to know. Later, she could read it again and decipher. But for now, she tilted her head at the three attached images, and clicked open image one. "What in the..." Her heartbeat increased, slow and steady at first until it raced and thudded in her skull.

Before her was a graphic of a sexy angel with flowing red hair, reminiscent of an old pinup from the '40s. She stood with a wink, biting into a glazed dripping doughnut. The image was fun and sexy, and hit on the key pieces of the creative brief.

Image two popped on the screen. A black-haired angel with a deep undercut, heavy emo-style makeup, and fire-red angel wings. She was lying on the floor on her belly, elbows propped up, blood-red fingernails gripping the doughnut. Sexy, edgy, smart—another requirement from the brief.

When she opened the third, it took all of five seconds for the image to register. Shaved head, lip ring, retro-rocker-style angel with fishnets, black fingernail polish, and a smirk rising at the corner of her lips. The angel held a glazed doughnut with the gum wall in the background.

She drew me? The picture was Sophie-esque. Her likeness at the very least. And the gum wall? Sophie's heart lifted and dipped so many times she got dizzy.

Did this mean they were okay? Was this Ella just throwing some things out there for the team? At this point, the *reasons* behind the images didn't matter.

She whipped the plug from her laptop and dashed across the floor. "Amanda!" she yelled to a senior project manager.

"Favor. Can you grab the leads and have them meet me in G-1. Urgent!"

"On it. G-1's booked, go to G-2," Amanda called while her fingers flew across the keyboard.

Sophie's eyes darted across the room. These graphics could work. Maybe. Ella was a painter, not a graphic designer. And these could be too artsy, but they differed from what the team had created, possibly in the right way. They could absolutely, maybe, dear sweet baby doughnut angels, be what the team needed.

"Erica!" She knocked on the window of a huddle room to grab a creative manager's attention."G-1—no, G-2—get your team, meet me there immediately. Please. Hot item just came in."

"Absolutely." Erica pulled out her cell phone and waved one of the leads her way.

Sophie's feet barely touched the floor as she sprinted through the hall, grabbing anyone she could find who had worked on this campaign. She searched for Malcolm, who was not in his office, and swore louder than she meant. Her breath came out in spurts. Yes, she needed to exercise more, but as long as she didn't pass out and waste any more time, she'd worry about cardio later.

"Malcolm!" she called out when she spotted him turn the corner.

"Hold up. Take a breath. I really do not want to perform mouth-to-mouth on you." He shoved his cell in his pocket. "What's going on?"

"Can you come to G-2?" Her words were frantic, nearly incoherent. She almost tripped over her feet as she walked backwards toward the room. Every cell in her body fired and needled at her skin.

"Something came in, I think... maybe we can pull this off. We'll need *everyone*, though."

Stupid projector lagging with the plug-in. What was this? 2004? *Come on!* She shoved it again and it roared to life. People shuffled in the room with a spectrum of curious, annoyed, and defeated looks. Her hands shook. Her limbs shook. Her breath shook. *Please, please*, let this work.

"Hey, all. Cutting to the chase here. We got a couple new images. Ella created them, and even though she's not a creative, I think they might work. Different direction than before, and you guys are the experts, but the imagery connects with the approved copy." She flipped to the first one and watched the raised eyebrow and murmured reactions.

"Second one." She clicked to the next. Other animated voices joined in as she allowed the team a moment to review.

"Third." The team's expressions didn't adjust much, until it seemed the image clicked for the entire room. Gazes flung her way, and she wanted to fan the burn from her ear.

"Huh. Sophie, who knew you doubled as a model?" Malcolm scratched at his beard. "These are all great. Team, thoughts?"

The room burst into conversation, teammates marveling at Sophie's angel picture, others talking about the colors and images, how they could be adjusted, or where the copy could lie. A few more moments passed before Sophie spoke. "All right. Thoughts here? I'd normally like to give you some time to think about it, but we have..." She glanced at her watch. "Two and a half hours. That's it."

"That's not enough time. George isn't around, the creative director is remote, there is—"

"Combine the images with copy and send it—"

"There's no chance we'll get this complete—"

The voices clamored for airspace, with some team members begging, some naysaying, some animated, and Sophie's insides trembling.

"We can do this. I'm sending the raw files now. Let's divide into teams of two, rapid-fire-style. Everyone, do a quick magic edit and modify directly in the platform. Take the existing head-line and add it to all three images. I know we can do this." The team stared at her.

"Now! Go. Please, we have to try."

A lead grabbed their laptop and started. "Gum wall has to go. Swap background from image one with image three."

And soon, a waterfall of direction occurred as the team sprung alive.

"Add shadow lines, not too much, to image two."

"Make hair white instead of red, change wings from black to red."

"Add tattoos to image one, black only."

"Reduce the copy font size by two and increase the highlights."

Sophie opened her notes app to help guide the team when Malcolm leaned over. "Quick chat in the hallway."

The words were definitely not a question. Sophie followed him out, scratching at her neck to go back inside. She didn't want to miss a word, a thought, anything, and cause even a second more of a delay. "What's up?"

"Ella created these images?"

"Yes, she emailed them just a few minutes ago."

Malcolm nodded. "They're good. I'll be interested to see what the team chooses." He stuffed his hands in his pocket. "I've gotta ask, though. She clearly used your image. I don't know if they're going to choose that one or not, but I need to know how you'll feel if they do. Your face will be plastered all over social, web, the parade..."

Sophie hadn't taken the time to really consider the ramifica-tions if they used her actual image for the ad.

"We'll need legal to draft something for you to sign, if they choose your face. I'm in full support of whatever you want. The image is great. But if you're not okay with it, say the word. I won't even tell the team that you're uncomfortable. I'll say I'm uncomfortable, or HR blocked it, or something. I'd feel terrible if you compromised yourself and regretted it later."

Sophie's heart swelled and tears prickled her eyes. Again. Crying her first week on the job, then not for six years, and now she was an emotional wreck.

Malcolm had always protected her, had her back. Hiring her on at eighteen, showing her the ropes, training her, guiding her. She loved her dad so much, but damn if Malcolm wasn't a solid work dad. She did something she'd never done before—she hugged him. Then promptly released.

"Damn. Consent much?" He laughed, then squeezed her back.

"I'm okay if they want to use it." Was she flattered? Yes, of course. Ella hadn't forgotten her completely, in fact she'd drawn an incredible picture of her. Was it a little weird to potentially have her face plastered all over Seattle? Yep. But right now, she would do just about anything to launch this campaign.

"Okay, then. You pop inside, do your thing. I'll call legal to preemptively draft a document. I'm going to call the client for an emergency meeting in, say"—he flicked his wrist to check his watch—"two hours from now. Four thirty, gives them ninety minutes before closing time to decide, but praying that they will stay late. They want this campaign launched as much as we do."

Malcolm already had the phone up to his ear before she retreated.

The energy back in the room was fierce. Sophie set the timer. "Seventy-five minutes until speed-round review," she called out. She captured notes, forgetting everything about a formalized project plan, and made sure all non-creatives were on high alert. A quick message was sent to the web production team, the SEO managers, the organic social people.

"Forty-five minutes!" Her fingers flew at a breakneck pace, and she typed like her life depended on it. Teams of two turned into two teams of four, and everyone made sure they weren't working against each other.

"Thirty minutes!" Sophie flexed her fingers, took one quick bathroom break, and slammed back water. She rushed to the breakroom, scooped granola bars and chips in her hand, returned to the room, and dumped them on the table.

"Fifteen minutes!"

People stood, paced, interlocked their fingers behind their necks. F-bombs and sighs and a few chuckles escaped. Her mouth was dry, her arms ached. She pushed her thumb into the tendon on her shoulder and rotated it. The timer screeched, cutting off her stretching. "Time! Everyone, upload to the shared drive. Remember, rapid-fire feedback."

The next hour flew, a tsunami of words and yells and clicking. Feedback flew: image back, image forward, shading on the left, increase font, decrease font, more prominent CTA, too sexy, not enough sex, less cleavage, more cleavage...

And then, then! They had it—or at least they had something to present. With five minutes to spare, the entire team voted, and even though it wasn't unanimous, it was pretty damn close. They chose the rocker outfit from the Sophie image, the face and hair of the undercut emo, and changed the wide smile to a shit-eating grin. And even though Sophie loved that Ella added the gum wall to the background, the team replaced it seamlessly with the background that had been approved by Devil's. The new rocker angel had a fishnet stocking-laden leg bent at the knee, her foot resting against the redbrick behind her, and her mouth poised to bite into a dripping doughnut. It was perfect.

A video conference call ensued. The Devil's team was as engaged as any partner could be, clear they'd been feeling the heat just like the Mahogany and Moon team.

More changes were requested from the Devil's team— bigger logo, remove the leather wristbands from the angel, change knee-high boots to Doc Martens replicas. Yawns and low energy and empty Thai takeout containers littered the conference room along with water bottles and half-dried markers. Even through the wide-screen monitor, the Devil's team's grogginess was evident. Malcolm left at nine, apologizing profusely, and explaining how unfair it was for his wife to care for the baby all day and then again all night. The VP dialed in, the executive assistant dropped off more food, and George messaged a note of encouragement.

Midnight came, and exhaustion seeped into the deepest part of Sophie's core. Even her eyebrows hurt. She looked up at the screen at the Devil's team, trying hard to read body language over video.

Finally, the Devil's Doughnuts creative director smiled and said the word they'd all been waiting for: "Approved!"

THIRTY

SOPHIE

Sophie hugged Maya goodbye, thanked her for the ride to the cruise dock, and looked up at the mammoth vessel resting on the Puget Sound. She'd seen cruise ships sailing by before, but she'd never been this close to one. The ship was as big as a city, the size almost incomprehensible.

Incomprehensible—like the last five days of her life. From the moment the client had approved, at the literal final second, everyone had pitched in—including people not assigned to the campaign. Various project managers covered meetings and consolidated notes for Sophie. The social team worked overnight to get everything ready for launch. The web team coded until five in the morning.

And this morning at exactly 1:01 a.m., the ad launched with minimal errors. Enough so that Malcolm said the team members not going on the cruise could cover whatever else was needed. Sophie had enough lingering adrenaline to pack, crash, and get to the ship.

For the next seven days, she didn't want to look at a phone, a laptop, a screen, anything even remotely digital. Her irises would shrivel up and fall out if she had to read anything that wasn't a smutty romance book. Her soul craved seeing the world outside of an open-floor concept office. And though she really liked her co-workers, and the cruise was supposed to be used for research, she planned on avoiding the team as much as humanly possible.

After waving off the deck to the cheering people on the pier —a bucket list item crossed off the list—Sophie strolled the ship. The cruise ship horn blasted goodbye to the land, and the sunshine-filled breeze hit her face as she made her way past shops and food, *so much food*, mini golf, pools, and spas. She was going to get a massage, join that damn knitting circle, and eat buckets of carb-laden food.

At the buffet, she plunked down at a table and filled herself with sashimi salmon, yakisoba, mangos, and two scoops of peppermint chocolate ice cream with shaved chocolate.

"God, this is delicious..." she said to a fellow traveler as she held her full belly.

She studied artwork on the wall, looked at jewelry from a vendor, and read the hypnotist performance schedule. When her belly settled, she returned to her room, and ordered more room service. Because, holy balls, room service was free! She could order anything she wanted, at any time, and they just brought it. Her inner child screamed with delight while her adult practical self tried to not be too gluttonous.

And then she slept. She slept so long she didn't even know the time. The rocking of the ship was peaceful, like an adult bassinet, pushing her into the type of sleep that seeped into her bones. Tucked away in a dark room, the only sounds surrounding her were wind and the ocean slurping against the vessel. She slept so long that when she woke up, the sky was black.

She wrapped a hooded sweatshirt around herself and slipped out onto the balcony. The sway of the ship put her in a trance, and the saltwater sprayed and misted her lips. She licked the salt from her mouth and stared at the moon and stars illuminating the sky.

The tension she'd carried for *years* slowly melted, allowing her brain to wander. For so long she'd chased the corporate dream, and now that she had it, was she truly happy? Did she want it? She wasn't *unhappy*, but she was aware that she wasn't living her best life.

The sound of the lapping waves continued. She retrieved a blanket and returned to the balcony, snuggling herself into the chair. She exhaled and tried to break down the key moments in her life that led her to where she was today.

For so long she'd wanted to find her soulmate. Or maybe, had wanted her soulmate to be dropped into her lap. And she *had*. She was ready to be in love, ready to open up her heart, and she knew Ella was the missing piece in her life. But Ella had not reached out, and clearly that meant Sophie felt more for Ella than the other way around. And yes, of course she understood that she didn't know what recovery from a seizure looked like. But it had been nearly two weeks. Wasn't that enough?

And yet... she wasn't ready to give up. Ella deserved more. *I deserve more.* Sophie would take these days, sleep good, eat good, and properly relax. She'd watch the sea, explore Alaska, and go hiking. And when she returned, she would try again to talk with Ella.

The fresh air and natural white noise made her yawn, and she moved back inside and curled under the covers. When she woke again, the sun was bright and full. She showered, taking the time to properly scrub. She put on a cute outfit, did her makeup, even polished her nails—everything she'd been neglecting, and everything that made her feel just a bit more human.

"Good afternoon." She smiled to the bellhop as she made her way to a restaurant.

At the buffet, she entered major decision fatigue. Smoked salmon, roasted potatoes, meats, cheeses, an omelette station, crepes, and hash browns. She loaded her plate with the fried deliciousness in honor of Ella. Her mouth salivated as she tucked herself away in a corner on the upper deck to face the ocean.

She'd always wanted to see the ocean like this, and it didn't disappoint. The ocean was both forgiving and unforgiving. This vast, powerful entity where you could throw in all your hopes and dreams, and it wouldn't judge you. The water could destroy you or give you life. Make you breathe or drown you.

Today, the ocean provided hope. She breathed in. The salty air prickled her nose with a delicious burn. She bit into the hash browns and grinned. They were delicious, probably made with grass-fed butter and flaky sea salt, but they would never beat the dive breakfast joint she and Ella went to. She closed her eyes, thinking of that day a lifetime ago, and blew a wish into the water that she'd take Ella there again.

Footsteps approached behind her, and she barely noticed among the travelers, silverware clanking, and servers rushing to clean tables. But when the shadow hovered, she almost turned around.

"These hash browns are good, for sure. But I know of a place in Green Lake that does them better."

No way. Maybe a conversation from a different table got stuck in the wind. Sophie was scared to turn around, scared to look, scared she was hallucinating.

But she did, and her heart leapt right into her throat.

THIRTY-ONE
ELLA

Ella didn't expect to be this nervous. She knew the decision to go on the cruise was impulsive. She had barely lifted from her seizure fog the other day when she'd sent the design samples and bought a ticket. When she arrived, she had no plans except to find Sophie. She assumed it would take an hour or so, not the near thirty-six hours she'd clocked searching this entire place.

She didn't realize Sophie would have her phone turned off. Nor did she expect security on the ship to be at a secret service level. They absolutely would not budge when she begged for Sophie's room number.

So, she'd been aimlessly wandering, knowing damn well that the likelihood of seeing Sophie on this mammoth eight-story ship was slim. But not impossible.

And finally, here she was.

Ella's hand slipped on condensation from the orange juice glass, and she wiped her palm on her jeans. She pointed to her bruised upper cheek and eye area that had faded to a terrible puke green by this morning. "You should see the other guy."

Sophie's mouth hadn't closed since Ella stepped behind her

a moment ago, but her jaw worked in a slow circle. "What are you doing here?"

Well, those words were not the reaction Ella hoped for, but it was better than "get the eff out of here." *What am I doing here?* A loaded, very good question, and she wasn't sure how to answer. "Can I sit?"

Sophie nodded and pointed to the chair. "Your dad told me you had a seizure. Are you okay?"

The words were kind, but the tone flat. Ella nodded and swallowed. "I think I have some explaining to do."

"Yes, you do." Sophie pushed the plate of food away from her and crossed her arms.

The wind blew Ella's hair and she tucked it behind her ears. The encounter with Jasmine and Sophie two weeks ago had crushed her. The level of betrayal she felt wasn't realistic, but it didn't matter. The news had destroyed her and made her question everything.

Ella wanted to explain what it was like never having genuine friends. How living in the shadows of her parents made her feel like she couldn't handle anything on her own. How she questioned her worth daily, but Sophie helped free her from that doubt, helped show her a world she didn't know existed. She wanted to tell her she'd fallen so hard, so deep, and that she was terrified that her actions after the Jasmine situation—and her unintentional ignoring post-seizure—ruined things for them.

But she froze, the words catching in her mouth, in her breath, and she shifted on the chair.

"I can understand what you found out was shocking, and really hurt." Sophie leaned back in her chair. "But going totally dark for two weeks? That's not how adults communicate. That's not how I communicate. And that's not the type of relationship that I want to be in."

Ouch.

Sophie twisted the ring on her finger. "Why did you run?"

Ella held her stare. "Why didn't you chase me?"

The words hung in the air, heavy and thick. So many moments passed Ella wasn't sure who'd break first.

"How much chasing did you want me to do?" Sophie asked. "I called. I texted. I even went to your house. Was that not enough?"

This conversation was absolutely not going the way Ella planned, but they had to get it out. When Ella lifted from the seizure fog, she'd seen the scattered texts and few voice messages. But then there was a full stop. And yes, maybe Ella had told Sophie to back off, but she was not in her proper frame of mind, and Sophie should have realized that. Her dad said she stopped by, but that was a week ago. Work took precedence, and Ella wanted more. She needed more. "Why did you totally stop? Maybe I didn't explain the post-seizure effects to the most detailed degree, but I did tell you I'm not myself."

Sophie's brows knitted together. "Are you serious?" She fiddled with the zipper on her sweatshirt. "Ella... I was working. We were down to the wire with the campaign. I was so busy. I don't remember ever being that busy in my life. And, well, you weren't there to help run things with me, so I had to pick up the slack."

The tone was softer than the words, but they still landed with a punch. Ella had let down the team. And work was more important. "A few months ago, you told me you hadn't had a relationship because you work too much. All these years you've put work first. Not yourself, not your relationships, and you did it again." Ella reached out and touched Sophie's arm. "You are worth more than your work."

Sophie inhaled a sharp, shaky breath and put her head in her hands. She wasn't crying, not that Ella saw, but Ella wanted to pull Sophie into her chest.

Sophie lifted her head. "I haven't been in a relationship since high school. I don't know what's right and what's wrong, or how to act." Her shoulders sunk, and she watched the water below. "I've only been out of work for a few days, but it's clear. I'm running myself down, and for what? Yes, I want to do a good job, of course. Yes, my work means a lot to me. But it's not worth sacrificing everything else that's important to me."

Ella scooted closer.

"So... you really are okay? Your face..." Sophie lifted her hand then dropped it in her lap.

"This one scared me more than most." Ella told Sophie everything from these last few weeks. After she saw Jasmine, and learned what happened, she was so angry and upset she couldn't think. She took an Uber home and spent the rest of the afternoon crying, angry, and feeling deserted.

Everyone thought she was at the office, Thomas was with her mom, and the staff didn't know she was home. "It was so eerie, so empty. My whole life I craved alone time. But then I got it, and everything was so dark and still." She sipped on juice and dabbed the corner of her mouth with her thumb. "After I stopped crying and pulled myself from my room, I made my way downstairs. After that, it's all blurry. My seizure triggered my watch alarm, which notified my parents, of course. I guess one of the staff found me, there was an ambulance, and then I was in the hospital."

The moments surrounding a seizure were blips, like a dream where you grasp to piece the fragmented chunks of what happened, but the harder you try and remember, the more they slip away. "It was a lot of chaos because I smacked my face pretty good, and my parents were beside themselves."

Sophie stroked the top of Ella's hand. "I'm so sorry. I can't even imagine how scary that was."

Ella shrugged. "It was, of course, but it always is. I may have had a hundred of these in my life, but it's scary every single time. It hadn't happened for a long time, and I had this hope that maybe it would never happen again. I know that it's rare that it would ever stop, but..." Ella played with Sophie's fingertips. "Honestly, though, it's not surprising it happened when it did."

Sophie froze. "God, I'm so sorry. The whole situation with your ex? Did I cause this?"

"You didn't *cause* this, Sophie. Do not ever think that. I was born like this, but I'll be honest. I was hiding things from myself, from you and my parents. I wasn't sleeping enough. My diet went to shit. I mean, how much pizza did we consume these last few weeks? The hours working, the project, the campaign..."

For so long, Ella had been desperate to prove she could do the same things other people could do. That she'd hack it in the real world, without her golden parachute. "But also, I refuse to blame myself. Yes, these things could have exacerbated the seizure, but it's also life, you know? I've also had seizures when I was painting, so..."

A gust of wind blew, and Sophie shivered. "Want to take a walk?"

Ella nodded and tentatively interlocked her fingers with Sophie's. They strolled toward the atrium and pulled up to a cushy seat facing an indoor garden.

"I'm sorry I never told you what happens after a seizure. I should have warned you." She slid closer to Sophie until she pressed against her. "But afterwards, I'm not myself. At all. It's a different version of me. I used to hate it, but I accept that this is just part of me. Every person with epilepsy in the world has unique experiences, right, just like anything else. But I go to a really dark place. While my mind rewires, I'm angry, and depressed, and I don't have the clarity I'd normally have."

She took a breath thinking of how best to describe that darkness that filled her after a seizure, where the world turned dull, like she was watching a movie filmed in grayish tones.

The only reason she had enough gumption to send the graphics was because it took her mind off the Sophie-Jasmine situation. "I didn't want to talk to you. I didn't want to see you. But I should have explained that in the beginning of our relationship so you would have been prepared."

Sophie licked at her lip ring. "And now? Do you want to talk and see me?"

Ella chortled through her nose. "You do realize that I'm halfway up the Pacific and spent all the money I'd saved, literally just to talk and see you."

"Wait, what? Didn't you end up just coming with the other team members?"

Ella flinched. "God, no. My dad was terrified someone would think he was playing favorites. My parents wouldn't give me the money for this."

A grimace flashed on Sophie's face. "Shit, that was really expensive."

"Sure was. But, you know, I've been saving up for months for a place of my own and now..." Ella waved her hand. Now she realized she had it pretty damn good. She lived in a restrictive home, but her parents loved her. And being alone when she had a seizure and the aftereffects shook her. "I'm kind of realizing maybe it's not the worst thing to live with my parents still."

"Oh yeah?"

"And do I really want to do my own laundry and dishes? Probably not." Ella laughed and grazed her hand over Sophie's.

Sophie shifted closer to Ella. "How do your parents feel about you going on this cruise unsupervised for a week? What if you hadn't found me?"

"Unsupervised?" Ella lifted a brow. "Yeah, um, no. Thomas is here with me."

"What?" Sophie looked around the room. "Where?"

"When I found you, he was like 'peace out, I'm hitting the pool.' That man has not had a proper vacation in a very long time."

Sophie grinned. "We should watch over the deck. Maybe he'll be the one who is pulled up on stage to dance."

God no. The last thing she wanted to see was Thomas dancing on a cruise ship and ruining the CIA-agent vibe he'd been carrying for years. "Nope, no thank you. What if he wears a Speedo or something? I'll be scarred for life. I've never seen him outside of a shirt and tie, and my brain has had enough activity for now. Not sure I need to see his bare chest. What if he waxes? What if he's super hairy? Both would be awful."

Sophie laughed and pinched the tip of her nose. "So where do you go from here? Are you coming back to work?"

"I am, but only part-time." She shifted to look at Sophie's face. "And I talked to my dad about maybe interning with the graphic department."

Sophie's face fell. "You don't want to work with me anymore?"

"That's not it. I just think that drafting project plans is not my passion... like at all. I want to do something art related. And I need to find a balance." Ella really hoped Sophie resonated with this message for her own well-being. "But the hours, the schedule, it's not healthy. And I'm prioritizing my health."

When Ella started, she didn't think she was ignoring her health. She took her medication every day, and somehow convinced herself that was enough, while knowing damn well the stress and lack of sleep were poison to her system. "I wanted the money for my own place and to prove to myself I could do it, and I did both. I earned respect. It was not just given to me based on my last name. And I'm going to take that with me."

Sophie nodded. "And the team loved your artwork. You created something fresh and new, and they ran with it. You're the reason that we are all here."

"No, I'm not." Being an only child with overbearing parents and artificial friends, she never grasped the concept of a work family. "I've never been on a team before, never understood team mentality, but now I get it. You all earned your spot on this vacation before I was hired. I was just a small part of the relay team bringing you all to the finish line."

A quietness fell over Sophie. She dug at her freshly polished manicure for a moment, then dropped her hands in her lap. "I'm really sorry about what happened with Jasmine and how I reacted. I never gave you the full grace to understand why you would be mad at me."

"I had no right to be that angry with you." Ella was so hurt when it happened but had some time to come down from the shock. The seizure interrupted her processing time, and she'd have to grapple with this more later, but it was clear Sophie didn't sleep with Jasmine to hurt her. "The only person here to blame is Jasmine. I couldn't see through my anger to separate you from what happened." She peeked back at the greenery, inhaling a warm breath. "I'm really sorry, too."

Sophie stood and motioned for Ella to follow. She interlocked her fingers with Ella's and escorted her off the deck. They made their way to another outdoor space on the top floor.

The breeze was fierce, even with the sun, but Ella was filled with warmth. She gripped the rail and absorbed Sophie, watching the ocean, her green eyes calm, her body relaxed. She looped her arm in Sophie's and rested her head on Sophie's shoulder. "So, what does this mean for us?"

"It means we can give ourselves some solid credit for having a mature grown-up conversation." Sophie's chest lifted. "You don't want us to end?"

"What?" Ella gripped Sophie's face, her heartbeat hammering. "No. Of course not. Do you?"

"I *never* want this to end." She kissed the top of Ella's head. "We don't know what the future holds, right? No one does. But what I know is I'm so grateful that we found each other."

Ella pressed her lips into Sophie's. "And I want to be with you."

Sophie kissed Ella back, soft, warm, and with intention, then pulled Ella into her arms.

When Ella started at her dad's company a couple months ago, she couldn't have predicted this would be the outcome. Sophie's tears that she flicked away, and her lip ring bouncing with her smile, and feeling the way she did when Sophie kissed her, confirmed everything she'd gone through was worth it. "I want one more thing. If you can do something for me?"

Sophie pulled back, her gaze sliding between Ella's eyes. "Anything."

"I really want some hash browns."

Sophie kissed Ella with the promise of tomorrow. Ella's heart lifted, soared, and then settled. This right here, being with Sophie, repairing her insides, knowing she was enough, was everything she needed. She didn't need to know what the rest of her life looked like, or where they'd go from here. But she was confident that together, they'd figure out the best agenda for themselves.

Sophie kissed Ella once more, then touched her forehead against Ella's. "Deal."

A LETTER FROM THE AUTHOR

Hey there!

Thanks so much for reading *So Not My Type*. I loved having you get to know Sophie more and introducing you to Ella. Much like most of my books, there is a little bit of me in each character. This story was so much fun to write, especially the snarky scenes. I am a sucker for the enemies-to-lovers trope, and hope you enjoy this as much as me.

As I continue to write my sparkly, upbeat romances celebrating queer joy, I'd love to keep you posted about my new releases and bonus content. Please sign up for my newsletter, below. I promise I won't spam you or sell your info.

www.stormpublishing.co/dana-hawkins

I'd be so grateful if you liked this book and wouldn't mind leaving a review. Even a short review can make all the difference in encouraging a reader to discover my books for the first time. Thank you so much!

While writing *So Not My Type*, my mind flashed back twenty-five-plus years ago when I stepped back into a college classroom as a young mom after taking several years off. I was scared and unsure of myself, and as a first-generation college student from a working-class background, I wasn't sure that I belonged. Here, I took my first (of many) courses with Dr. Heather Hackman, who changed how I viewed the world while introducing me to concepts I didn't know existed—heterosexism, identity fluidity, equity, social justice, implicit bias... the list goes on.

From day one, I started on a journey of learning invaluable life lessons, including celebrating and affirming the differences in one another. I continue to try and apply those principles in my daily life. But also, I learned what it felt like to be on the receiving end of someone embracing and respecting folks with various socioeconomic statuses and identities.

In her class, Dr. Hackman told us we were welcome to use her first name, Heather. It was the first time in my life that a teacher had offered the use of their first name, and it broke down a bit of an "us vs. them" wall I had built inside. Another moment I will never forget was when I saw Heather at an event, and she introduced me to her friend as a colleague. *An equal.* Something about this introduction deeply struck me and started a process of erasing a power imbalance I had built in my head based on my background.

With her dynamic speaking abilities, empathy, and incredible sense of humor, Heather created the ultimate safe space for her students to learn and absorb. I wanted to emulate for readers that same safe-space feeling I had in her classes. I consciously choose to write stories where coming out is not an "issue" and that being LGBTQIA+ is nothing to "overcome." Creating a world where my characters live in a safe, affirming, celebratory space while navigating their relationships and real-life issues fills my heart. I am keenly aware the queer community continues to live in fear and is subject to discrimination, violence, anti-inclusive legislation, and more. I write novels that create a reality I want to be a part of—a hate-free world.

Thanks again for being part of this amazing journey with me! Please stay in touch—I have so many more stories and can't wait to share them with you.

KEEP IN TOUCH WITH THE AUTHOR

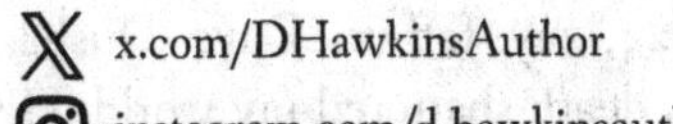

x.com/DHawkinsAuthor

instagram.com/d.hawkinsauthor

ACKNOWLEDGMENTS

In March of 2024, my father, Dave Dusha, passed away unexpectedly. His death shattered my world. He was the kindest, warmest, funniest man you could ever know. He was also the humblest—except when he spoke about his children and grandchildren. He would brag to anyone who would listen about our accomplishments. I felt my father's pride in everything I did. And my gosh, when I published my first book, he was thrilled for me. I will forever cherish the picture of him reading my debut novel. I will also be continually grateful that we mutually decided he would skip over any spicy scenes!

After my dad's death, I wasn't sure if I would write again. I felt a tremendous amount of guilt when I focused on anything but the sadness I felt from losing him. But my incredible family, including my mother, Esther Dusha—an absolute rock—encouraged me to continue. And I am so glad I did. I was able to finish this book and have a creative outlet to derail from my heartbreak. So first and foremost, I need to honor my father's legacy, encouragement, love, and firm belief that his children could do anything they set their minds to. And I want to thank my mom for continuing to carry that encouragement torch, even through her own heartbreak, and telling everyone she meets that her daughter is an author (and that they need to buy my books!).

I want to thank the following people. These tiny sentences below will never fully express how much you all mean to me.

To my spouse, "My Forever." You continue to amaze me with your unwavering support and encouragement. The sacrifices you make so I can fulfill my dreams are beyond the call of duty. I love you, and I am counting the days until we take our solo road trip!

Jennifer Gatewood. My phenomenal critique partner and dear friend. I could never do this without you! Thank you for your guidance, help, critiques, and support. I will shoulder shimmy with you forever!

Katherine Bost. Your attention to detail with critiques and your freakish ability to remember so much from past work never ceases to amaze me. Thank you so much for helping me to develop these characters to their fullest.

S.E. Reed. Thank you for dreaming big with me and being with me on all my writing journeys. I cannot wait for our secret squirrel project to be released!

Dana Renee Green. Your friendship, guidance, transparency, and encouragement over the years have meant everything. Thank you for letting me into your world.

Amy Nielsen. Thank you for your constant support in everything I do.

I have the best family in the world. Truly. Thank you to my kids, Tanner, Kianna, and Joey, for having so much patience with me while I am in my "writing hole." To my brothers, Ryan and Dustin, thank you for your constant encouragement and support. Double thank you for bringing your families to my book signing to help settle my nerves! To Mollie and Erica, the best sisters-in-law in the world, and all the kids in the family—Amanda, Megan, Alex, Teague, Lola, and Kai, who always support their Auntie Grummie. I love you all.

I want to thank all the people who bravely shared their stories with me about what it is like to live with epilepsy or care for someone with epilepsy. I am completely in awe of you and your strength. Your collective willingness to share such deeply personal stories was beyond anything I have ever seen. I really hope I did you proud with Ella's story. Sharing their names with permission. Thank you to: Trevor Harris (@patchcomedy310), Frankie, Sam Longhair, Gillian Sapia, Caroline Maston, and JEdwards (@epilepsieaaargh).

To the Storm team, especially Emily Gowers. Thank you so much for your continued support and encouragement. I love being part of the Storm family!

And to those who are still reading these acknowledgments... thank you for sticking with me!